SEVENTH CITY

EMILY HAYSE

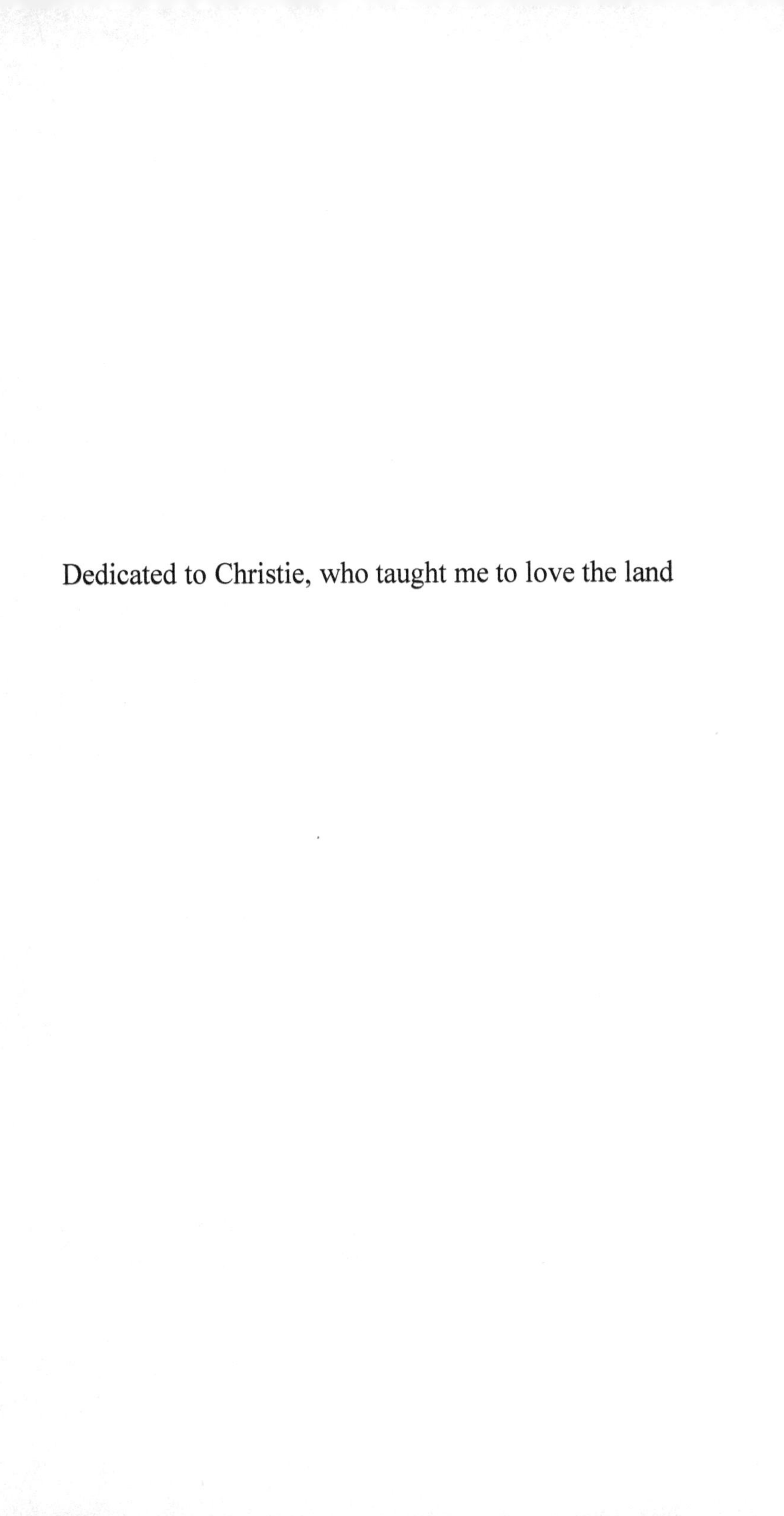

Dedicated to Christie, who taught me to love the land

TABLE OF CONTENTS

TANSILET

The last time I saw my mother, she told me a story.

I was five the summer the nomads came to camp near Tansilet. Rangy men, most of them, occasionally with a wife: solemn-faced women with braids, some dark, some fair, but all with that restless, hooded-eyed look that the traveling people wore.

I mistrusted and envied them at the same time. I did not have to be old to know that my own family was unhappy. Especially my mother, since I did not have a father.

One of the nomads came to visit us—a tall fellow with a face that was almost handsome, despite his large chin—and I was tired and restless after he left.

Tsanu was out hunting.

My mother took me on her lap because I was cross. I still remember the sweet smell of her neck and her breath as she spoke. "Little one, why are you so unhappy?"

"I want a story," I told her.

"Then I shall tell you my favorite."

I settled in, leaning against her soft shoulder, the skin of her neck cool against my face. The day was warm and I was glad that we were inside, in the shade.

"Long ago, there were six great cities in Uniap'nik, rich with silver and whale oil and *nanuk* furs, but there were legends told of a seventh, greater than them all—the place where the heroes dwell. It was called Inik Katsuk, and it was closed to all but those who proved themselves worthy."

"What is it like?" I asked.

She leaned back and closed her eyes as if she could see it.

"Beautiful!"

"How beautiful?"

Her hands, warm and gentle, played in my hair, twisting it into little braids. "As bright as the stars in the sky, as shining as the sun on the stream, as vast as the far mountains. It was a place that all men wished to find, but few did."

"And the good people live there?"

"Yes." Her voice was very soft. "The good live there."

I reached up and touched her face. My mother was beautiful, with her soft skin and dark eyes and full lips. I wanted to look like her when I grew up.

"Someday, I will go to Inik Katsuk," I declared.

She looked down at me and her face was wistful. I did not know why then, but the memory of it now still hurts deep inside me. "Will you, little one?"

I nodded. Adventures were my favorite thing at that age. "Will you be there, *Aaga?*" I asked.

Her hand caressed my face. "To be sure, little one."

I snuggled further into her arms.

"We will go together . . . ."

The sun was warm, and she hummed to me under her breath, and that is the last memory I have of my mother.

I sensed the difference the moment I woke up. The sun was still shining, but I felt the change in the day. It was nearing evening, and I could smell meat cooking.

"*Aaga,* what is supper?" I remember asking before I came around the side of the hides we had stacked on a basket. "*Aaga?*"

She was not there. It was my brother Tsanu who knelt in front of the fire, feeding it with sticks to keep the flame strong.

"Maki! You are awake!" He turned and reached out his arms to me in a kind, protective way. I knew immediately that something was wrong.

"Where is *Aaga?*" I demanded, drawing back from him.

A cloud crossed his proud, twelve-year-old face and he only gestured with his hand. I stood my ground, panic welling up in me. "Where is *Aaga?*"

His eyes went my face and then dropped to the skins of the two rabbits he had brought back. "She is—gone, Maki."

"Gone? Where?"

He shrugged. There was finality in his tone, and I knew that wherever she had gone, she was not coming back.

I turned and ran out of the house, shouting for my mother, hoping that if I just ran fast enough, I would catch her. I ran into the camp of nomads, searching around their smoking fires, calling for her, calling and calling her name.

One of the women came over, looking at me with faint concern. "It must be the child of the woman who left with Tassit," she said, crouching down to look into my face, her long arm draped over her knee. "They say her man was killed by the Invaders on the coast five years ago."

"Where is my *aaga?* Have you seen her?" I screamed, panic making me hysterical.

She leaned closer, speaking louder as if that would help. "Do not blame your *aaga.* It's a rough life, losing your man, being alone."

I did not understand her. I only knew that my mother was gone and I had to find her.

"Maki!" It was Tsanu, looking for me. I ran to him.

I remember crying. I do not remember being hysterical, as Tsanu said I was. But I remember his strong arms around me as my tears soaked his shoulder, his smell that of the wild air and pine he had been hunting in all day, his voice vibrating against me as he spoke. "Maki, I am sorry. Maki, I am so, so sorry." I clung to him tighter, and his arms pressed me closer. "I tried to stop her, I went after her—but—she had to go."

He peeled me off him and looked me in the eyes. I had to wipe the tears away just to see him.

"Maki, I swear to you that I will not leave you. Do you hear me? And you will not starve." His voice cracked, but there were no tears.

It was only in hindsight that I realized he was trying not to cry himself.

"We will survive. You and me. Together."

THE INVADERS

ONE

To Glory

I watch a pair of mounted soldiers pass on the dirt path in front of me, and as soon as their backs are to me, I spit. I was a baby when *they* came to our wide land of Uniap'nik. Just a baby. It is because of them that I never knew my father, that my grandma stopped talking and died soon after, that my mother ran off to the hinterlands with the nomad because she couldn't stand living in Tansilet anymore.

But Tsanu tells me about life before them. Of the dances in the village square where women wore skirts of every color imaginable. Of the trials of the young men—of the freedom we once enjoyed. I wonder sometimes: If our young warriors were as good as Tsanu said they were, why were we so soundly defeated?

I never ask him that, though. I think it would hurt his pride. *They* have weapons that are stronger and shoot farther than any of our spears or arrows. I call them strike-locks. It does not take any skill to kill with a strike-lock. Any fool can do it.

"What are you thinking of, Maki?" A hand tugs my braid and I slap it.

"Nothing." I pull the braid out of reach. "What are you supposed to be doing, Tsanu?"

He looks around him carefully, like a fox before it enters a clearing.

"Nothing, little wolf."

I have been too loud. I see now there is a guarded look in his eyes as he watches the Invaders pass.

"Nothing at all?" I squint up at him and shift to make his tall head block the sun. He is dressed in caribou hide for hunting.

Another pair of horses passes near. I do not spit this time, but one of the men glances down at us, and Tsanu looks away. His narrow face is closed, hiding thought and emotion from the Invader.

They pass us by, but the troubled look does not leave Tsanu's dark eyes. He reaches down, presses something into my hand, and disappears back into the trees.

I open my hand just a crack and see that it is a river pebble, blue and shot through with clear streaks.

It is our signal to each other, one we have had since I was six. It means a place. Safe, away from the eyes and ears of the Invaders that are ever swarming our village and the paths around it.

I glance down the dirt path that the Invaders are taking and give their backs one last dark glance. Then I back slowly into the pines and follow Tsanu.

We walk in silence, he a couple paces ahead of me, for nearly an hour, and he tells me nothing. But the woods are telling us many things. Spring is here, waking slowly, like a dog yawning and stretching and looking around. There is food to be gathered and much to be done. The animals are talking too; there is a minx or weasel somewhere nearby, and the birds are nervous. A herd of deer lies within two lengths of a thrown stone.

At last Tsanu stops. We are at the hollow beside the river, the same place he took me when the Invaders first came to our village. He was afraid I would try to fight them. I would have, even though I was six.

He stares down into the running water, his hands clasped behind his back as he thinks. I watch him, thinking he will speak any moment now, but he does not.

I seat myself in the sun-warmed dirt of the hollow and watch the reflection of the pines blur in the swift stream. His silence gnaws at me. He is often silent, but in the time it takes him to find the words he wants, my mind can imagine any number of dire things that may be in his mind.

"Maki." His voice is low, blending with the wind in the trees. "The wolf pack goes out tonight. And Kavik leads us."

Hope leaps in my heart. I like to run with the wolf pack, and I like Kavik. He was a grown man when the Invaders first came, and sometimes he leads the men of the village in raids against the camp that lives in and around our village. We do not have enough men for full fights, and the youngest of our warriors are only half trained, because we cannot train under the eye of the Invaders. But we carry out small attacks to cause them trouble. If they are annoyed enough, they may leave, as a bear leaves if too many bees pierce his fur.

Tsanu reads my thoughts in my face. "I wonder if I may borrow your spear," he says at last. "They took my good ones after the last attack, you remember."

I do. I was very angry. They did it when I was not home, and it has bothered me since. If only I had been home, I could have hidden the spears or talked the Invaders out of doing it. I am still young enough that I can sometimes sway them with sad, innocent looks.

I push away the unpleasant thoughts. "Which?"

"The fishing spear. It is the only one strong enough with the length I need."

My fishing spear is my pride and joy. "You must not break it," I warn.

"You know me, Maki. I swear I shall not."

"What if you lose it?" I do not know why I am dragging my feet over this. Perhaps it is because he has not asked me to come along.

"I have never lost a spear in my life, Maki!"

"You cannot be too careful."

"Look. If a put a scratch on your spear, something that cannot be mended in an afternoon's work, I will make you a new one—a fine, light hunting spear. I swear it." He sets his hand on the inside of his leg just above the knee to make the oath.

I can see it in my mind: a new hunting spear, all my own. It may be worth the sacrifice to hope ill upon my own beloved spear. There is a sudden splash in the water—a fisher perhaps, hunting the young trout. Tsanu waits for me, for an answer.

"Yes, Tsanu. The spear is yours for tonight."

He grins, his dark eyes flashing. "You are a shrewd thing. But I thank you."

"But Tsanu, one question."

His eyes grow sober to show me that he listens.

"Why has Kavik not asked me this night? Will you do more than raid their bacon and scare the hornless beasts?"

He bites his lip grimly. "Did you see the new company that rode through town two days ago?"

I do remember this. I did not see their faces, but I saw forty or fifty come in from a distance. There was good deal of noise in the camp that night.

Tsanu's face tightens. "It is a new captain."

"Oh." That is why they must attack. Every time the Invaders grow comfortable or make any new show of force, Kavik is sure to lead a disturbance to remind them that though we may be trapped, we are not tamed.

"It is our duty to greet him warmly. But my little wolf cub cannot take harm—that I have sworn."

I growl a little under my breath. I am too old for such names. "I am not afraid of taking harm, you know that."

"It does not mean I wish it. You are small, Maki."

I draw myself up as tall as I can, hurt by his words. It is true that I am small, but I hope to grow more. I wish to be tall and lithe and iron-muscled like Tsanu and the pack. One day I will be. But I still have at least two hand-heights to grow before I reach even Kavik's height—and Kavik is smaller than most.

Tsanu's face is bewildered. He knows he has hurt me but does not know how to mend it.

I take my chance. "May I follow your pack tonight? In the woods?"

He brightens. "I shall speak to Kavik. I daresay if you scrambled up a tree no man would see you, nor could get you down even if he did."

"So long as he—" I stop before I step into dangerous territory. An Invader could sight me and reach me with his strike-lock—then I would be doomed as a snared partridge. But I want to go, not think of reasons why I cannot.

"So long as he what?" Tsanu eyes me slowly.

"Nothing." I kick the pebbles by my feet. "What will you make my new spear of?"

"Ash, if you wish it. But I do not intend to bring any harm to your spear." He reaches over and tweaks my braid gently.

"Three glass beads says you will."

"Now then!" He laughs and makes a dive for me which I do not quite escape. He wraps his arms around me and I fight him, just for the principle of the thing. "No more bartering! I have promised you a new spear, and that is all!"

I only laugh; I know I am beaten. He laughs too, throwing his head back. His eyes are slits, black as a starling's wing. I get a strange feeling that he was trying to make me laugh. The thought sits oddly with me—he does not tease me much these days.

But I love to see him laugh. He does not do it as often as he should. I keep laughing, hoping he will continue, and he does. Our laughter echoes loudly in the safety of the wilderness.

The birds hush, but Tsanu and I are such a piece of this strip of river that a massive antlered *tuttik*, with bearded chin and drooping nose, does not even look at us twice as he wades into the river with long, knobby-kneed legs.

But Tsanu notices, and he stops. His chest rises and falls in ragged breaths against my shoulder. He jerks a piece of hair out of his eyes with a tiny flick of his head and tilts his face to the sky. "We should go now, Maki. We must eat, and then I must make ready." He releases me.

"As you say." I speak with more cheer than I feel. The thought comes to me, unusually strong, that I do not want him to go tonight.

I take this thought and hold it at arm's length to examine it. After all, not many minutes ago I wanted to go myself. But the river runs too loud and sweet in my ears—I lose the thought and with it the reason for my feelings. All I have now is a vague dread.

I start down the path so Tsanu cannot see my face darken.

Dinner is *pantak*—dried meat—and berries that I picked yesterday. I am always hungry, but I hold back deliberately so Tsanu will eat more.

He eats, but he leaves three thick strips of meat and two fistfuls of berries for me.

"Not hungry, Maki?" Brief worry lines trace his brow. "You are always hungry."

I flash him a quick smile and dip my meat in the oil to soften it. He is too alert tonight. I take this as an encouraging sign; he will not be easy to take down in a fight.

He watches me to make sure I eat it all and then lets his breath out slowly through his nose.

"Maki, will you bring my *mudi*?"

I jump up, eager for this task. I take a clay pot down from the shelf and set it upon the table across the room, beside a fine mirror and an armband of jay feathers.

The mirror was a present to me from Tsanu. He either traded for it or stole it. I have never asked which, for it was a gift. When he is good enough to bring me things he thinks I will like, I accept with thanks. To ask would be ungrateful.

Tsanu gets up, wiping his oily fingers on his trousers, and pulls a low stool over in front of the table. I say nothing as he lifts the lid from the clay pot and thrusts two fingers into the paint. Tsanu smears lines of bright blue across his face, drawing out the brown of his eyes. There is something strong and warm inside my chest tonight. He is dearer to me than usual.

I squeeze one hand until my nails cut into my palm. Perhaps these thoughts are an omen. If I don't have them, the evil cannot happen.

I dip my fingers into the *mudi* and start a design on his arm. The branches of a stag's antlers form under my fingers. Stags are a symbol of protection.

It is rare also that he leaves his arms bare. They are scarred in places now, some from previous attacks and others from hunting, but the Invaders do not know the difference. He covers them all to be safe when we are in the village.

But tonight it is as if he has no fear.

"So solemn, Maki." He pauses in his work. "Are you still sore about the spear? Or is it that you are not going?"

"Neither." I shake my head. "Only that the discussion has put bitterness in my mind."

"Put it out of your mind, then." He reaches up and makes a long blue streak down my cheek.

I smile at him, but my usual laughter is not here.

"Maki, what is it?"

He is like a mosquito that will not die. Why can't I fool him?

"I wish you would not hunt with the pack and leave me here tonight. We do not know who this new commander is. What if he is a great fighter?"

"He is a pig, so I hear." Tsanu gets up with a lopsided grin.

"Easy, then." I can feel a grin growing, mirroring his.

"Nothing to worry over." Tsanu leans down and presses his nose gently against mine. "I will be back before the first moon fades."

He speaks as if it is a short time, but the fading of the first moon and the rising of the second is more than halfway through the night. He is expecting more fighting than usual.

"May I come to the gathering? I will bring Iki if you wish."

Tsanu pauses, his hand on my spear. Perhaps there is a good reason he does not want me along.

But he jerks his head to me, and I follow.

The woods are swiftly darkening around us. I see through the shadowy branches a gleam of green and pink—the beginning of the *kitya nitkas*, the summer lights. When I was little, I used to run among them with the other village children, trying to grab the thick gleaming light. But it is like a fog; you cannot grasp it, no matter how sure you are that you can.

Iki pads silently beside me, pale in the darkness. I am often amazed that an animal so large can walk so quietly. If he reaches his head high, he can almost lick my face. Even some of the men of the village avoid him, for he carries blood from a dangerous strain of wolf—larger, the kind that rarely comes as far south as Tansilet. But I have never been afraid of him.

The lights creep across the forest floor towards us, making our faces glow. Tsanu's black hair is brushed back away from his face, his jaw grim-set. Every muscle in his body is taut, his eyes keen like an eagle's, scanning the trees around us for danger as we walk. Over his back he wears a bow and arrows, at his thigh is his knife, and in his hand he carries my spear. The paint obscures his face just enough to give him a raw, untamed look. But I can see the goodness in him by the tilt of his head when he looks down at me. He drops a long arm over my shoulders and his eyes gentle.

"You are hardly a girl anymore, Maki," he says.

Warm pride starts up between my ribs. "I can hunt *pannik* just as well as anyone." I do not know what else to say.

"You will be all right tonight." He rubs the top of my head.

And I will. I have on my waist a knife, and Iki, my wolf-dog, is at my side. I will have no trouble tonight.

Three men are standing in the wooded circle when we arrive, leaning on their spears. But the one I notice is Kavik.

He is lean like a birch tree, with iron eyes like blue river-gems and hands that are strong like an eagle's talons. When the Invaders came to Uniap'nik, Kavik was one of the youngest warriors from our village who answered the call to help fight them on the coast.

And he was one of the few survivors to return.

But unlike the others, he was not broken or made old by the defeat. He recovered, he made something of Tansilet. He trained the young men in secret, at great danger to himself.

For almost as long as I can remember, I have admired Kavik.

"Welcome, Tsanu." Kavik steps forward and clasps Tsanu's tanned arm. My brother leans my spear in the crook of his arm to clasp Kavik's shoulder in his other hand.

"All is well, my brother."

"Good." Kavik's jewel-blue eyes are grim. "It will be fine hunting tonight."

A white grin flashes onto my brother's face. His eyes are keen, like a wolf's. "I depend upon it."

"Is that—is that your spear?" Kavik looks at me when he says this.

My heart flames up with pride. When a spear is noticed, it means the hunter has done well with it.

I lift my chin. "Yes, it is. My best."

"It is fine and straight," Kavik says, and leaves it at that.

The clearing is filling, filling with people I have known all my life, with the stragglers and squatters who make up the rest of the village. The faithful village, that is. There are some who are outcasts because they have befriended the Invaders.

I refuse to look at them anymore.

"Maki, you should go now." Tsanu moves close, his voice low, just for me. I press my forehead against his in farewell, and he lingers a moment before drawing back, adjusting the strap of the quiver across his chest.

As the last of the pack gathers, I find myself a seat out of the way, partway up a pine. The wind blows the stray hairs that have come free from my braids west and a little north.

It is a fine, quiet evening. Perfect for a hunt.

I have always liked Kavik's voice, with its odd inflections, but from where I sit I cannot hear what he is saying. I think Tsanu sent me away because he did not wish for me to hear it.

Kavik's voice, still distant, breaks the night. "Good hunting, my brothers!"

"To glory!" From thirty throats the answer comes as one.

I do not even hear them leave. They are silent as wolves.

It is dark enough that my hand in front of my face is just a blurred shadow as I approach the camp. From across the clearing, just under the trees, a gleam of summer lights rises and dies. I hear a low sigh and rumble from of one of the hornless beasts the Invaders keep in their camp.

Despite my dislike for the Invaders, I find myself drawn to these beasts. I envy how happy and strong the men look astride the tall, muscular animals. They move swiftly over the ground, shaking it—like when the herds run.

I can imagine the feeling of that much power beneath me, the way my hair would stream back, the way I would appear as one with the animal, the way I would be seen by the Invaders. They would be impressed, and perhaps they would give me one to keep.

I shake off this silly dream. I hate them. They are my enemies, and I do not want to impress them. Besides, it is impossible.

A long-drawn howl sounds. Iki does not stiffen beside me, so I know it is the pack, not real wolves. But the Invaders do not know the difference.

One of the hornless beasts raises its head and gives a nervous snort. A couple men by a nearby fire look up—for the Invaders build fires just as we do, and they sit around them for warmth and companionship, as we do—and briefly, separate from their swift stream of low talking, I catch their word for wolf.

I settle in the brush and draw my knees up to my chin as Iki settles on the ground beside me. This is not very near to the place the pack will hunt tonight, but it is near enough that I will be able to hear the shouts and feel the thunder of the beasts' hooves. The lieutenant—their second in power, I understand—pitches his *tupaak* here, but the captain does not.

The captain is a pig, so his *tupaak* is in the center of the camp.

I lean my back against a pine, feel a familiar stickiness. I turn and get my braid in it. I pull my braid free and pick a thickened clump of resin. Chewing it will keep me alert.

A shout is the first indication that there is something more than a wolf pack abroad. I grin and thrust my fingers deeper into Iki's thick fur.

I cannot be with them, but that does not mean I will not enjoy myself tonight.

TWO

What the Stars Saw

The fight is swift. I do not see any of it, though I hear plenty. Shouts and swearing, sounds of wood splintering, and the stampeding of the hornless beasts.

That is my favorite part. The ground fairly shakes with the sound of their hooves.

My joy falters at the sound of one man's voice. He pleads with his beast to be calm and stay with him, while all around the others break free and run in terror. It is too dark to see whether his animal remains faithful, but it is strange how much I want him to keep his beast. A lump thickens in my throat.

The noise is dying down. The fight is ended and the pack is slinking away by twos and threes back into the woods. It will be an hour or more before they all are together again—this way they cannot be easily tracked back to the clearing in the woods.

I hear a long-drawn howl with a familiar taunting in the tone. I shrug off the thought of the pleading man and his hornless beast and smile. It is a joy to me that my brother is one of the cleverest of them all.

"I say—over here!" cries one of the Invaders. I stiffen. They are not talking about me, but there is a great scuffle happening just out of my sight. I climb a few feet up the pine. Four or five of our pack are fighting an ever-increasing crowd of men.

Below me, Iki takes a couple stiff steps forward, his hackles risen like a mountain ridge across his back. "*Tss.* Stay, Iki." I cannot have him give us away, and he is no match for strike-locks.

One of the pack breaks free and streaks for the woods. Pursuit is vain. I think it is Sila, two years older than me and taller than a female *tuttik* at her shoulder. In watching his escape, I lose track of the scuffle.

It is finishing now. They are holding someone—just one—in their midst.

"We have one!" An Invader shoves the captive forward. It is not thin enough to be Kavik, but it is the right build to be Tsanu. My chest tightens.

"Take his knife, fool!" Another man dives forward and seizes a knife out of the prisoner's belt.

I glance around the trees, searching for moving shadows. One of the pack may know who it is, or I will sight Tsanu and my fears will be put to rest.

I see nothing.

They bring the unfortunate man nearer to me. I can see how he walks, how he stands, and something drops in me, down to my very feet. I scramble further up the tree, almost blind with panic. After gaining about six more feet, I settle on a branch and strain my eyes. They have brought him before the fire on the edge of camp. The light falls upon the faces of the hateful soldiers and their captive. Blood runs down his face from the fight.

It is Tsanu.

But it can't be. He is the best of them all. How could he be caught? The question runs around in my mind like a ptarmigan until it comes to rest on the truth.

Many of our men were in the skirmish—now there was Tsanu alone. He had given them the chance to get away.

"Speak now, *savet*," snarls a soldier. "Or do you not understand us?" He is tall, the same height as Tsanu. Another, much shorter, stands beside him.

Tsanu's face is hard and blank as one of the masks we wear on festival days. Only his eyes burn. He does not want to speak. Once they know you understand, they can ask you questions, and sometimes in nasty ways.

I have certainly never let on that I understand them.

The shorter of the two interrogators strikes Tsanu and shouts something I do not recognize. I want to go to my brother, but they are wearing strike-locks. Nothing I have, not even courage, stands a chance against strike-locks.

Tsanu spits and shakes his hair out of his face. "I understand you, *kannuq*."

I would smile if I was not so frightened. Tsanu, too, has words they do not understand.

"Then hear this: we know your village is small. It will only be a matter of time before every criminal and thieving dog among you is rooted out. Save yourself and tell us your leader's name."

Tsanu lifts his head proudly. I know he will not speak.

"Speak!" One of them twists his arm. Nothing shows on my brother's face. Twisting arms hurt, but the boys of Tansilet used to do it just to see who could keep their face straight the longest. It was a stupid game, but Tsanu always won. Only the boys played that game—it made me glad to be a girl.

I grip the tree so hard that my palm is on the edge of cutting. Sweat has broken out on Tsanu's face, joining the blood.

They will break his arm if they keep on much longer.

The soldier lets go with a sudden gasp of breath as if it was his arm being twisted. Tsanu's face has not changed one shade.

"Perhaps fire?" suggests his companion.

A third man joins them. "Fire? What for?"

"We caught this—*savet*—" Tsanu's captor accompanies these words with a cuff— "in the attack on the camp. We are trying to get information out of him."

"That's a job for the captain, not for you."

"Aww, give that jaw to someone else!" snaps the short man.

"I'm going now, and I'd better not hear a word more about this. I'll find the lieutenant or the camp-leader." The man strode off.

"There's no sense in this," says a new voice—a man sitting at the fire who has done nothing as of yet.

Now he rises. "This kind don't do pain. Not the way we do. They train it straight out of them. I say we do away with him before wind of this gets to the lieutenant. At least then we'll get some satisfaction."

"Kill him?"

"Why not? He killed today, no doubt. It'll only be giving him what he has coming to him."

"The lieutenant will be angry."

"Perhaps, but who'll be able to prove he was taken alive?"

I sense something rising among these men. I have seen it in the village dogs when a savage mood comes on them. They get killing on their minds and they are not satisfied until there has been blood. Sometimes lots of it.

I have never seen this in people before—just dogs—and it makes my hair rise.

"All right," says the tall man, stretching the word out as if buying time to think. "This coyote's not fit to live. But it was your idea. On your head if the lieutenant finds out."

Tsanu's face doesn't change. I wish that it would just a little. He cannot die shut off like a closed door, closed to even me.

I saw a man killed once before. Tsanu and I were walking home late and two men were brawling in the street, mad with their fire spirits. They had fallen out of the drink-house, neither quite right in the head, and one stuck the other with a knife. I still cannot get the picture out of my head—the way the man stopped short, sagging over the knife in his side, and fell, limp as a dead fish.

They cannot do this to Tsanu.

Two men grip his arms, holding him. The third draws a knife. My limbs are frozen. I want to move, but horror paralyzes me.

I find myself a split moment later. I am gripping my knife, running at the men. None of them are holding their strike-locks—I may stand a chance.

"Halt!" a voice screams, not my own.

I halt as if the words are for me.

A tall fellow, taller than Tsanu, runs up, seizing the man with the knife and throwing him down. "What are you doing?" The firelight plays in the hollows of his cheeks, and his dark hair is unkempt.

"It's a local fellow. Making trouble. He's not worth anything."

"I daresay that is not for you to decide."

"Willow," says another man, "go back to your tent. You are too ill to be up yet."

"Perhaps, but unless I mistake myself, you are about to kill someone in cold blood."

The silence is uncomfortable.

"Take him to the lieutenant," says the man named Willow. "I will not say it again."

"The lieutenant will not care."

"I say he will." Willow throws back his head—a gesture my brother has made time and again.

The man with the knife picks himself up, a little dazed but brimming with the fighting spirit of a thrown dog. "Just this once, Willow!"

"This man has but one life. The fight is done. Do not commit a thing deemed a crime."

"He was attacking us." The taller of the men holding Tsanu gives him a shake.

I have sometimes seen a lone dog cower and crouch very still when he is outnumbered, hoping that his enemies will leave him rather than tear him apart. Tsanu is very still right now, and he does not speak.

The man named Willow unbuckles his strike-lock from his waist and lets it fall. His hand goes to the knife in his belt. "I will fight you, then. One at a time."

"You are ill yet. I see fever in your eyes," the short man says.

"Then we had better get on with it."

The tall man holding my brother spits a couple nasty-sounding words and shoves him to his knees. He looks up with an ugly glint in his eyes. "I will remember this, Willow Tam."

"As will I," says Willow, stepping between Tsanu and the men.

Tsanu's shoulders tense. Even bound, he stands a better chance running than staying with these men. And I am here. I can free him in the time it takes a hawk to swoop.

Willow takes another step, and the men slink back like rogue wolves. Tsanu launches to his feet.

Willow reaches out and seizes him by the collar. "Not so fast."

My insides tighten and I clench my fist. *Fight, Tsanu, fight.*

Tsanu fights like a cornered lynx, twisting and kicking and biting, but his wrists are tied. That is a great disadvantage, even against a man who is supposedly sick. Willow's friends come to help him, and Tsanu is caught again.

I clench my hand hard around my knife, imagining running at the men, but I know if I do, I will only be caught too. And I cannot save Tsanu with my own wrists tied.

"I will take him to the lieutenant." Willow jerks his head to the men who hold Tsanu fast. They haul him off in the direction of the lieutenant's *tupaak.*

The blood pounds in my ears. *Kavik.* I must find Kavik.

I burst into the clearing, my lungs on fire. Kavik is there, tying a strip of cloth over a skin-wound on one of the young men.

"Kavik!"

He glances up like startled deer and catches me as I fling myself at him. It is a relief to have his strong arms around me.

"What is it, Maki? Take a breath."

I don't. I pant and barely get the words out. "It's Tsanu. They caught him and took him to their—their lieutenant. They almost killed him. I am afraid the captain will have him shot with a strike-lock."

Kavik's face tightens, sharpens. His jaw clenches. "How is it that he was taken?"

"There were many," I say lamely, the words and reasons flying from me like a scattered flock of geese.

"There was a thick fight." One of the young men raises his voice. "He gave us a chance to run."

"Better than death," Kavik mutters with a bitter shrug. He takes up his bow, testing the tautness with his thumb, then looks to me.

His face is grim but the hand he puts on my shoulder is gentle. "Do not worry, Maki. I will have him back by the second moon." He lifts his head and whistles like he is calling dogs. Four of our young village men come, taking up their spears.

"Tsanu is captive," he says. "Come."

"Thank you, Kavik."

He gives me a curt nod. When he is preparing to do a hard task, he has little use for words.

"Kavik, may I come with you?"

He shifts his jaw, a thing he does when he is thinking. "No, Maki."

"But I may be of help—"

He starts to stride away from me. "No, Maki," he says again, grimmer, louder. "There may be killing. I do not want you there."

It burns my heart to sit by and do nothing, but I cannot argue with Kavik.

"I will send him home to you," Kavik promises. "Do not wait for us."

I stand, my fists balled in tight knots, watching Kavik and the four disappear into the shadows.

The forest is alive with the calls of the night creatures.

I have never been afraid of them unless I hear a wolf pack or stumble upon a *tuttik*. Most of the creatures would rather be about their business; we are like distant kin that move near but not with each other. I hear the cry of an owl, the grunt of a bull elk, the drawn-out cry of a wolf from afar.

A real wolf, not Kavik and his kind. The night is growing colder and the blue of the first moon is fading, giving way to the red of the second moon. I must hurry back to Tansilet.

The village is ominously still, save for the occasional bark of a dog. I think the sounds of the attack must have reached it, because this stillness is not one of peace. Our house is near the middle of the village, made by my father's father. The other dogs outside raise their heads as I tie Iki to the stake in the yard.

I slip inside and light a glim by feel. The house is horribly empty, and for the first time in my life—at least, since I was three—I wish I had Iki in the house with me.

Deep dread settles over me. I want to sleep—I am so very tired—but I cannot when at this moment Tsanu could be fighting for his life.

I go to the bear rug in the corner and wrap it around me, settling against the wall. I will sit here like some proud elder until he returns. I will not abandon him by sleeping.

Time goes on. Once in a while the dogs bark.

This time he will come.

But he does not, not any of the times I hear dogs.

My head is heavy. I feel myself drifting away. *He will return and see me sitting up in the bearskin rug, and he will tease me, but I won't mind. I will not mind so long as he is home and safe . . . .*

I wake to sun in my eyes. It is morning—not just morning, but late morning. I look to the wolf rug in the corner where Tsanu sleeps. He is not there.

My stomach tightens. I must find Kavik—if he is still alive.

Dread makes me sick, hardly able to see as I run my fingers over my hair, tucking back the locks that have escaped my braids. I glance down at them, black and glossy, hanging to my waist. They are filled with twigs and leaves, but there is not time to re-braid them. I run out into the morning, throwing the dogs each a joint, apologizing to them for the lateness.

The streets are astir—some of our own people, but mostly the Invaders, riding their hornless beasts. Some carry supplies and strings of dried trout upon their backs. Several unharnessed beasts pass by, dancing and snorting, driven by a handful of Invaders. These must be the ones set loose by the raid last night.

The Invaders have not acted thus for many seasons, not since I was just a girl. They act like they are leaving.

I ought to be overjoyed. But without Tsanu and Kavik, it means little.

When I reach the house of Kavik, his mother is sitting outside. "Where is Kavik?" I ask.

She looks up from the raw hide she is cleaning and her face turns grim.

"What is it, Maki? What want you with my son?"

"Is he home? I want to speak with him."

Her face is hard to read, but I know she is troubled.

"Please, *Aaga* Karima. I must speak with him."

She jerks a thumb over her shoulder to the hut, her wrinkled face still dark with brooding. "He is within."

I duck beneath the door, a flap of hide hung by bone hooks.

Kavik is lying beside the wall under a caribou rug. He is still, though his chest rises and falls. I step softly toward him. Tsanu says that within a house, I am like a *tuttik*—no sense of stepping carefully.

"Kavik?"

He twists his head to look at me, but he does not move his body. His face is haggard. His black hair, usually tousled, is oddly straight, as if it is a little wet.

"Maki." His face is a jumble of many things, but I can recognize two: he is in pain, and he is searching for the words to tell me something bad.

My panic overtakes me. I cannot be subtle. "Where is Tsanu?"

Kavik casts about, tries to find words.

"Where is Tsanu?" I demand louder. "Is he dead?"

"No, no. He is not dead," Kavik manages. "But Maki, we failed."

"They have him still?" I settle back on my heels. I can bear anything so long as Tsanu is still alive.

"Yes. We went where you said, but there were many men there, and we were discovered. Yikaq and Inukuk are dead. I was shot twice with a strike-lock."

Strike-lock wounds are dangerous. Many men die from them, and those who survive are sometimes changed forever. Kavik went because I asked him to, and now he is hurt badly. Yet all he feels is sorrow for me because he failed. "Kavik, I am sorry. Will you recover?"

He gives a forced little smile that is meant to reassure me. "I know I shall. It is my shoulder and leg. But I will not hunt for a long time."

I wish I could take his pain away. "I think they are leaving."

"Indeed?" He lays his head back down, facing away from me. "I wonder what that means." He does not try to speak again.

His wounds must be paining him a great deal. This is news he has wished to hear for ten long years.

I should leave him alone, but I cannot. "Did you see him?"

"Yes." Kavik does not turn his face back to me, so I have only his voice by which to judge the situation. "He was with the lieutenant."

The panic fights its way back up my chest. "Are you sure he is not dead?"

"Sila came to me an hour ago. He lives."

Relief spreads over me. Things are bad, but not beyond fixing. "But he is captive."

"Yes. I am sorry, Maki."

I do not know what to do, but I do not want him to be sorry. There has been so much trouble—so much went wrong last night. And he is hurt. "Do not worry, Kavik. It is I who am sorry that you were shot."

The corner of his mouth lifts slightly. He is trying to accept it, but he has little strength. For all his brave words, he is not well.

I must not tax him. He talks as though he will recover, but any wound may go bad and bring death. And strike-lock wounds are slow to heal. I sit, wondering what to say, until his eyes close. I hope he will sleep.

"Do not worry, Kavik," I whisper. "You did well. I will bring Tsanu home myself."

His eyes snap open. "You will not, Maki."

I shrug. "I must try."

"Promise me you will not."

I lean my arms on my knees. My legs are getting tired of crouching, and I want to stand up. "Someone must, and you cannot. Do not worry, Kavik. Your best warrior will be home again before the buds turn to leaves."

"Maki . . . ." His voice trails off. I feel guilty for arguing with him, but my mind is made up.

"I will bring him home," I whisper defiantly, so low that he cannot hear.

I push myself up out of the dirt, and instead of the traditional nose-to-nose farewell, I press my fist to my chest. "Be well," I say softly.

He looks smaller than usual, his eyes closed and the edges of his hair sweat-soaked. The sight sits low and cold in my stomach.

I will get Tsanu and I will bring him home. I will fix all of this, even if it takes everything I have.

"He is very ill," says Aaga Karima defensively when I step outside. She is sewing a *mukluk* now.

I stand in the warm sunlight, blinking down at her. Her quick fingers somehow capture me, flitting in and around the beads and leather. For a moment I have stepped outside of time and feeling.

I hear my voice answering her. "He is strong. He will recover."

She says nothing. Her fingers fly no faster or slower than before.

"I am sorry, *Aaga*. It was I who asked him to save my brother."

She shrugs her wide shoulders. I always wonder how Kavik stayed small, as thin as if he had grown within a fishing sluice, when he had a mother like her.

"It is as life runs," she says. "I am sorry about Tsanu."

I nod.

"Do you want chicory tea?" Her voice is like a peace offering, held out to me.

I shake my head. "I must go. I will have tea another day."

I flick my braid behind my back as I set my face toward the Invader camp. I have a job to do.

The camp is humming, men coming and going rapidly. As I reach its outskirts, I do not even know where to start.

Courage, Maki.

I run up to one of the Invaders, putting on my most innocent girl's face. They do not mistrust me as they would the young men. For once, I am glad for my age and my small stature.

"What is this?" My heart is in my throat. "Are you leaving?"

"We break camp tomorrow and march north." He speaks with the abandon of one who has been offered glory.

"For what?" I cock my head innocently.

"We have taken a man who has seen the greatest of the jeweled cities. He will lead us to it."

Tsanu? It has to be. But why would he use that story?

My heart crumples inside me. "And you will go to it? What—what happens if you do not find it?"

"The captain has his heart set upon it. If the dog is lying, he will die."

The legend of Inik Katsuk seems fated to come between me and my family. There is no city of jewels. I know this, Tsanu knows this, everyone in Tansilet and all of Uniap'nik knows. Tsanu must have been desperate to have sold his life for this tale.

The man walks away, figuring he has said enough, and for once, one of the dirty muskrats is right. He has said enough. He will be sorry that he said anything at all.

My mind races with thoughts, ideas for rescuing Tsanu, none of them suitable. But one thing I know: I cannot let him out of my sight. If I have to follow them away from Tansilet, I will.

By evening, I have two sets of Tsanu's clothes cut down to my size and his pack filled with the most important items for a journey: *pantak*, a knife, Tsanu's *mudi*, a bone needle, sinew thread, hooks, and a fire stone. But I do not want to leave.

I do not want any of this to have happened. I want Tsanu to come back, to be happy in Tansilet, to never have to bid our home farewell. I want the sun to run backwards, to take me to the time before it all went wrong.

I close my eyes. Our cottage is dark and smells of dried meat and preserves and root vegetables. It is the smell of home, our home.

Reaching into the basket where we keep our tools, I find the whetstone. It lies cool and smooth in my hand, like a threat. I draw my knife—the thin one I keep in my belt, not the wide one for cleaning animals. My fingers shake a little as I draw the blade over the stone in long, sweeping strokes.

It has to be sharp. Sharp enough to cut instantly.

I sharpen a little longer than I must. I know I am putting it off. But once I do this, I cannot go back. Finally, I lift the knife and test the edge. It is sharper than the edge of a fresh clam.

I do not want to do this. My braids are my pride. To cut them off will be like killing a friend. But I have to. I *have* to.

I can wait no longer. I take one of my braids in my hand and lift my knife.

My hands hesitate.

For Tsanu.

I pull my braid taut and slash through it before I can stop myself. I feel a sudden lightness as the braid slithers to the floor. It lies there, and I feel the place where it was and is no longer. A short stump of hair remains.

Tears fill my eyes. I look away from the braid, force myself not to think on it. It is like seeing a loved one lying on the floor. This is the same hair my mother braided before she left. And now it is gone forever.

I close my eyes. Tears run down my face and off the end of my chin. I take in a shuddering breath, slash again. It does not cut through entirely. I slash again and the braid falls.

Breathe, Maki.

I stoop to pick them up tenderly, and press them to my face, and cry.

I have cut open animals, ended life, all with the understanding of the need to survive; yet I feel the pain of it in this moment as I never have before.

The braids are gone. I am gone.

Courage, I whisper to myself. *This is for Tsanu. You would cut off your hand for Tsanu.*

This is true. I must not grieve like a child for what cannot be helped.

I go to the mirror that Tsanu gave me as a gift, bracing myself for the sight. I look strange without the braids, but not as strange as I feared. A few minutes of careful work trims my hair into a rough version of a boy's haircut.

I put on Tsanu's clothes and take up the mirror, drawing it up and down to see my whole self.

I look like a boy. What would those in Tansilet say if they saw?

It is time to leave, but my hands and feet drag. I do not want to leave this home empty, perhaps never again to be filled with our happiness.

Enough, Maki. You must stop thinking such things.

I blow out the light.

"I will return, I promise," I whisper to our little home. It says nothing, but its silence is answer enough. I shut the door and run out into the bluish light of the first moon.

The stars are bright tonight. I see the dogs tethered outside the hut, lying on their sides, stretched out on the cool ground.

My heart squeezes. I wish suddenly that I could take them all. I swallow back the tears and thickness in my nose.

"Iki," I whisper, snapping my fingers. He wakes and lifts his head. His yellow wolf-eyes watch me warily for a moment. My smell is right, but I look much different. He gets to his feet silently and shoves his nose against my hand.

That is all he needs. His tail gives an agreeable wag as I tie a rope around the thick ruff of his neck, and he falls into step beside me, his pads almost silent on the pebbly ground.

This is goodbye.

I refuse to look back as I head toward the camp. I look up at the stars instead and wonder what they think, seeing everyone who goes about in the night.

They would not know what to think of me, a small girl in boy's clothes, leading a wolf-dog almost as tall as herself.

THREE

Fire and Ash

The camp is alive, even at night. I take off my knife and stash it in my bag so I will not be seen as a threat. I rub a little dirt into my face. I even duck my head down to look—I hope—a little meek.

I walk right up to the nearest camp fire, hoping to be seen. There is no acknowledgment from the men as I approach. I am almost beyond the fire when a voice rings out. "Where do you think you are going with that wolf, boy?"

I start, then curse myself for a fool. I must not react. I must be straight-faced, like Tsanu.

"I hear you are leaving." I draw myself up a little. "I want to be a horse-boy."

"And where did you hear that? What concern is it of yours?"

"I want to work." I raise my voice enough to be heard. "I like the hornless beasts."

"The hornless beasts?" One of the other men howls with laughter. My cheeks warm, and I am glad they cannot see it in the dark.

"Quiet, Basher."

For a moment, it seems the first man is on my side. Then he gets up and comes over to me. He is tall and lean and looks like he has become strong by work. "We do not need another horse-boy."

"I like the beasts," I counter stubbornly. "This is my only chance."

"Sure it is." He folds his arms and leans his head back. I do not quite understand his words, but I understand his mocking tone well enough. It is all I can do not to pitch into him.

"You are not in charge, are you?"

"Enough, I am."

A smattering of laughter rises from the men.

I ball up my fists and step up to him, close enough to smell smoke and fire spirits and roasted meat on him. The hackles on Iki's neck rise.

"Want to fight me, do you?" He is amused, and when I swing at him, he catches my thin wrist. *Ai,* his hands hurt. I struggle against him, lapsing into my Tansilet dialect to give him some names I dare not call him in his tongue. Iki snarls, and it takes all my willpower to order him down. I would like to see this man put in his place. But I need the job.

"Rutter, what is this?" A quiet, matter-of-fact voice interrupts, the tone carrying a hint of reprimand.

Rutter lets me go and I turn to face the speaker, a solemn-eyed, bearded man.

The lieutenant. I swallow hard. I have never seen him up close before. His dark hair is streaked with gray, a thing you do not see from afar. Nor does one see the weariness beneath his eyes.

His eyes are jewel-blue, like Kavik's.

"This lad wants a job as a horse-boy. I was just turning him away. He'll only cut the tethers at night."

"I will not." I square my shoulders proudly.

"Why do you want to be a horse-boy?"

The lieutenant fixes me with his keen eyes.

I set my hand on my heart. "The hornl—the horses, they fill my heart when they run. It is as the sound of many *pannik.* I want to be near them. And I—" My voice quivers a little despite my effort. "I need the work. The pay."

The lieutenant flicks his eyes to Rutter and then back. I swallow, afraid those eyes will see to the bottom of me. "What about the wolf?"

"He is a wolf-dog. Not the same," I answer. "He will be no trouble."

The lieutenant holds out the back of his hand. Iki gives it a brief sniff all over, then returns to whatever his mind was on before. I do not know if I should be relieved or annoyed that he sees nothing wrong with the man.

"I will give you the job. There is not much pay to be had—" he says this as if they are all poor— "but pay you will have, and food."

He holds out his hand, and I almost recoil. I catch myself and grasp it, trying not to shudder.

But his hand is much like that of any other man, cool and firm and—if it can be—friendly.

"I am Lieutenant Ransom. If you cannot remember all that, call me Ransom."

"Ransom," I echo.

He smiles suddenly, wing lines appearing at the corners of his weary eyes. "Rutter, show him what we need. If there is misconduct on your part, I will be sure to hear of it."

Rutter agrees, tongue-tied, and Ransom turns and strides away. I watch his retreating back, straight and held up by firm, even shoulders. My heart warms with a throb of gratitude.

Fool! The thought follows instantly. I hate every one of them.

I snap my fingers to Iki. My bag slips off my shoulder and slams into the crook of my arm. Iki shies off, setting his yellow eyes on me with a look of reproach.

I haul the bag back onto my shoulder and duck my head under the strap so it will stay. "Quiet, Iki."

Rutter looks back at me as if hoping I have changed my mind. I start toward him, which reminds him he has somewhere to be. Muttering, he starts out toward the place where the horses are. Iki scents the air and quivers at my side.

"There are three hundred horse," Rutter says over his shoulder as we walk. "Do you understand?"

"Many," I echo.

"Yes, many. I suppose you have never seen a camp of war?"

I shake my head.

I tolerate his rambling talk as we approach our destination, but my eyes are for the horses. This is one thing I do not have to hide from Rutter or the lieutenant: I am fascinated by the animals, even though they so often bear the men I hate. There is something about their proud necks, longer and more graceful than that of any deer or *tuttik*, and their strong, lean legs. Their heads are long and shapely, with just enough nose and eyes—not overgrown like the *tuttik* or small and wedge-shaped like the deer.

One horse reaches out its head curiously, its ears swiveling toward me. Even in the dim light, I can see it is pale gray, almost glowing in the starlight. It snorts gently in my face. Its breath is warm and sweet. No warning of territory, no erratic threat of sudden death, just curiosity. I reach out hesitantly to touch it, and it does not shy from my hand.

"You've a quiet hand for a lad." Rutter raises his eyebrows. I wish he would stop talking. "But then again, that's a good 'un. She's a favorite of mine."

I wish she wasn't a favorite of his. I do not like him.

"Name's Rosita," he volunteers. "Means rose."

"Rosita," I echo softly. She blows into my outstretched hand, and I rub her nose gently. It is soft, with tiny hairs more delicate than anything I have felt on an animal before. Not like the leathery noses of the deer. This is warm and intimate and so very alive.

Rutter sighs loudly and Rosita pulls her head back. He has broken the magic.

"Come along. I'll show you where to sleep." Rutter strikes out in the direction of a cluster of tents. "No use hanging around the horses before daybreak."

I make a sign against evil behind his back, not to protect myself, but because he probably deserves it.

Morning comes and Rutter's rough hand shakes me. I am awake already, waiting for him. Without him, I would not know what to do with myself in a strange camp surrounded by rough men.

I shove the sleep gruffly out of my eyes. "I am up."

He leans back, his hands on his knees, and grins. "All right, all right, I see that."

He seems less impatient now that he does not smell like fire spirits.

I go to tuck my hair back and remember that it is not there. Instead, I let my fingers comb through my shorn locks, like a boy. A pang of loss shoots through me.

"Come now, lad! The horses won't wait all day."

I follow him out of the tent into the dark morning. The horses tethered on their picket line move restlessly, reminding me of our dogs at home. Perhaps they are hungry, or perhaps they sense change in the air.

Rosita is on the line, picking at grass that is not there. The area near the horses is eaten clean to the ground.

"You haven't had much to do with horses, have you?"

I hesitate, then shake my head.

"Just as well. I can teach you everything my way."

I draw myself up and eye the horses quietly.

"Don't startle them—they kick."

"I know that," I say. "Many beasts kick when they are startled."

"These kick out every which way," he answers dryly. "Don't suppose your deer can do that, can they?"

"They do."

"Not with bloomin' huge hooves, they don't." A spark of amusement enters his eyes.

I fold my arms.

I will be careful not to approach them from the rear or side.

"You can go up to their head or shoulder, and they like that just fine." Rutter sets a firm hand on the shoulder of the nearest beast.

I put out the back of my hand and the horse touches it briefly. It seems unsure of what I mean by holding out my hand—not like a dog. But it does not shy back.

"All right, follow close." Rutter heads down the line. I hurry to keep up with his long stride.

At the end of the line, he picks up a canvas bag and pulls out a couple brushes. "Here, I'll show you." He goes to the nearest horse and starts brushing down its back and sides with long, sweeping strokes. "Have you seen saddles?"

I nod.

"Good. We leave soon, so just brush around the saddle area, and down here—behind the front legs. Gentle, they can be touchy about that."

I nod again.

"When we're on the march, some of the men'll do their own horses, but today, we do 'em all. Start here, and I'll call you if I need you."

He shoves the brush into my ready hand, and I get to work. The better a worker I am, the less they will look at me sideways. I will need to hide my anger, for I must gain their trust. Nothing is more important than Tsanu's freedom.

✦

I am twelve horses down the line—and enjoying the company of these hornless beasts far more than I expected—when a figure catches the corner of my eye.

I stop short. It is Willow Tam, who saved Tsanu's life.

He is young—well, older than I am, but as young as Tsanu, perhaps younger. I look away quickly, lest he catch me staring, and rub my hands together to rid them of the dry, gray grime that covers them. I move to the next horse, Rosita.

She looks at me mildly over her shoulder, then blows into my trouser pocket. Her breath is warm and it tickles. I giggle before I remember that I am a boy and push her head gently away.

"I see you have made Rosita's acquaintance."

I glance over and stiffen. Willow Tam has come up almost beside me and is stroking Rosita's face. Her eyes close and she stretches out her head towards him.

Why does she have to like him better than me? If he hadn't been there last night, Tsanu might be free.

Of course, if he hadn't been there, Tsanu might be dead, too. But I shove the thought away. For now, it is enough to be angry.

I give Willow Tam a long stare and then return to my work. I do not want to reply. He does look wasted and ill, though—I can see the toll of the fever better in the daylight.

"It's not catching," he says softly.

"I do not care about that." I move past Rosita and to the next horse.

The grass rustles as he follows me. "You can take your time."

"Are you a horseman?"

"One of the horses is mine," he admits. "But that is not what I mean."

I scowl back at him. "What do you mean, then?"

"You live in the village, don't you?"

"No, I live in the camp. I'm a horse-boy."

He raises his eyebrows. "Is that so? Since when?"

He is asking too many questions. I round on him, trying not to look like an annoyed girl. I have seen girls act like this in the village, trying to be coy.

I toss my short hair out of my eyes and scratch my head with a dirty finger. The rising sun is in my eyes, and I can hardly see him. "Do you want something from me?"

He shakes his head slowly, debating how to answer. "No." But he looks long at me before he turns and leaves.

It is bright morning by the time the horses are finished. I must have brushed nearly thirty of them. Some three or four dozen men take their horses and ride off.

"Where are they going?"

Rutter shrugs his shoulders. "They rarely tell me."

"I thought we were leaving today."

He drops onto a log with a long breath. "So did I, lad, but as I said, what do I know? C'mere and I'll teach you to repair tack."

Rutter grabs a torn jumble of leather and metal and holds it up with one hand. "This here's a bridle. Goes over the head. Bit goes in the mouth, headstall over the ears, fastens below, and there you are."

I watch as he points out the parts, but I will have to see it done before I know it for certain. He lays it over his knee and unbuckles one of the straps.

"This is an easy one." He holds up the broken part for me to see. "The stitching's come out. It needs to be resewn."

He reaches into his jacket pocket and pulls out a leather kit. Inside he carries a needle, some odd, sharp-looking tools, and thread, thinner than the sinews I use.

"This here's a needle. Have you used a needle?"

I open my mouth to reply, but he says quickly with a sheepish laugh, "Ah, no. I forgot. You menfolk hunt, your women sew."

I shut my mouth and nod. He has unwittingly saved me. I must be more careful.

"Well, this is the needle we use. You thread it like so."

He thrusts the threaded needle into the cloth of his trousers and opens the kit again.

"With cloth, the needle slides smoothly, but this leather is thick. We pierce it with an awl first." He pulls out a sharp, pointed tool.

I touch it briefly—not on the sharp end. He thrusts it through the leather. It slides in easily and he pulls it back out. "Here, try—but watch yourself. One slip and you've gone clean through your finger."

I take it and pierce the leather promptly.

"Not bad." He sounds impressed. "Now the next one."

I do the next few, and he takes over to finish.

"And now for the stitching—"

He shows me how to do this, and I pretend to look a little dumb. I fumble it slightly so he does not think me too experienced. At last the bridle is done. He holds it up with one finger, satisfied. "Not bad for a first time, lad."

He glances at me with genuine pleasure. I simply fold my arms and stare.

The wind picks up, bringing a hot crackle and the smell of smoke. I whip around.

"What is that?"

I raise myself on tiptoes, which does nothing to help. Rutter's brow knits as he peers in the same direction. "Reckon it's a fire."

"It is not the season," I answer, even as a wave of dread hits me.

I run to the nearest pine and scramble up the branches. Rutter calls after me, but I do not heed him. I cannot tell what he is shouting anyway in the blur around me.

The pine branches scratch my hands as I scale higher and higher, sending a couple flocks of lover-birds flapping hastily out of my way.

A thick, pulsing tower of smoke rises slowly upward, dark gray.

Tansilet burns.

I am near enough to hear shouts and screams, the ragged barking of dogs, the smashing of wood and pottery. This cannot be happening. It is a nightmare.

But the smoke stings my eyes and throat even from here, proving that I do not sleep.

"No!" I scream. "They are burning it!"

I can see the blur of my cottage. I cannot see if it is standing or fallen or neither, but I must assume that it is burning with the rest. The little house I just bade goodnight and promised a homecoming—it is a thing of memory now.

My dogs. My mirror. My pottery, crafted by my grandmother for my parents' wedding. Kavik, trapped in his house with two wounds from a strike-lock, unable to defend himself or move.

My people, my kin, my clan.

I descend, my heart hammering in my throat. "No! They can't!"

I run headlong towards Tansilet. Nothing is clear in my mind, only an instinct to get as close to the hurt as I can, to save something or to fix it somehow.

"Wait, lad!" Long arms grab me, wrap around me, and drag me back. I sink my teeth into them, reaching back with my nails and running them deep into the side of a face or a neck.

"Ah—!" Rutter drops me with an oath, then seizes my wrist. I bite that too, but this time he doesn't let go. "Stop, boy! You can't run over there!"

"I will, you *kannuk!*" I shout.

"If it's burning, you could be killed."

"I don't care!"

"You will tomorrow—" He howls as I flail at his face with my free hand and catch his face.

"Serves you right, you son of a devil's antler!"

"Drucker!" he roars. "Give me some help over here!"

Moments later another hand, large and long-fingered, seizes my wrist, but it does not pinch. I notice the gentleness even through the red haze that fills my eyes.

I fight it anyway.

"Enough, stop!" The order is clear but not angry.

I jerk my wrist to no avail, but I stop, shoving the front of my short hair out of my eyes.

A man towers over me, a long, strong-jawed face and a brown-and-gray beard. His eyes are stern, but they hold a glint of concern. "Easy there," he says, as if talking to a hornless beast.

The man smells strange, like fire spirits and something else sharp and unpleasant. But he is neat and clean, not like a drunk.

I let out a long breath and raise one corner of my lip in a snarl. My rage simmers down to strong, strong hate.

I hate them. I *hate them.* I want to run at them, to hurt them, to make them all sorry. Sorry that they have ruined my life, ruined Tsanu's, and ended the life of my village.

But I cannot pull my wrist out of this man's strong, gentle hand.

So I stand still, waiting for him to relax his grip, still snarling.

"What is it?" It is not clear to me whether he asks this of me or of Rutter.

"The village," supplies Rutter softly. His cheek has two bloody stripes down it.

A wave of hate and pain washes over me and a surge of energy nearly knocks me down in a faint.

"Ah . . . ." The newcomer looks slowly at me with eyes that are deep, that I cannot quite read. He releases my wrist and I stand a moment longer, looking at him.

Then I turn and flee.

No one comes after me, but I have been ruined. The recklessness in me is drained out. I flee to the far hill that overlooks the burning village, throw myself down, and sob.

Everything except Tsanu is gone now. And I have no promise of his safety. Since yesterday, I have held in my mind the single hope of bringing Tsanu home, of seeing the approval in Kavik's face, of being a hero in Tansilet.

All of that is gone. What hope is there now?

I watch the village burn, sobs racking my shoulders until I can barely breathe. I tear up fistfuls of grass, ripping them in the vain hope that it will soothe the flaming rage in me. I want to run back down the hill and hit Rutter, hit him until he is sorry and calls off the men who are burning my home. I long to get my hands on that pig of a captain—he is the one responsible for this. He is the one who must pay.

All of them must pay.

"Boy, what is your name?"

I whip around and let my fists fly. The man throws up a hand to protect his face, but he does not fight back or grab me.

It is Willow Tam, and I stop only because he still looks sick.

I shoot him the ugliest look I can conjure. But he just sits there, looking at me with troubled eyes. I wrap my arms around myself and tuck my head down.

"Come, now. I do not mean to hurt you."

I whirl on him with a snarl and spit at him. It lands on the front of his shirt. I continue to stare him down, one corner of my lip raised, showing him the full force of my anger.

"You are not a boy, you are a bobcat!"

He says it more like a compliment than an insult. I stop short, shocked for one brief moment out of my anger, though not out of my grief.

He calmly wipes the spit off his shirt, his eyes on me. "It was wrong to burn your village," he says slowly. "The captain was wrong to order it."

"It was evil to do it!" I grind out. "You are all evil! *Evil!*" I lean into his face to throw that last word at him.

His eyebrows knit and he opens his mouth, as if forming words in his head. He does not say anything, but he does not close his mouth either.

Tears fill my eyes and I jerk my head away so that he cannot see. Let him think I am angry and not crying.

"I would have refused to do it. Even if I was not sick."

"Lies!" My voice is thicker than I intended. I had better not talk any more.

Willow Tam settles on the ground beside me. I look at him under my arm so he cannot tell I am watching.

"I don't know Captain Innes, so I cannot speak for him. But in the three months our company was stationed here, we did not hurt your village or steal a thing. Yet you attacked us last night. Some would believe it a just retaliation."

I make a scoffing sound.

"Many of us do not approve of these methods, mind, but we are still bound by oath to follow our captains."

"You said you would have refused."

Willow Tam puts his arm over his knee. "In this case, I would have."

I raise my head and stare long and hard at his sharp-boned face. "I do not believe you. Why would you cross him if you took an oath?"

"There is such a thing as right and wrong, my lad." He speaks like an older brother, teaching me a thing I do not know.

"I know it," I say quickly. I care deeply about justice and right.

Which is why I hate him.

"What is your name?" he asks again.

I stare at the burning village. Part of me is glad that I am not down there dying—the other part feels that I am, even up here. Part of me is dying.

Three or four minutes pass. At last, Willow pushes up off the ground and leaves. I am alone, alone with the crackle of the fire, with the growing sounds of the company making ready to leave behind me.

Ashes fly on the wind, like gray snow falling the wrong direction.

"Lad, where are you?"

It is Rutter's voice, calling me.

I cannot give up now. I must bring Tsanu home, even if I have to build a new one with my own hands. We will live and we will be well again.

I rise, wiping the tears out of my eyes with the heel of my hand. I catch at the ash in the air, capturing a few pieces in my hand.

I open the pouch I carry around my neck and tip the ash inside.

A part of the village will always be with me now. I will need every ounce of courage it can give me.

Rutter's voice comes again, husky and insistent. I press my fist to my chest and bid Tansilet farewell.

FOUR

In the Camp of the Enemy

We move out that same hour. I am glad the soldiers have no time to revel in their conquest; I will lose my calm if we look any longer upon my ruined village.

I ride in one of the wagons, while Rutter gets a horse of his own. I ask for one, but he looks at me like I am crazy. "I wasn't born yesterday," he scoffs. I do not understand what he means, but I will not argue right now. I cannot afford trouble.

I shift into a more comfortable position and trail my legs out the back of the canvas-covered wagon. I would rather walk, but our pace is too swift for me to keep up on foot. The road is rough, and every bump and dip of the wagon bruises my legs and jars my spine.

A broad swath of meadow stretches out on either side of us, and the place goes quiet and still in fear of the Invaders. There are ground-dwelling birds among these rocks and deer crouched in the tall grass, but only the wind dares carry on as usual, heedless of the passing wagons. My heart aches. These are the hunting grounds where Tsanu taught me everything I know. Just there, beyond that hillock, I made my first kill, a fine doe fat with the sweet fall grasses.

I was proud of that kill. She was in her prime, with an autumn coat of rich, warm fur. Kavik's *aaga* made the hide over for me, since my mother was long gone. And though Tsanu did not say he was proud, he told me it was well done, and that was as good as saying he was proud.

I look down between my knees. The ground, grass-patched and rocky, passes below me. The wagon jolts as it hits the rock, reminding me that every bump takes me further and further from the patch of forest and river I call home. For good, probably.

The wagon jerks to a stop. I drop off the end onto the cool spring grass and crane my neck to see why. I should have stayed on the wagon—I cannot see a thing.

"Just a pause, lad." The driver unhooks a pair of small canvas bags from the side of the wagon. "Stretch your legs while you can, and don't go far."

I do not give him the honor of an answer. But I have no intention of straying far. I have more important worries.

The quiet wind still smells vaguely of smoke—it takes a long time for a blaze that large to die down and for the air to clear. The birds can smell it too. They are quiet and anxious, their calls quick and short. The Invaders around me are so calm, so carefree, it is maddening. The fools cannot read the birds. I clench my fists.

Well, I will be quicker and smarter than they are. I will use what I know—and they do not—to stay ahead of them. I will make them all sorry when Tsanu and I run away, never to be found.

"What are you smiling about, little *savef*?" The driver comes around the side of wagon, looking surprised to find me there.

"Nothing. I wasn't smiling." My smile disappears instantly.

"You were. I saw you." He looks amused, as if he talks to a young child.

I glower at him and stalk away.

"Don't wander off. After these horses are done eating, we'll be on our way."

I don't answer. Let him worry a little.

The camp is rowdier on the march than when it was staked. Men mill about, shouting to one another, laughing loudly, leaning against their horses, and spitting smoke out of their mouths. I have heard of this smoking, but it seems odd that anyone would enjoy a fire in one's mouth.

I pass through them mostly unseen. They are too busy talking and laughing to notice me. That is good. The less they see me, the freer I am to move about and make plans.

I spot Rosita a little way from me, ridden by a man I have not seen before. My heart rises defensively. He had better treat her well.

Somewhere a thin, tinny horn sounds. I quicken my steps back to my wagon. Thankfully, it is easy to tell from the others. The horses are splashed white, as if with *mud*, and someone has sketched a fish, rough and blue, along the side of the canvas.

The thought of fish makes my stomach rumble.

"So you're back," says the driver in a loud, grating voice.

I shrug, jump back onto the wagon, and grip the side. It jolts almost immediately into motion.

We do not stop again until the first stars are showing over the sunset. The wagon in front of us rumbles to a slow stop, and ours does likewise a long ten counts later. A man on a rangy-looking horse rides down the line to my wagon and draws rein alongside us.

My driver hails him. "We stopping or no?"

"There is a little—ehrm—indecision up front. We'll know presently." He drops his voice confidentially, but he is still loud. It seems to be a habit with these Invaders. "Captain don't want to stop."

"Oh he don't?" The wagoner creaks forward on the seat.

"No, he don't. Wants to press on another three, four hours, past dark."

"And who contests?"

"Drucker and the lieutenant. Lieutenant thinks the men won't be able to set up well after dark—too much risk of stepping off a riverbank or getting lost in the dark. The scouts bring back reports of varied land."

That is true enough. These hills are full of small, twisty creeks and lakes, not to mention wolf dens. I imagine the wagons foundering in the dark and the Invaders running from the wolves, and a little knot of satisfaction settles in my stomach. It would serve them right.

"And Drucker?"

"Too many sick still. We have a few men that really should have been left in Tansilet, if it hadn't been burned." The man's horse fidgets and he pulls its head over, away from the wagon horses.

"Gotta go pass the word. It might be a few minutes before it's sorted."

The sun is gone behind the mountains, but I gaze after the lingering light. I do not have the feeling I sometimes get—the great weight of destiny. I am only tired and my head hurts from cutting my hair, but I know that this is a day I will not forget. From this day on, nothing will be the same again.

I am still watching the fading light over the mountains when the wagon lurches forward. The captain must have won. I swing my legs over the back and hum a little, a tune as old as the hills. My mother gave it to me the day she left, along with a blanket, bad feelings, and the legend of Inik Katsuk.

If she couldn't bear to stay in Tansilet, why would she leave us there?

Tsanu never talks about her, but he always stops me from speaking ill of her. Perhaps she was too crushed by my father's death to be blamed for what she did.

If Father was anything like Tsanu, I think I would have liked him very much.

The light has faded almost entirely and the stars are growing pinpricks in the pale night. If I were not surrounded by enemies, my brother a hostage, and moving further and further from the ruins of my burned home, it could almost be peaceful.

A shout echoes down the line and the wagon comes to a halt.

"Get down, lad. This is it for the day."

So the captain only got half his way. A smug warmth nestles between my ribs.

"Hey, lad!" Rutter materializes out of the dusky air. I fold my arms instinctively and a glare starts between my eyebrows.

Rutter stops in front of me, his hands on his hips. "Time to work, lad. Let's see how well you earn your keep."

I slide off the back of the wagon onto the ground, jamming my arm up into my shoulder. I forgot the drop was much taller than my elbow. My arm tingles with the jolt, and I rub it.

"Don't hurt yourself," Rutter chuckles over his shoulder.

All around the Invaders are settling for the night, pitching tents, starting fires. The tantalizing smell of food creeps through the air.

But *smoke*. A sick feeling rises in me. The smell of smoke makes me angry right now.

"We'll eat after we work." Rutter shoves his hands in his pockets as he walks. "Horses eat first."

"Horses eat first," I mutter. I bet he will set me to work and go feed himself, the pig.

"Once we're on the march, the men'll mostly take care of their own. We only brush down the wagon horses and officers' horses."

Half a dozen men are rigging lines from the branches of one tree to another, and already men are bringing their horses and tying them to the line with lengths of rope.

"We'll start on this end." Rutter grabs the horse on the end and pulls its head up. "A few of the officers do their own—Lieutenant's one of 'em. But you'll learn soon enough when you get to them and they're done. Won't take long, that, unless you're a dunce."

He slings the bag of brushes off his shoulder and reaches in, handing me a brush and a curved pick for the hooves.

"Get to work on these. I'll show you the grain later."

I start on the nearest horse—one of the officers' mounts. He is a black fellow with a woefully short tail. I reach down to clean his nearest hoof, and he stiffens his leg so that I have to use all my strength to pry it off the ground. But he pays almost no attention as I brush the saddle mark off his back, and he pauses only briefly to look at me when I brush his belly.

In two minutes, only sweat remains where the saddle and girth were. I move on to the next horse.

My hands are covered in dirt and sweat and horse hair when Rutter comes by with three other horse-boys and a hand cart full of sacks.

"Every horse's got a nose bag or a bucket." Rutter digs a wooden scoop into one of the sacks. "All of these get a scoop, the big ones get a little more."

Rutter moves down the line much quicker than I do. Soon I am surrounded by the quiet dark, brushing horses to the contented sound of their munching. They sound like the herds of caribou that roam the meadows near Tansilet.

So much is wrong with the world today, but somehow this is a comfort.

When I am done, I will sneak around and try to get a glimpse of Tsanu. I have only Kavik's word to tell me he is alive; I have not seen him.

I must know how he is. I must know the worst, and perhaps it will not be as bad as I fear.

I work quickly—I am used to caring for our dogs, so I know how to work fast. Every minute I save is one more I can spend looking for Tsanu before I am supposed to be in the tent, asleep.

Just as I am finishing the last horse, Rutter trudges up to me, the ruddy light of the fire playing on his hard cheek.

"This one done?"

I nod. I am not afraid of him, nor am I angry, but my mouth is glued shut. I will not say a word more to these Invaders than I must.

"Good work, lad." He draws from his pocket a small bundle. "Here's your ration."

Ration must mean food. I can see, plain as day, a piece of hard bread and jerky.

I want food, but not from him.

I suck in a deep breath and knock it out of his hands. "I will not take food from you." I stare defiantly into his surprised face.

He looks long at me. "How else will you eat?" His voice takes on a sharp edge.

"I am not hungry tonight."

"Look here, lad, I know it's been a devil of a day, but where we're going, you'll be regretting turning anything down."

I crouch down, still staring him defiantly in the eye, and pick up the food. I take a slow, deliberate bite, and swallow.

I make a guttural choking sound to let him know what I think of his food.

"Didn't say it was fancy grub." He turns and leaves me.

Rutter does not come back and he leaves no instructions, so I tie Iki to one of the wagons. He noses my hand as I crouch beside him. He knows I am sad and angry.

"Stay, Iki." He curls up dutifully and watches me as I steal through the shadows towards the center of the camp.

I stay in the shadows but try not to look suspicious. If I am spotted, I must have at least three good excuses. Even glimpsing Tsanu is not worth drawing attention to myself.

The wind is low and quiet, and I relax. I can hear everything, every footfall. Back on the picket line a horse blows, and near at hand one of the men burns himself while stirring a pan of food over the fire. His cursing is drowned out by loud laughter from his companions.

I must be nearing the center of the camp. It is quieter here, and I see the captain's tent just ahead. Ducking behind a wagon, I watch the dancing light of the fire play on the tent, crossed by a shadow now and again a shadow.

My ears strain toward the captain's fire, and I hear meat sizzling. Something scrapes against a metal pan, and a voice speaks—it sounds like the lieutenant. I slip out from behind the wagon, keeping my foot silent as it settles into the grass. Step by step I near the campfire.

Four or five men sit around the fire. Another half-dozen stand. These men hold themselves with an air of authority, like the elders or the strongest warriors of a village. They are wreathed in smoke, some of them breathing it out like hunters on a frozen day. Standing by the lieutenant is the long man with the gentle hands who stopped me from running back to Tansilet this morning—the man who smelled oddly of spirits.

A man with his back to me shifts a little, and I see the sleeve of his coat in the firelight. I may not know the captain's face, but I know the marks that denote a captain.

"Sergeant Nolan has been with me for three campaigns," the captain was saying. His voice is deep, but has a charming reserve, as if he is saving strength under it. "He dragged me three days across a desert when I couldn't stand on my own."

There is an appreciative murmur around the circle, and a couple men slap another—Nolan, I presume—on the shoulder.

But this Sergeant Nolan is of no concern. As the circle's attention shifts to him, I leave my eyes on Captain Innes.

He is tall, with hair that is sleek and kept far better than the former captain's. His face is smooth, but the firelight catches and plays off his long nose. His features, sharp like a hawk's, transform suddenly as he grins and then laughs in answer to another man's words.

"And I intend to," he says, holding out his glass for the fire spirits, which are being passed generously round by someone in the circle. "Inik

Katsuk will be the crowning achievement of my career."

One of the men takes a swallow and lowers his glass. "With all due respect, sir—"

"You don't know him, son," interrupts Nolan with a laugh.

"No, no," chides the captain. "Let him have his say."

"Isn't this Inik Katsuk a bit of a long chance, sir?"

"Have you ever heard the legends, Corporal?" The captain's face is gently amused, lit briefly by the glow of a smoke-stick as he thrusts it between his lips and then pulls it away between his fingers.

"That it is a city of gold, sir."

"And you shall have your fair share when we find it." The captain smiles. "In my company, every man benefits."

"So you are that sure that it exists?"

"Legends don't come from nowhere, Corporal. And with the Tansilet man's life in my hands, I shall have a sure guide."

"Do you trust him?" This question was accompanied by a guffaw.

"Not as far as a shotgun's length," the captain allows with a laugh. "But he is not the first man I've had to weigh and sift. He'll learn to tell me the truth, if he hasn't already."

I clench my fists. He doesn't know Tsanu. Tsanu can tell the truth and still send his enemy in the wrong direction. *Just wait and see, Captain. It is you who will learn, not Tsanu.*

"There's another in the camp," says the long man with the gentle hands, sitting heavily upon the log and running a hand through his graying hair.

"Another what?" The captain drops the stub of his smoke-stick and grinds it out with the heel of his boot.

"Native lad. Younger, more impressionable."

"Really? How long's he been with us?"

"A couple days. He's from Tansilet."

"Hmm." Captain Innes swings his gaze outside the circle, and I draw back into the shadows, heart hammering. Why should he choose this moment to look out beyond the fire?

In another moment, he returns his attention to someone who has come over to speak to him. I snatch up the chance and slink back towards the picket line.

"Where you been, lad?" Rutter greets me as I slip between two drab brown horses.

"Just looking around," I say, loud and clear. If I mutter, I may look suspicious.

"Well, you'd better turn in. We'll be up hours before dawn." He shoves a rolled blanket at me—it is colorless and scratchy. "Quartermaster's compliments."

FIVE

The Spear of Tslaniq

Iki's cold, damp nose shoves me awake. It is still dark. On the other side of the tent, Rutter is stumbling about, his boots as loud and careless as always. He must have let Iki into the tent.

I shove Iki off and rub the sleep hastily out of my eyes. My leg twinges and I rub fiercely at the knot in the muscle. I must have slept on a stone.

I duck out of the tent. The morning is cool and still, with not even a trace of light hanging on the eastern horizon. Iki presses against my leg. The fires all around the camp hang low, coals barely glowing. A big man stirs the closest fire, rousing it a little. He clangs a kettle over the coals and draws his coat closer around his neck.

I chuckle to myself. The man is weak—it is not cold.

Behind me a loud rustle sounds, and Iki whirls around, slamming his bony hip into my legs. Rutter emerges from the tent, scowling into the darkness, and sees me.

"You are up." He looks surprised.

My nod is probably lost in the dark.

"Have a seat." He gestures roughly to a log someone has dragged up to the fire. "Laramie will fix you something hot."

I sit down on the rough bark. The end of the log is scarred with fresh hatchet marks, evidence that it served as firewood last night.

"First time on the march, lad?" The one called Laramie grins up at me. He is an older man, built like a lean pine, who moves with an odd swing in his step, like a long-legged *tuttik*. A mustache hides most of his mouth, but his eyes gleam in the firelight.

"Aye," I say, imitating the reply I have heard from some of the men.

"Coffee'll be ready in just a minute. Best to take it piping hot."

I fold my arms on my knees and watch him work. I've never had coffee. Some of the travelers who passed through Tansilet over the years, like Sakka and Barbarian, drank it. But I wasn't even curious then. I remember thinking it looked dark and smelled bitter, and I was much more interested in playing with the dogs or hunting for berries. But I recognize the aroma that is stealing through the air, cutting the crisp smell of the morning.

Laramie plunks down three tin mugs and lifts the pot with his leather-gloved hand, pouring a black, steaming stream into each. "Drink hearty."

I pick up the mug and take a slow, hesitant sip. It is scalding hot and bitter and watery. But a second later a wonderful warmth seeps into my veins, and I take another sip.

"First time, lad?" Laramie raises an eyebrow and fixes me with a twinkling eye.

I nod, and he bursts into laughter. I fix my face stubbornly and take another swallow. I don't know what is so funny.

"Well, drink it while it's hot. Even in summer the air here has a nip." He takes a long swallow of his own, then stops. "Though I don't suppose you notice it any?"

"It is not cold." I take a longer drink, imitating him.

He watches me drink deep and nods, satisfied. "This stuff will make you a man. Want more?"

For answer I hold out my tin cup, and he refills it.

Rutter stumps up and crouches beside the fire. "Got any for me, bub?"

Laramie passes the coffee and Rutter downs his first cup fast. "You still have the touch, Laramie," he manages through tightly-shut teeth. I cannot tell if it is a compliment or an insult. Either way, he pours another cup straight away and downs that too.

"All right, lad." He slaps me hard on the leg and gets up. "Plenty of work to be had this morning."

Lieutenant Ransom is by the officers' horses when we arrive, sweet-talking his mare and brushing her down.

"Morning, Rutter," says Ransom.

"Morning, sir."

As we pass by, I hear a snatch of a cheerful tune.

Rutter slaps the nearest horse on the rump. "Start here," he orders brusquely, and stalks on through the wet grass to a dark, fidgety horse.

A moment later, he gives a loud oath, followed by a couple other words spit out too low to hear. Ransom lifts his head to look over the backs of the horses at Rutter.

But Rutter is not paying attention. He's leaning down, touching the dark horse with great care. The horse throws his head and kicks out.

"Easy, easy." Rutter strokes him at the high point where the mane and back meet. "I'll not hurt you. Not like that devil."

He clicks to the horse, pausing now and again from his swift, deliberate brush strokes to rub its mane soothingly. The beast stamps hard and jerks its handsome head violently up and down. I wonder that it doesn't snap its head off the end of its big neck.

I break my gaze and get back to work on my own horse. Ransom walks past, his horse's saddle over his arms, still whistling that funny, cheerful tune. It is hard to see the dirt with only firelight and the beginnings of the dawn to help, so I reach up and feel my horse's back and girth line with my bare hand. It is clean. I move to the next horse quickly, hoping to reach Rosita before one of the other horse-boys gets to her.

A tall figure passes close, almost brushing my sleeve. I sense rather than see him: a long, firm stride, the air of authority radiating from him like a wolf. I can hear him breathing as he passes.

"Rutter!" a voice barks out. I jump, and the horse I am brushing starts. "Is Fredrico ready?"

"Yes, sir." Rutter's voice is clipped, respectful. Ransom's whistling has stopped.

A quiver of something—not quite fear—twinges up my middle and I peer around the horse to watch. It is the captain.

Rutter is holding the dark horse—Fredrico, I guess—as he dances nervously about.

"Careful, sir. He's sore. You shouldn't use the spur till he's healed. Otherwise he'll be a trick to ride."

"I think I know how to handle a horse, Corporal Rutter. I once caught a stallion on the Rythian plains, broke it, and rode it to the nearest post. *After* I was left for dead."

"A horse is spoiled for great things who feels the spur on smallest occasions."

"Do not quote the ancient general to me, Corporal. Have you not heard that a disobedient horse is as useless as a disobedient army, and often twice the rogue?"

Rutter's mouth twitches angrily, but he turns the dancing horse around the right way again.

Captain Innes does not hesitate. He grasps the saddle, shoves a shining boot into the stirrup, and lands easily in the seat.

Fredrico springs free of Rutter's grasp and whips around at the captain's touch. The firelight reflects off the polished leather of boot and saddle; the stirrup is glowing, flickering red.

"When will the rest of the horses be ready? I do not want to wait for daybreak."

"Shouldn't be long, sir." Rutter sounds sullen.

"It won't be." His voice is both confidence and warning.

"Yes, Captain."

"How many do you have on the task? I see not all the teams are hitched yet."

"They will be soon. I have half a dozen on the job."

"I thought I told you to put more men on it."

"Two are ill. I hired a new boy."

"Did you?"

My stomach jolts. The captain searches for me from the vantage point of Fredrico's tall back.

"You, lad," calls Rutter. "Step out."

My heart clogs my throat. I step out from behind the chestnut I am grooming, but my eyes feel left behind. Everything swims a little.

"Ah. Native boy."

I swear the world goes silent. I hear nothing save my own quiet breath, in and out.

"Name?"

I do not answer—I think he's still addressing Rutter.

"Name!" His voice cuts through the air like a knife.

"Maki." My voice comes to me immediately. I am thinking clearly and calmly again.

"Hmm."

"He's a good worker," offers Rutter. I almost feel sorry for him. In the presence of the captain, he has shrunk considerably.

"Come here." Captain Innes pulls off a leather glove and crooks a long finger at me. Fredrico is still throwing a fit beneath him, but he rides it out like it is nothing.

I step out slowly from the safety of the horse into the open grass. Fredrico lunges forward, throws his head, backs a step. He is as wary as I am.

Captain Innes has not taken his eye off me. "Were you from that village?"

"Tansilet." I fight to keep my voice dry, measured.

"A little closer. Fredrico can't hurt you."

I come close, though I doubt that very much. Fredrico is jigging his head back, white showing in his eye.

Even in the weak dawn, the lines of the captain's face are clear and sharp. His mouth is determined, his shoulders strong.

Their captain is a pig. I can hear the laughter in Tsanu's voice still. If this man is a pig, I have never seen a warrior.

"Have you heard of a place called Inik Katsuk?" The world seems to have gone quiet again.

Inik Katsuk, the Seventh City.

I nod.

"Have you seen it?"

"I have only heard of it in tales."

"And do you believe them, these tales?"

My throat is dry. What do I say? Say no and throw Tsanu's story into doubt? Say yes and put myself in the same danger as my brother?

"Believe them?" A voice laughs. "A lad like him?"

Captain Innes's attention breaks away from me. He glances up with anger sparking in his eyes. "I did not ask you, Willow Tam."

I turn without thinking, see his bony frame standing just beyond the line of horses. Willow clears his throat and opens his mouth to speak, but nothing comes out. Suddenly I know he was trying to divert the captain's attention, give me a moment to think. To what purpose, I cannot guess.

"It is a legend we have," I say quickly. "But I have rarely left Tansilet since I was born—I know little but the tales."

Fredrico jerks his head again, stamping hard.

"Enough." The captain jerks the horse's mouth impatiently.

Fredrico lunges. Suddenly I am on the ground, my chest empty and painful, my head ringing, voices shouting above me, clamoring.

It is quiet in a split second. Have I blacked out? Hooves thunder away, and faces hover swimming over me.

"Back off!" Rutter bawls, shoving one or two of the horse-boys back, but it is Ransom who reaches out a hand to help me up.

I grasp it, pull hard, and only make it halfway to my feet. My lungs ache, and every ounce of breath drags in painfully.

"There now, laddie." Ransom hangs onto my arm. "Breathe slow. You got the wind knocked out of you pretty hard."

The captain is holding Fredrico, dancing still, at a distance.

"He's not dead?" His voice is brisk, businesslike.

"No, sir," Rutter answers loudly, but he will not turn to look at the captain.

I stagger upright and shove off Ransom's hand. "I am not hurt." Anger wells hot in my chest. If I am to pit myself against Captain Innes, he must see that I am strong.

A quick smile lights the captain's face and he gives a short laugh. "I like this one." He lets Fredrico go, and they shoot away in a swift rumble of hooves.

I have been breathing a little while and the other boys have dispersed when Rutter finally stops glaring at the place where the captain disappeared. He sighs and scratches his head. "Back to work, lad."

Everything hurts. I limp back to the chestnut horse and see with disgust that another boy is already brushing Rosita.

Oh, well. What do I care for Rosita? She's Rutter's favorite—that does not make her mine.

I set to picking the horse's hooves out, my chest protesting. I finish as quickly as I can. It feels like a bear is lying on my lungs. I straighten, letting the air flood back in, and stop short.

Willow Tam is looking at me.

A little bit of me wants to like him for trying to save me—and for saving Tsanu two nights ago. The rest of me hates him in spite of it.

Ungrateful, a little voice nags.

I want to turn away and ignore him, but I find myself looking over at him instead. It is a mistake. He takes it as an invitation and comes over.

My eyes are on the brush and the grimy coat of the horse under my hands. "What do you want?" I snap.

"I hope you aren't hurt. The captain didn't mean anything. His horse is not used to this land yet, I think. All the new smells." He gives a little laugh, shaky.

I grit my teeth. "I am fine, as you see."

Willow drapes his arm over the rump of the horse. "I mean it."

I glance up at him. His dark-circled eyes are lit with genuine concern. A little corner of my anger melts.

"I will be all right," I say grudgingly, brushing faster. "I'm just a little bruised."

"Good."

Instead of being grateful, I am annoyed. "Why should you care?" I must be careful, or I will begin not to hate him.

"Because—" He lifts his head to look over the horse's back. Then he lowers it close, his nose wrinkled in a look of confidence. "Because you're not a boy, are you?"

A shock runs through me, like when I touch Iki on a stormy day.

"I—what do you mean?" I've ruined it all.

Stupid Maki, found out on the second day.

"Don't worry," he whispers. "I don't think anyone else knows."

"What do you mean?" I repeat stubbornly, straightening my shoulders, drawing myself taller.

"I saw you in the village four days ago. With braids."

Oh. That is a bit hard to explain away.

"You cannot tell a soul," I hiss, drawing my finger down the side of my throat.

He does not look threatened. His gaunt face softens, like he is afraid of scaring me. "I wouldn't."

I start brushing the horse harder, my heart pounding. I race through the possibilities: who else could have seen me, what will happen if anyone else finds out, how long I can really keep up my disguise, what I will do if Willow proves untrustworthy.

"I won't tell a soul." Willow leans more heavily on the horse's rump. "But you have to watch yourself. I will watch out for you too."

"Why should you care? I can take care of myself."

He shrugs. "I don't know. Because you are alone, I suppose."

It's a fair reason. Especially alone in an army camp full of my sworn enemies.

"And you won't tell anyone?"

"I already said I wouldn't."

"Then . . . it is all right if you watch out for me."

A smile bursts out on his bony face and he holds out his hand. "I'm Willow. What is your name—for real?"

"I am Maki. My name is the same. They can't tell either way."

He grins at that, and I cannot hate him as I should.

"Good day, Willow Tam." I move on to the next horse and he does not follow me, but I am not alone now, and it makes me happy, just a little, deep down.

"Captain's a bit tetched." Laramie the cook touches the side of his head with a gnarled finger.

I dig a piece of meat out of the beans on my tin plate and feed it to Iki. The fire feels good on my aching legs. After a day on the road and an army of horses to brush down, I cannot afford to turn down a hot meal.

"Since he's hit this forsaken land—no offense, lad—what's your name, again?—he's thought of nothing but finding those lost cities."

"All brilliant men are a little touched, I find," drawls one of the others, the one I have heard them call Jeremiah. He lies on his side in the grass, tracing patterns in the dirt beside the fire with a stick. He is the maker of maps for the army—a tall, granite-faced young man with a deep voice and secretive gray eyes. He is the only one, I have noticed, who knows how to move quietly and listen to the land. For an Invader, he seems to have some sense.

Laramie guffaws. "Not old Tracer Puckett. Any of you fellows knew Tracer Puckett?" He stops and looks around the circle. There are some half-dozen of us, including Rutter, gathered around for the night.

No one speaks up for the memory of Tracer Puckett. As for my name, which he can never seem to remember, too much time has passed for me to supply it. But Laramie doesn't seem to care.

"That man was as tetched as an inside-out cat. Thought the world was ending every time the sun went down, shod his horse backwards, tried to eat his leather boots once. Nothing brilliant about him."

Jeremiah does not seem bothered by this contradiction; he is more interested in the pattern he is drawing in the dirt.

"Do you believe there is no city, then?" I bury my cold fingers in Iki's ruff.

"Me? Nah." Laramie laughs. "Who believes in such things?"

"The captain," says Jeremiah without looking up. I cannot tell whether or not he means it to be humorous.

"But a city of gold and jewels?" Laramie clatters the ladle in the pot. "It's too much."

"I'll believe it when I see it," puts in Rutter from his log. "And not before."

Jeremiah's pattern is coming clear. I recognize in precise, deft lines the winding rivers and sloping hills of this region. I watch his hands, mesmerized.

"But not every man is Captain Innes," puts in the oldest of the horse-boys. "You've heard the stories about how he brought twenty men through Yarnat pass alive, or how he charted the south sector of the Dernes and fought off tree dragons besides. If there is a city of jewels, he'll be the man to find it."

Grunts and grudging agreement went round.

"What's it called again?" asks Rutter. "Inuk—Inik—?"

"Inik Katsuk," I supply quietly. This talk bothers me, and I am not sure why.

"What's that mean?"

"Highest mountain."

Rutter leans his elbows his knees, skeptical. "So it's up a mountain?"

I shrug. "It sounds so. I've only heard tales. Even among our people, the tales are different." The thought of my people is a pain inside me, keen and lingering.

"Do you believe them?"

I look up quickly. Willow at the edge of the fire.

How long has he been here?

I look down and ruffle Iki's ears. "Maybe. As I said, they are only legends. None of us are fool-brained enough to leave our homes and go looking. Passing travelers say it is real—though they have other reasons for believing it. The better stories they tell, the better their supper is."

An appreciative laugh rises. The men understand this motive well.

Laramie gets up, waving Willow into the circle. "Willow, you're hardly back on your feet. Sit by the fire, it's warmer here."

With a reluctant smile, Willow heeds and sits down across the fire from me. He glances warmly my way.

I do not quite smile back, but I do not frown, either. He saved Tsanu's life, after all. When I free Tsanu and we run away together, I will remember Willow's courage. If there is one Invader I can forgive, it will be Willow Tam.

"And what do you think of Inik Katsuk?" I ask, curious.

"I don't think it exists," says Willow. "But that does not mean I wish ill on this journey. Perhaps it will be useful in its own way."

Laramie grunts. "If we don't get led off a cliff because that native *savet* says the Inik place is over the edge."

Laughter sounds here and there around the circle, dry and bitter.

"No, not this captain," says the horse-boy. "He knows how to handle men, including that *savet*."

I stiffen and edge further from the fire, an angry flush starting in my face, but a new voice breaks the night air from outside the circle. "I heard a rumor that the captain's horse ran someone down." There is an immediate stir of respect, like dogs when the leader of the pack approaches. The long man with the gentle hands and the gray-brown beard is coming.

I freeze inside, and my fingers clench in Iki's coat.

"It's Drucker," hisses one man.

An uncertain mutter runs through the men. A couple of them look uncertainly at me and then at the newcomer.

Jeremiah, lying practically on my feet since his map has grown, seems to sense my nervousness and murmurs, "It's the doctor. Medicine man."

Oh. Nothing wrong with that. All the same, I can't let him look too close.

"I am fine." I get up as easily as I can with my bruised back and sore chest. "Not hurt."

Drucker folds his long arms, looking me up and down. "You sure about that?" His voice is curt.

I nod.

He steps forward and lays his hand on my flat chest. "Breathe. Deep," he orders, and I do so. Then he lays his ear beside my chest and orders me to do it again.

"I am not hurt," I insist.

"Very well." He straightens and looks down at me sternly. "Just had to do my duty. But you come if you feel pain in your bones or anything sharp—like a knife, you understand?"

I nod again.

"Goodnight, boys." He strides away and leaves the circle strangely quiet.

"Well, lad," says Jeremiah in his deep, lazy voice, his stick still tracing new hills and plains. "As you have heard the legends, why don't you tell us what they are?"

I lean my arms on my knees and stare into the fire. A pain sits low in my chest. My mother's soft arms and sweet voice are as clear in my memory as if it was yesterday, but I do not want to think of her. Instead, I try to remember the look on Aaga Tiqa's face the nights she told this story.

I remember burrowing in furs, lying upside down on the floorboards of her house. Aaga Tiqa had a nice house with a wooden floor. She would tell it during the deep of winter, when our fathers—not mine, for he was dead already—were out hunting seals and storms were blowing in from the sea. She knew the best thing to drive worry from our minds.

With a deep breath, I lower my thoughts into the tale alone.

"Let me tell you a story that happened so long ago that only the hills and rivers can remember the time. The land lay differently: some cliffs were steeper, some hills were flat. And in that time, there was one man who was greater than all the others. His name was Tslaniq."

Iki raises his head and whines into the night.

"Hush, Iki," I soothe, and reach down to scratch his head.

"There was nothing that Tslaniq did not have. He was strong in battle, he was fair to look on, and his gold and silver, it was said, could be poured out into a river and not be carried away, but stop it from flowing."

Rutter gave a long, approving whistle.

"But Tslaniq was proud," I continue. "Not the pride that comes with doing right and leading your people well, but the kind that leads your people to destruction because greatness has blinded you."

Willow leans forward on his arms, intrigued. A touch of happiness wicks up inside me.

"He was a great conqueror. He ruled well and justly, and every place he ruled grew prosperous under his hand. But because he was proud, he was not satisfied, and he desired the one thing he could not have: Inik Katsuk."

"Why couldn't he have Inik Katsuk?" Jeremiah narrows his eyes.

"Because Inik Katsuk was different. It was for the brave and the good. It was not the sort of place that can be found by conquest. It was found when a man was tested and found pure—when he sought it not for himself, but for someone else."

Willow's eyes hunger in his thin face. "Did Tslaniq know this?"

"He knew, so the legend goes, but he was proud, and like many, did not see his pride as a flaw. He thought by might anything could be attained. So he set out to find Inik Katsuk, taking with him only his faithful friend, Nanik. Now Nanik was a good man and content to do good without being seen, and in this way, he was the better man." My gaze strays to Willow, who is watching me intently. I take a deep breath, past the ache in my ribs.

"Many long weeks of travel they passed together, and many dangers they encountered—windstorms, wolves, lightning, sickness—when a deep suspicion took hold in Tslaniq's mind, and he began to distrust his friend. He feared that Nanik had only come to take his glory."

"But he hadn't," says Rutter.

"No, not Nanik. Yet Tslaniq began to treat him badly, keeping him away from the maps, watching him of nights, speaking ill and not good to his face. He forgot how faithful Nanik had been in their hardships, risking himself as much as ever Tslaniq did. At last they fell to arguing, and Tslaniq, as lord of the lands, sent Nanik away, swearing he wanted never to see his face again."

Here I always asked Aaga Tiqa what happened next. Whatever I thought of the rest of the legend, I loved Nanik's loyalty.

"But Nanik, when he had gone a little way from that place, called to mind the oath he had sworn in friendship to Tslaniq: 'Friend I am to you, and naught shall change it. I will follow, through ice and through fire if need be.' And he spoke his oath again in the darkness, with only the stars to witness, and turned around and followed him. The way was hard, and Nanik was beset with many trials. He was hunted by the *ska-ana*, great monsters of the sea who followed him and tried to snatch him from where he traversed the ice and the shore. Wolves followed him, and he fought a great white *nanuk* on his way. Many times he wished to turn and go back to his home, but he did not. He pressed on after his lord, hoping to find him, for a great foreboding had fallen upon him."

"And I bet something bad happens now," says Jeremiah, smoothing the dirt with the side of his hand and starting afresh.

He has good instincts, this Jeremiah.

"As for Tslaniq, he came to a dark place through which he had to pass to reach the Seventh City. He was not afraid, for he was proud, and thus far nothing had withstood him. So he entered boldly, as if to challenge the evil that lay within. But once within the dark place, he heard a great sound—like a *nanuk*, but far greater."

"Was it a dragon?" Rutter leans forward, hopeful.

"A dragon?" I scoff. "It was a beast far more terrible than dragons. The Tiriarnaq, the weasel-bear—a savage white beast that towered over all bear-kind and had not their lumbering way but went swift and lithe like a weasel. Yet even this did not frighten Tslaniq, for he thought only of the glory he would gain if he killed the beast. A great combat ensued, and hours passed as they fought. And now, at last, there came into Tslaniq's mind the thought that he would lose this battle and the evil Tiriarnaq would be victor. But even as he shouted aloud the ancient words, that he might be ready for death to take him, Nanik came to him and threw himself also into the battle against the beast."

There is silence around the fire except for the scratch of Jeremiah's stick. Even that stops now as he looks up, wondering why I have paused.

"And thus it happened that together, Nanik and Tslaniq slew the king of the bear-kind. And when the thing was ended, Nanik fell to the ground, covered in many wounds. Stricken, Tslaniq knew then that he had been a fool, and he begged forgiveness of his friend, which Nanik granted even as he died. And as if through a mist of rain, Tslaniq looked up and beheld before him, on a far hill, the great city Inik Katsuk."

The men's faces are still and the snapping fire makes the only sound. Even Iki is listening.

"But Tslaniq knew then that he was not worthy to gain that city. He went only to its gates, asking their keepers to accept his friend and bury him as a hero within. Then he went to a hill outside the city and there carved for Nanik a memorial, a great *totem* raised for all to see. And he went to his home in mourning, and once every ten years, he would journey again to the gates of the city, bringing a portion of his vast riches as tribute. And he was ever after known as a great king."

Rutter lets out a low whistle. "Now then, that's a downer."

"It is not." I lift my head, indignant. "It is a story of greatness."

"Greatness is as greatness does." Laramie gives a short laugh. "I'd rather stay alive, I would."

"Leave be, Laramie." Jeremiah rolls over and sits up to look at both Laramie and myself. "I like a good hero-story. I daresay more men would be men if they took them to heart."

He jabs his stick in my direction. "Just you keep believing those, lad."

Not many days afterward, the captain comes to the picket line and takes Rutter aside.

I hope Rutter has done something wrong. That way both of them will be inconvenienced.

From a distance, I spy the captain gesturing toward me. Rutter's voice carries across the line of horses. "Sure, Captain. He is just here."

I freeze. The captain is looking for me.

Innes gives Rutter a brusque nod and strides down the line in my direction. I duck behind the horse I am brushing, hoping he will miss me in the dim light.

It is too late. He has seen me.

"Boy, have you eaten yet?"

"No. We are not even finished with the animals."

"Rutter has orders to bring you to my tent when you are finished. And—" He gives a hard sniff. "Wash up."

I spit after his retreating back.

SIX

A Trick of Fame

Despite my defiance, I wash and take care with my appearance before I go to the captain. After all, I want to avoid trouble, not seek it. And if luck is with me, I may get a glimpse of Tsanu.

"Lucky lad, invited to dine with the captain," Rutter grins, dusting the horsehair off his hands and tossing his brush into the bag. "Most men never get the chance, and you aren't even in the service!"

I think he just envies the food.

"I do not want to."

He folds his arms and clucks his tongue in mock reproof. "You have little choice in the matter, lad. Just go, eat. And tell me how it tasted."

I was right. It is the food he is thinking of.

Rutter leaves me in the doorway of the tent, nodding at the two soldiers who stand watch. I push through the flap with my shoulder and squint in the sudden brightness.

"Ah, the lad!" The captain sets down a book and comes toward me.

In the lamplight he is fair to look on. His black hair is neatly brushed, and his teeth show white inside a smile like the sun. He is a fine man, I admit to myself grudgingly.

But he has my brother, and for that I cannot forgive him.

"Tell me your name again, lad."

"Maki."

"Maki." He thrusts his hand out to me, friendly-like. "Roger Innes." He clears his throat and gives a start like he has forgotten his manners.

"Come! Come, sit down."

I move silently to the seat he indicates and sit down stiffly on the edge.

He puts a smoke-stick in his teeth and holds it as he lights it. The end glows briefly with fire, then disappears in a puff of smoke. He pulls it out, holding it between two fingers, and looks up with a pleasant expression.

He wants something from me.

A gust of cold air enters and Lieutenant Ransom ducks in, giving a "sir" to the captain and a nod to me.

"Is Drucker coming?" asks the captain.

"He is." Ransom takes a seat beside me.

Drucker pushes the tent flap aside and I sense a hush in the other men. "Venison smells good," he says, striding across the room to the table and jerking out the chair next to mine. "That man from Tansilet, you feeding him?" Drucker's look to the captain is sharp.

"Yes."

"He doesn't look it."

"Him? He is never hungry."

Drucker looks unconvinced.

"The truth is, Surgeon, he refuses to eat much of the time. There is nothing I can do about that." He cuts a thick slab of meat and drags it onto his plate. "Help yourselves."

Ransom serves himself and then hands the tools to me. I am not used to these eating-tools of the Invaders—at least not the pronged tool you eat and serve with—but I do my best.

Instead of eating, the captain leans back, resting the hand with the smoke-stick on the table. "So, Maki. You've lived a bit."

I do not know how to answer. I think he means to flatter me, but I am not sure how. A person can only live as long as he has lived.

"I suppose," I answer stiffly.

"I was impressed with you the other morning. Lads like you are just the sort that make a name for themselves in my company."

"I am not part of your company."

He dismisses this with a wave. "Enlisted or no, that is a small matter. What makes the real difference is whether you are willing to be of service. Why, I had a lad along not much older than you—a mapmaker—when I was scouting the Parmyla jungle, and not only did he earn the distinction of making the only comprehensive survey of the territory, he earned himself favors from our king and queen for saving the life of their grand-nephew, a gentleman adventurer. And all because he kept his eyes sharp."

I wonder if he is speaking of Jeremiah.

The captain takes a break from his talk to eat a few bites, and there is a silence at the table.

"I trust the food is to your liking?" Ransom addresses me. "Our cook was taught how to prepare the venison by an old hunter from Kuypuk. A fine man, that hunter."

I stare at him a moment, surprised that he would speak of a man like that as a friend. But there is no lie in his eyes.

I lift my chin a little. "The food is better than the provisions I have had here."

Drucker clears his throat loudly.

"You tell stories, you and your friends in the village?" asks the captain, changing the subject.

"Yes."

His smoke is going to waste, winding lazily upward from the stick.

"What sort?"

I know what he is after. I will play his game the wrong way.

"How the Hawk Got His Sight," I say with utmost solemnity. "How the Sea Became the Color of the Sky, The Berry-Picker, The Athssan—"

"Those are children's stories." The disgust in Captain Innes's voice is supposed to shame me and make me want to prove myself a man.

"The Athssan is not for children," I protest. "It is as terrible and real as the night sky. Do you not know any stories, captain? What do you want of me?"

"Listen well and you will hear. I have heard from the men that you told them the story of Tslaniq and his quest. A story of Inik Katsuk, the seventh and greatest city of Uniap'nik."

"Perhaps in the past Uniap'nik had great cities." I look at him intently. "But no longer. You will not find any now."

The captain leans forward as if about to share something great and dear to him. His brown eyes light with an eager glow.

"Everywhere I have gone, I have sought and triumphed: the Nuvian frontier, the jungles of Havast, the uncharted territory west of the river Rein. But of all places that I have set in my sights, Inik Katsuk is the greatest. I have heard tell of the great cities of Uniap'nik, and I have passed through many places which claim to have once been one of the great cities, but no one—until this captive from your village—told me he could lead me there. It is more than fate, lad. It is destiny."

I swallow, trying not to let him see me do it. Tsanu has run himself into deep trouble. And so have I.

The captain sets the smoke-stick between his lips and takes a deep breath. He blows the smoke from his mouth, then grinds out the fire on the edge of the table, leaving a ruined stub. "Do you know anything about this Inik Katsuk?"

I do this for Tsanu—I must not hesitate. I lean forward and meet his sharp, direct gaze.

"Only in legend."

A small smile starts on his face. If it were not for what he has done to my brother, I could almost like that smile.

"I'll take it."

Fredrico throws his head back, shaking it and rearing off the ground.

"Now, now—easy, boy!" Rutter reaches up with a flat palm and pats the horse's neck. He drops his voice. "Bloody fool. Maki, fetch me some rags and water."

I set down my curry brush and pick up a wooden bucket. We camped near a stream last night, and it is not a long walk from here. But I will have to walk near the captain's tent. I have been avoiding him all week, ever since the dinner.

As I pass the tent, larger than the others and brightly lit in the dark morning, a flash of familiar movement catches my eye. I know it by instinct, as a baby senses the difference between its mother's arms and a stranger's, as one recognizes one's brother in a crowd from his back alone.

It is Tsanu, chained to the axle of the nearest wagon. His face is bruised. There is a cut just below his unkempt hair and another along his cheekbone, but he still looks strong. In the dim light, I can just make out on his arm the remnants of the stag that I painted on his arm the night of the attack. Our warriors always washed off the evidence after a fight, so I never knew how long the *mudi* would last. But there it is, a sign of hope.

And he is alone.

I step out of the shadows, into view. At first, I think, he doesn't believe it is me.

"Maki?" He starts partway up, as far as the chains will let him go.

I take another step forward, almost shy. I can feel the wind blowing on my bare neck—if he has not noticed the changes, he will in a moment.

"Why are you here? What are you doing?" Tsanu's gaze sweeps me up and down, from my shorn head to his clothes, hemmed and cut down to my size.

He wears the same look he gave me once when I accidentally broke up a training fight with the warriors—like I have ruined some plan of his.

I crouch down beside him. "I came with the Invaders as a horse-boy, taking care of the hornless beasts." My voice is dry and I am having trouble getting the words out. "I have come so that we can run away, when we get the chance."

"Maki, Maki—"

His hands—are they thinner than before, or am I misremembering?— grip my arms firmly. His dark eyes bore into mine. "What you have done is rash. I want you to collect your things and leave. We are not so far from Tansilet—"

I shake my head, my throat filling with a dozen strong protests. One bursts out on its own. "You cannot send me back." My voice catches in my throat. "They burned Tansilet."

Tsanu's face goes blank. "What?"

"They burned it. The day we left."

"Is—did you—?"

"I don't know, Tsanu." My voice catches. "We might be all that's left."

I wish I had not said that. His face is stricken and he has no words. I am not used to seeing him like this.

I lean forward. "Tsanu, one of these days I am going to free you, and we will run. I just have to find the right time."

"No, no." In the darkness I cannot tell if there are tears in his eyes, but his voice is thick. "You cannot stay, Maki."

"I came so that we could escape. Besides, we are many days away from any settlements."

"I do not care. The wilderness is safer for you than this camp."

"They think I'm a boy. They are paying me—a little."

"But if they discover you are girl, what then? This is no place for you, and if they find out you are my sister—"

"They will not. I swear it."

"Maki, no. Swearing it is not enough. You must leave."

"I cannot, Tsanu." I begin to back away. No one has noticed us yet, by some wonder, but I cannot count on it any further. The more the camp wakes, the greater chance we have of being caught.

"Maki, come back, please."

I hesitate. If something happens to one of us, I will never forgive myself for parting from him like this. "You cannot stop me," I say softly. "I am doing this for you. You will understand one day, when the time comes and we flee together in the night. I am not leaving you."

"I would rather die than have it go ill with you, Maki."

I know that.

I am annoyed that he thinks he must say it, and especially that he has mentioned dying.

My voice turns gruff. "Peace, brother. Trust me."

"Maki, please."

"Our time will come, Tsanu. "

He lets his breath out slowly, and I see his shoulders sag. We never fight—and now, when he probably has to fight the captain or his guards every day, I fight with him.

"I am sorry, Tsanu." I crouch back down beside him.

He takes my hands in his. "Use caution. Do not be rash."

"I will try."

He grips my hands harder; he is almost stern. "You must promise me."

I hesitate, because to be rash is my way, and sometimes, though not always, it has helped me. Even so . . . .

"I promise." I set my hand on my leg above the knee to swear. He relaxes just a little.

"Farewell, Maki. Do not come to me unless it is absolutely safe."

"I will not." I lean my head against his and we press our noses together for a long moment. "Be well."

"Be well," he echoes softly.

I turn and run to the stream to make up the time. Rutter is surely noticing by now that I have been gone too long.

Raised voices reach me before I reach the line. In the dim light of dawn, I see the captain's tall figure standing beside Fredrico.

I should have hurried with the water.

"It is not bad." I recognize the flippant voice as Innes's.

"I am telling you, sir, it is. It's three weeks I've been treating him. He will settle if you don't put the bent don on him and use dull spurs."

I set the bucket down. My arm is sore and I do not want to walk into the center of this discussion. Innes stands by Fredrico's flank, tapping his whip impatiently against his high, polished black boots. Rutter's hand is on the horse's mane, and he leans forward with mussed hair and his shirt open at the front. I can almost feel the air crackling between them.

"Nonsense! I do not have time to coddle him. He is obstinate, and more time will be lost in coaxing him. A horse is to be mastered, not reasoned with."

"He's like that because you have a bit that pinches and spurs that cut. If you ease up on him, I swear he will be better."

"Corporal, I have handled both man and beast under conditions where minds break and wills crack. Have you kept horses alive on sawgrass and dust, or men in jungles so dense that the sunlight only lightens the darkness six hours out of the day?"

"No, sir."

"You see, then."

Rutter shakes his head. "I only see one thing, sir. That sawgrass and jungles did not teach you how to treat a nervous horse."

"Corporal." The captain speaks with a show of great humor and patience. "You seem to forget that my duty is to lead this company to greatness, yours is to keep us mounted."

Rutter's fist closes tightly on Fredrico's mane. The horse shifts uneasily.

"Sir." His voice is soft and very controlled. "If you cannot treat the horse as he should be treated, then you can bloody well find a new horse, because a man can speak for himself, but a beast can't."

Dead silence follows.

Captain Innes takes a step forward, and he is no longer smiling. "I see that my problem here, Corporal, is not the horse, but the man. You will no longer lay a finger on him, on pain of court-martial."

Rutter's face goes blank. "Sir—"

"Enough. I do not want to hear a word."

Rutter shuts his mouth and clamps his jaw tight. Much as I dislike Rutter and his rough ways, I think it is not quite fair of the captain.

Captain Innes turns and finds me gaping like a trout.

"Lad, come here."

I pick up the bucket and obey.

"See this animal? He's your responsibility now. When he is finished, you may go on to the other horses, but not before." He smiles and roughs my shoulder with his hand. "Consider yourself lucky."

Behind the captain, I see Rutter's face. He is a little white, and anger and shock sit on his face like two jagged edges of a broken bone, not quite fitting together.

I suck in my breath and set the bucket down. "Yes, sir."

"I will return in five minutes. I want him ready." The captain leaves, and I eye Fredrico as warily as he eyes me.

There is little time for anything but putting the saddle straight on. I heft it over, barely able to reach his back. I must go around his other side to tug the saddle down into place.

I am tightening the girth, wondering how I will get the bridle on fast enough, when I sense Rutter behind me.

He holds out his jar of ointment.

"Just a little. It'll do better than none at all."

He puts it in my hand and trudges away from me as if his feet were of stone.

SEVEN

The Fishing Spear

"You do not seem yourself, Maki." Willow checks his horse slightly beside me and leans down over the horn of his saddle.

I do not like that he has noticed a change. Ever since yesterday, when I saw Tsanu and took charge of the captain's horse, I have been thinking hard.

We must escape, and the sooner the better.

"There is nothing the matter," I mumble, stroking the shifting shoulder of his horse as I walk alongside.

Willow leans back in the saddle and lifts wise eyebrows. "Well, if you change your mind and decide there is something the matter, remember I'm happy to help."

I know he wants to be kind. He does not want me to feel alone. But my plans to escape with Tsanu are something I cannot trust anyone with, not even him.

I wish I could be up near the front of the company, where Tsanu guides them. I just want to be near him and away from the wagons and all these strangers smelling of smoke and sweat and salted meat.

"Maki!" Laramie's voice startles me. He is cupping his hands around his mouth, waving to catch my attention. "We've got a problem with a couple wheels—we may need to stop and make a repair. Run up and tell the lieutenant."

I nod and set off for the front at a lope. I do not mind this task. Ransom never shouts at me, and he looks directly at me when I speak, as if what I say is important.

I spy Ransom's gray mare near the front and Fredrico about ten paces beyond, the tall captain astride him. I cannot see Tsanu.

"Ransom!" I call. I am the only one—other than the captain—who is allowed to call him Ransom, so I do it as often as I can. He does not know that I can pronounce the word "lieutenant."

He pulls his horse aside and slows it so that I can walk at a comfortable pace beside him.

"There are some problems with the wagons in the back." He bends in the saddle to hear me. "I think some broken wheels. We may need to stop for repairs."

His eyes sober, but the rest of his face does not change. "I will ride back and see."

He turns his horse out of the way and trots back down the line. I fall in step beside Jeremiah's horse, near the front but out of sight of the captain. I want to see Tsanu if I can.

Jeremiah's horse is tall, like he is, so I can watch from under its neck. The map-maker looks down at me, removes the pencil from his teeth, and gives a nod, as though I must be up to something important that is not his business. Then he goes back to looking at the land and sketching in his books.

I like that about him.

Peering sideways beneath the neck of Jeremiah's horse, I can see Tsanu. He walks beside Fredrico, within an arm's length of the captain. He leans on a tall staff as we would a hunting spear, and the chains I saw before are gone. There is no need for them in the daytime—with the strike-locks, escaping in daylight would be sure death.

My brother's eyes are cool and proud. He is strong, but his face is too thin. My simmering irritation with the Invaders flares up into fury.

They took both Kavik and Tsanu from me, and they don't care.

They go on as if nothing happened.

I miss Tsanu. I miss Kavik and Tansilet and our old life. Nothing will be the same again. The ache in my chest grows strong, and with it the determination that I must not fail Tsanu. I must save him if it takes everything I have.

Ransom comes up the line, riding fast, and pulls up beside the captain. Tsanu is inches from the pounding hooves, but he does not flinch. He has nerves like a glacier.

"The ground we are covering today is too hard for the wagons at this pace." Ransom talks loudly—I can hear him from many paces away. "We have two wagons disabled, possibly a third."

"Can we leave them behind?" The captain glances over his shoulder.

"I would not advise it. The repairs can be made within a day. We can stop now, or we can slow our pace to let them catch up overnight."

The captain jerks off one of his gloves with an impatient gesture and spits some words I do not recognize. "How much farther can we go at this pace?"

"We are approaching a wide flat valley." It is Tsanu who answers. "We could make it across, maybe. Camp on the other side. But the weather is fair. We would be in no danger camping in the middle of it."

The captain turns to consult with Ransom, and the two talk quietly.

"We will camp in the valley." The captain slaps his glove fiercely against his leg. "It is an ill thing, though, for the weather is fair."

Ransom nods in mild agreement. "I will tell them to make the repairs and catch up as they can." He turns to the nearest man and sends him off to the back of the line with the news.

The captain shoves his hand back into his glove and kicks Fredrico. The horse pins his ears and rolls back against the bit in protest before springing forward like a shot.

"There you are!" I jump at the sound of Willow's voice and turn to find his horse nearly upon me. I should have heard him approach, but these

Invaders make so much noise that a bellowing *tuttik* could hardly be heard among them.

Ransom brings his mare alongside Willow's. "I say it is a fine thing we must stop. Those horses are about blown. And you, young man, are looking better than you have in months."

Willow grins. He does look less bony than before. "The air here is good for me. Better than the settlement camps down south, for sure."

"Are the settlement camps large?" I look up at him. This company— some two hundred horse—is the largest I have ever seen.

He looks down at me, and his smile is touched by none of the sadness that usually lingers about his eyes. "Yes, Maki. Twenty and thirty times this."

That is more people than I have seen in all my life. Too many. No wonder Willow was ill.

"Why are they here?"

"Many reasons," says Ransom. "Some are here to explore or settle, others to conquer."

"Innes is here to conquer," I say, soft and sullen. "Why would you come with him?"

Ransom looks at me directly, and I regret the bitterness in my tone. "There are many ways to react to the wrong we see in the world, Maki. Some run away from it, have nothing to do with it. Others ignore it—I cannot speak for them. It is the coward's way. And still others brave it to its face and try, in their way, to make it better. To make things different than they would have been. To hold back the evil from having its way." He gives me a shrewd look. "Not all of us are here to oppress your people."

I am not sure what to say. I stick my fingers in the mane of Willow's horse and shrug.

Willow draws rein and stops short. "What is this?" There is awe in his voice.

We stop at the crest of a hill that falls down into a wide, rolling meadow, full of long grass and darting birds. Across the meadow, a great distance away, are more hills, covered in shivering birch, and beyond that the faint blue lines of distant mountains. I had forgotten how much I love this part of the land.

"I knew this land was fair." Willow stands in the stirrups and takes a deep breath of the air. "But I did not know that it was so very fair."

I smile. I know. And to stand beside someone who has never seen it, who does not know it better than I, is a wondrous thing. I feel a lift of pride, the way one might feel after a great kill.

"What do you call this part of land?" asks Ransom.

"Auta-qui-tarniq," I say. "It means 'the grasses move like sea waves.'"

Ransom's beard splits in a smile. "I like that."

My fingers play in the long hairs of Willow's horse. She is white, splashed with gray like spring mud. I wish I could ride her. Someday I will ride a horse.

"You have been here before, then?" Willow looks down at me.

"Yes. My brother and his—his friends, came here for summer hunting. I would follow them sometimes when they did. But we do not come here in the winter."

"Why not?"

I laugh. "Have you not seen our winters?"

Willow shakes his head. "I have been here only a few months. But I have heard some tales."

"When winter comes, the snow lays so thick here that one must fashion wide shoes out of branches to keep from sinking. If you sink, it goes over your head."

Willow does not answer. I have shocked him into silence.

But Ransom is intrigued by the practical details. "You fashion shoes out of branches? How is that possible?"

I shrug. It is too complicated to explain.

"Will you show me sometime?" he persists.

"If one night you give to me eight thongs of rawhide and two switches of ash, man-height, I will show you."

"I will remember that."

"Halloo!" The captain is looking down into the valley, shouting with his hands cupped around his mouth. I stretch on my toes to see whom he hails, but I cannot.

"There is someone down there," says Willow, standing in his stirrups.

The someone is a hermit I once knew: a man our people call Barbarian, for he came out of the north—from where, no one knows. He cannot be much older than Tsanu, and he is pale, with brown hair that curls and blue eyes that look like the sky. He is accompanied by roughly thirty of his dogs, all barking and howling as we approach. Our horses snort and blow. It feels as if we are about to have a great fight on our hands.

"Hush! Sa now!" Barbarian calls to the dogs. Even now he is not loud, as if his throat is unused to speaking, let alone shouting.

The dogs settle in an instant. The captain knees Fredrico toward Barbarian through the silent, watching dogs, keeping a masterful hand on the reins. "Greetings, fellow traveler! Who are you and where do you come from, walking so far from any settlements?"

It is a silly question to ask. Out here, no one asks why someone is far from settlements. For men like Barbarian, it is the reason for being here.

Barbarian does not answer right away. Then he gives a little smile and says very softly, "I am Barbarian. And I do not live near settlements."

I have always been scared of Barbarian. He has a front—a small, shy smile he puts on when he is asked hard questions. I do not know what to do with a man like that.

"You live here?"

"Hereabouts." He looks like he is humoring an ignorant child.

"How long have you lived in these parts?"

Barbarian gives that odd, shy little smile again. "Oh, most of my life."

"And you have lived alone for all that time?"

"The last ten years or so."

"To what purpose?"

"To be alone."

"What other purpose?"

Barbarian's smile stiffens a little and he spreads out his hands. "I want to be alone."

I nearly laugh, watching them. Barbarian answers every question with the fewest words possible, and the captain is not used to meeting such resistance.

"We would like to camp in the valley today. Is there water to be had?"

"It is out of the way, but there is a good stream two miles that way." Barbarian lifts his arm and gestures to the east.

"It is well." Captain Innes smiles with his flashing teeth. "We would be glad of your company tonight."

"That is very fine," says Barbarian, not smiling. "But I will move on."

"But you must, I insist. I will feed you well, and your dogs too."

Barbarian shakes his head. "I intend to camp beyond the valley today."

"One more night can do you no harm. I wish to know of this area."

Barbarian looks at the group with sudden, half-hidden alarm. "You want to settle?"

"No, no!" In this, Captain Innes is more than pleased to soothe his fear.

"We are just passing through. We are looking for a place called Inik Katsuk."

Barbarian laughs and shakes his head. "You are in for disappointment. There is no Inik Katsuk."

Captain Innes gives a sly half-smile. Perhaps he thinks Barbarian is trying to fool him. "No matter. Show us this good stream."

He urges Fredrico a few steps to the side, giving the dogs a wide berth. With the captain no longer standing between us, Barbarian sees me. A tiny crease of confusion appears his eyebrows.

I must tell him before he lets anything slip.

I run to him, clasping his arm and pressing my forehead to his in greeting.

"I am Maki-boy to them." I give him a steely look and draw a finger down the side of my neck. "Tss."

Barbarian gives me his small smile. "Hello again, Maki."

I step back. He gazes mildly at me, then looks up to the captain.

"You know him?" Captain Innes graces me with a keen look, and I give it right back.

Barbarian only nods, stooping to untangle a couple of his dogs, who grow restless with this delay. "From a village called Tansilet. A nice little one."

A strong silence falls.

"They burned it," I say, loud enough for everyone to hear.

Captain Innes gives me a sharp look, but I pay him no attention.

"They burned it?" Barbarian glances from me to the captain. He clicks his tongue. "That is too bad. A mistake, that was."

"Are you ready yet?" A touch of impatience steels the captain's voice.

Barbarian does not answer, but continues to wade among his dogs, parting them as methodically as a woman unweaving the strands of her braids. Then, with an odd, mild glance at the captain and back to me, he leads the way eastward.

✦

The sun filters gently through the trees onto the swift-moving water of the stream. Barbarian knows of what he speaks. It is one of the best streams I have seen, full of fat trout. But I have no way to obtain the trout. A net might work—a spear would be best.

I turn and head back through the mass of wagons, the wagoners still unhitching the horses. We are halting early, and I refuse to be put to work yet. One of the wagons has spare weapons and tools, and I am determined to find something I can use to fish.

I wait until the wagoner leads his horses away and climb up the tailboard. Inside is a jumbled pile of broken strike-locks, both short and long, beside stacks of perfectly whole ones.

And then I see it.

Tucked into a sheaf of spears is my own fishing spear, my pride and joy that Tsanu lost when he was taken. I put one foot inside the wagon to reach it.

"What is this? Get down, boy!"

I am jerked down by the collar of my shirt. I swing at my attacker.

"Now then!" The man shakes me until I can't see straight.

"I want to fish."

"Fish with what? A gun?"

I shake my shaggy hair out of my eyes. "No, *piku,* a spear."

"A spear?" He reaches in with a not-so-nice grin and pulls out the whole sheaf. He admires one, red and white with barbs on the end. "I wonder what damage could be done with this."

I don't answer. He is trying to provoke me, and I refuse to be provoked. The lure of fresh, sweet trout is too strong to give it up now.

He pulls my spear out with his dirty Invader fingers, and something in me roils at the sight. I muster my sweetest—but still boyish—voice.

"May I—have that?" I hold out my hand for my spear. It needs a bit of care, but the jay feathers are just as blue as the day I put it into Tsanu's hand.

The man looks from the spear to me.

"It is a fishing spear," I explain, as if to a child. "I will not use it on you."

"That guide of ours, he tried to use it on us." The man smiles slyly, thinking he has caught me in a deception.

I hesitate for a split second. "Then he was a fool," I say, inwardly asking Tsanu's forgiveness. "It is clearly for trout."

I hold out my hand again.

Reluctantly, he sets the spear in my open palm. A thrill runs through me as my fingers close around it. I almost forget that I hate where I am, that Tsanu is a hostage, and that we are no longer in Tansilet. The fish in the running water flash silver and brown and red, and I can taste them now, fresh and sweet and hot from the fire. The fish will be mine, to eat and to dry, and the Invaders can barter with me if they want any.

I wade in slowly, letting my feet become part of the riverbed, the rest of me swaying naturally with the flow of the water. "Out of your great number, I ask only what is needful," I say to the fish, as Tsanu taught me when I was small. "This is the oath I make." I raise my spear, keeping the sun to my front so that I do not cast a shadow.

A fat trout slides by, and for a moment the world stops.

I stab and feel the satisfying resistance of the fish against my spear. I bring him up before he can bleed into the water, and I toss him, flopping, up onto the bank.

"Amazing!" A few of the men have come up behind me and are watching, fascinated. "I could not see your arm, so fast it moved!"

"Do not touch the fish," I warn. "It is mine."

I wait. The river sometimes holds its breath a moment after a disturbance, but the fish always resume their flow within minutes.

Another fish, large and brown-speckled, flashes past, but I am faster. He joins the fat trout on the bank. Two more, and I can tell the men are watching hungrily.

Let them watch. I want to get a good trade.

"What's this?"

I glance back. Willow crouches on the bank beside my four fish.

"I am fishing," I throw over my shoulder. "Do not distract me."

I spear another and another until nine fish are flopping and gleaming on the bank.

"Are you going to stop soon?" Laughter fills Willow's voice. "They say all these are for you."

I give him a severe look, for he is distracting me again. "They are all *mine*. I intend to trade the ones I do not eat."

"Ah. Shrewd."

"Now let me get back to work."

"Let me ask one more thing."

I sigh, but I am surprised to find that my heart does not mind. It even enjoys it.

"How many do you intend to catch?"

"Many." With my arms I indicate a wide span. "The river is long and the fish-kind are many. They do not mind if I take many of them."

"They do not mind? You ask them?"

It is another question, but I answer him. "Always. The animals live in the land as we do, and we eat them to live. But we do not want them all to die. If we ate them all, we would die too." I shrug. "But there are many. So they do not mind."

Willow does not ask more questions after this.

At fourteen fish, I stop. I will only eat one, perhaps two myself, and dry a few for the future. I could not possibly keep all the things the Invaders might trade me if I caught thirty.

I wade out of the water, soaked to my waist, grinning at Willow. "Do not tell me you could have done better without a net."

I crouch beside the glowing coals and turn the fish onto its other side. It will char, leaving the inside perfect. Part of me wants to eat it raw, but I do not want to shock Willow too much.

I break a big, flat piece of bark off the nearest birch log, glance at Willow, who is feeding the fire with a small pile of snapped twigs, and then break a smaller piece off the bark.

Preparing for journey, I scratch into it with my fingernail. *Be ready. Have horse. Where shall we go. Wait for right time.*

I slide the smaller piece of birch bark under the wide one and hold it in place with my finger. My message was hastily scrawled, but Tsanu will know what I mean.

As for Barbarian, I know him well enough to be sure that he will pass it on to my brother without showing it to the captain.

I pull the first fish out of the fire and heap the birch bark with the steaming white meat. My mouth waters, and I recklessly wish I could keep this fish as well as the two in the fire and eat all three myself. But there is too much at stake, and the price of a trout is one I am willing to pay.

"Where are you going with that?" Willow looks up from cleaning his own trout.

"A present for our guest. Watch the fish, do not let it burn."

He grins and salutes.

It is not hard to find Barbarian. The captain's tent is already pitched, rising slightly above the rest of the camp, and there are dogs milling everywhere around it.

A fire crackles nearby—the only place conspicuously free of dogs—and beyond it, surrounded by hounds, sit Barbarian and the captain. A handful of others stand nearby, listening.

I step over an amiably panting dog and straight into their circle.

"But what is the terrain like—?"

Barbarian holds up a hand to quiet the captain. "*Kitaya*, Maki."

"*Kitaya*." I hold out the fish. I was not afraid when I first thought of using Barbarian to pass a message, but now my heart pounds out of my chest.

He looks at me with that slight smile. "Is this for me?"

"A present of welcome, kin to kin." Barbarian isn't my kin, of course, but he is so much a part of the land now that it does not matter.

He takes the slab of birch from me with a nod of thanks.

I can feel the eyes of the others on me. I nod in return, heat rising in my face, and leave.

It is in his hands now.

EIGHT

Spark and Tinder

I wake in the small hours of the morning and Barbarian is already up, packing his things—he and his dogs are accustomed to rising early. Rain spatters on the tops of the tents, and I can hear the captain's voice issuing orders. He is anxious to make headway, as is Barbarian, though in the opposite direction.

Mist fills the camp, and somewhere far off, a wolf howls in the dark morning. Two or three of Barbarian's dogs lift their heads and howl back, while others growl and bark, the hackles rising on their necks.

Iki sits beside me as I groom Fredrico. The two have come to an odd truce. Iki stares at Fredrico as he stands, and Fredrico stares back, neither seeming to mind the other's presence. Strangely enough, Fredrico is calmer when Iki is there.

I brush the dust off of his dark back, avoiding the sores, which are beginning to heal. I have avoided Rutter since the day I took over—I do not know if he angry with me about it, and I have done some things since that I do not want him to know about.

First, I hid the captain's sharp spurs. Innes left them on the saddle one day, and I hid them inside Laramie's box of soap. They should be safe there. Laramie never uses soap.

I went to the captain right away and told him the spurs were missing—I am no fool, and I did not want to be accused of stealing them. He railed about it and ordered Rutter to have his horse-boys search the grass, but he did not accuse me of touching the lost pair. He remembered leaving them on the saddle.

A careless mistake. But fortunate for Fredrico.

Fredrico stomps as I try to pick up his hooves, and I mutter at him.

Ungrateful beast, I do not know why I have gone to such lengths to help him.

The second thing I did was switch the sharp bit. I put it on Drucker's bridle instead, because Drucker does not pay attention to such things. In fact, he hardly pays attention to his horse at all when he is in the saddle. He usually leaves his reins on the horse's neck, forgets his spurs, and stands so long in one place that his horse falls asleep.

But Fredrico has noticed the difference.

Iki whines a little, hearing Barbarian's dogs.

"Easy, boy. We will be done soon," I soothe, running my hand along Fredrico's face as I slip the reins over his neck.

I open his mouth and slide the straight-bar bit in between his teeth. When I first took over grooming him, he fought me every time. Now he stands with reluctance, but he stands.

I lead him to the edge of camp where the captain and a handful of the officers are seeing Barbarian off. The captain has a bottle of fire spirits which he offers as a gift.

Barbarian accepts it with a shy smile. I do not know what life did to him to make him meet all things with that smile, but I do not always think it means he is happy.

"Good journey," says the captain.

"And a good one to you," Barbarian replies. I think he does wish us a good journey, so long as it is away from him. I almost wish I could go with him.

To my surprise, he comes over to see me.

"You still have your Iki," he says with a smile. "I wish I could have his bloodlines."

"One day, perhaps."

"Perhaps. May light shine upon your path, Maki." He takes my hand and presses something into it.

It is a blue river pebble, shot through with clear streaks. I look up swiftly, but he is already ten paces away, passing between the last tents.

Barbarian stops just outside the picket line and calls his dogs. They appear from around camp where they have been exploring on their own, surging around him in a great, milling pack. Iki trots over, his tail raised a little, his head stretched out to sniff the others. Barbarian gives a long, loud whistle, and his dogs move out with him.

Iki lunges toward them. I grab him by the scruff, hauling him back, my arms wrapped around his neck to keep him from following. We watch as they disappear into the mist, and my heart reaches out after them.

I want to go along, to disappear into the mist and be back in my old life. I am sick of being in this dirty, foul-smelling camp full of rude, rough foreigners. Tears tighten my throat. I cannot wait to escape this place.

"Those dogs of his look like wolves."

I look up at Willow, swallowing my annoyance and my sadness. "Well, some of them are. At least half."

"Wolves?"

"Half-breed. The rest of their blood is hound, probably."

Willow stoops to scratch Iki's ear. "What about Iki?"

"He is half wolf. Ts—my brother got him for me from a den the day he was born, and we nursed him off one of our female dogs."

"How do you know he is half?"

I grab one of Iki's paws and hold it up at an angle where the firelight falls on it. "It is hard to see in the light, but there is a little pink in the pads. Wolves are all black."

"Did his mother die?"

I nod.

"And your brother went into the den?"

"He knew the pups were there. The mother was in milk."

"Isn't that dangerous?"

I shrug. "Yes. Wolves are dangerous."

"But you are not afraid of them." Willow scratches absently along Iki's back.

"I was raised to survive with them. You were not."

Willow studies his hand, buried in Iki's fur, with an odd intensity. "Can someone learn?"

I shrug. "Perhaps. Sometimes I think it can be learned." I get up, snapping my fingers for Iki to follow.

"Where are you off to?" Willow calls after me as I go back into the trees.

"Going to cut myself some long switches. The captain—" I pause to make sure Innes is not within earshot— "is impatient to leave."

"Switches? What for?" He takes a step like he wants to follow me.

I shrug. "You'll see."

We make our way out of the valley that day and the next and start winding the long way over the foothills and around the mountain. The grass is beginning to turn, gaining a ruddy hue where it had been full green only a week ago.

We stop early on the fourth day out from the valley, a couple hours before dark. The days are already beginning to shorten. At last I have time to sit down with my switches and rawhide and work on my snowshoes. I must finish them soon, or there will not be time enough for them to harden before the snow falls.

Ransom has been by a few times since I started making them, and he asks many questions. I think he likes to learn about our ways. What he does not know is that all the things he asks about are things I am preparing for our escape. The dried fish, the snowshoes, the rope I am weaving for traps, the hides I am curing for fletching arrows and patching clothing.

"What are those?"

I look up. A small, wiry man of middle age sneers down at me, rubbing the half-hearted scruff on his face.

I smell danger all over this man. He is a little too thin, like one who does not care for himself because of laziness and vice, and even from a distance, his breath smells like rotten fire spirits. And I do not like the glint in his green eyes.

"*Tapinan*," I say, purposely using my own dialect. We used to use the foreigners' tongue in the same way around the younger Tansilet children, to keep them from knowing when we had gotten our hands on fresh fruit. I will admit that was not very kind.

"And what are *tapinan*?" His voice is unashamedly mocking.

"Shoes for walking in snow." I grip my knife a little tighter.

"With just those branches?"

I do not answer him. I want to end this conversation, not continue it. My hands work steadily, weaving the rawhide around the frame.

"Looks like fine work. Are they only for little boys like you?"

I pretend not to hear him.

"Listen, *savet*, when I am talking to you!" He swoops down and grabs my collar, almost choking me.

"Put me down!" I brandish my knife in his face, and he drops me like I have camp fever.

"The wolf pup has teeth, does it?"

I snarl at him. At the beginning of the summer, the name would have angered me, but now I take it as a compliment.

He snatches up the snowshoe I have finished and looks it over. "This is an oddity. I think I will keep it."

"You give it back!" I swipe at it, but he whisks it out of reach. Alas for the height I do not yet have. I cannot lose my shoe—I must be ready to leave at any time.

I try again, but he holds it too high for me. I sink my teeth into his arm. He howls and hits me full in the face with his fist.

The world spins and goes in and out for a moment, and I find myself on the ground. I am embarrassed, but I am also angry. My head and my nose throb, and I cannot see straight for the tears.

My fingernails scratch a furrow down his arm and his fist piles into me again, though this time I dodge, and it hits my shoulder instead. I am halfway between red rage and dizzying pain, sick to the pit of my stomach.

But I charge at him again, this time jumping onto his back. I sink my fingernails into his shoulder and my teeth into his ear.

He lets loose a string of profanities so rapid I cannot discern a one—all ugly sounds that carry the full weight of his pain. I dig my fingernails deeper. His head smashes into my face.

I wake on the ground, blood in my mouth, with Drucker's long face looking down into mine.

"He's come to," he assures someone slowly. "Thank goodness."

I sit up and the world shifts and spins. I feel in the whirl one steady thing: Drucker's large hand behind my shoulders. As I lay back down, the world returns to its rightful place.

"What did you mean by picking a fight with someone twice your size?" Drucker is half scolding and half amused. I sense that he is impressed, and warmth surges through me, dimming the pain a little.

"He picked it." Stars, my mouth is swollen. I run my tongue over my teeth. All there still.

"What for?"

"My snowshoes. The dimwit was looking for trouble."

"And he found it. My assistant put three stitches in his ear."

I try to hide how much this cheers me, but it sneaks out of my eyes. Thankfully, Drucker has turned away, reaching into his black leather bag.

"He bloodied you up a bit, lad—what is your name again?"

"Maki," I mumble. My mouth is getting worse.

"Maki." He takes a cloth out of his bag and presses it against the lip of a bottle of clear liquid. "Easy there. This may sting a little."

He presses the wet cloth against the worst part of my mouth. It is deliciously cool for a moment before it begins to sting sharply.

"It will help it heal." He transfers the cloth to my hand and turns back to his bag.

I leave the cloth against my mouth, even press it a little closer. I probably look as swollen-nosed as a *tuttik* right now, and I cannot wait for it to stop.

"Does he have my snowshoes?" I ask, half muffled against the cloth.

"I doubt it." Drucker glances around as if to look for them. "He is with my assistant still. But if he does, I'll see you get them back."

"What's his name?"

He looks at me with wry reproach. "Are you taking names so young, boy?"

"I am not going to fight him again, but he is my enemy."

"Good. He's from the wrong end of camp, and a boy like you shouldn't go near the likes of him. How old are you, anyway?"

"Uki-qui," I mumble, hoping this will put him off. I do not want to tell him my age. I must pass as younger than I am, since they think I am boy.

"Well, you're older than you look, I reckon. Or perhaps they start young in your village."

I close my eyes. The swimming has come to my head even lying down, and I want to sleep.

A gentle slap hits my hand and my eyes snap open. "You can't sleep after you're hit in the head. Not for a while, at least." Drucker's hand draws me up and he looks intently into my eyes.

"Looks like you haven't taken too much damage. You're coherent—that's something." He pulls a strange, ticking gold amulet out of his pocket and peers at the glass face closely, all while holding my wrist pinched in his fingers. I do not know how it can possibly be helping to cure me.

It makes me nervous, but I do not pull away. Medicine men do strange things.

"A bit fast." He holds onto me a bit longer, then mutters something to himself, setting my wrist down. "A bit of excitement, my lad. That must be it."

"Uhhuh," I mumble through the cloth and my swollen mouth.

He checks my head and my face, my shoulder where the punch landed, my hands and arms.

"Anything else hurt?"

I shake my head. Besides the uncommonly bad headache and swollen face, I am feeling quite well, and I do not want him to look any closer. Last thing I want is for my secret to be discovered.

The very thought brings a cold sweat to my neck. Ransom and Rutter remember how desperate I was to join, and they are not so dim as not to wonder why a girl would want so terribly to be a horse-boy. And then they might draw rightful conclusions about Tsanu and I. After all, we are blood. Surely someone in this camp has eyes to see it.

"Let me carry you to the hospital. You can spend the rest of the day there. Don't worry, I won't put you anywhere near Pulhem."

I assume this is the man's name. I make a wry face. I do not want to spend any time in the hospital, but then again, I do not want to get sicker, because that will assuredly bring on closer inspection.

Drucker lifts me easily and carries me through the camp. I lay stiff in his arms like any boy of the village might, aloof and offended. The bed is a cot, nicer than the blanket and spare pack of Rutter's that I normally sleep on, and just this once I am grateful for the comfort. It makes me think of the fur rugs we have to sleep on at home.

But there is no such thing as home anymore.

Bitterness creeps up my throat. I want to make Captain Innes sorry. I want to make all of them sorry.

After a while, Drucker's assistant brings me my snowshoes and the supplies.

One shoe is crushed beyond repair. Alas, for I put many hours into its making.

But I cannot spend time being sorry over it. I set back to work crafting the half-finished one. I will rebuild the other later—I will have to get more switches.

I am almost done with the undamaged shoe when Rutter comes striding through the hospital, bold and brash, like it is his picket.

"Maki!" He gives his large, lopsided grin. "You look bloody good! I asked them where you were and I got the whole tale from someone who saw most of it. Took on an old toughie, eh?"

If he was angry about me taking Fredrico, he is no longer.

I grin, which hurts, but I do not care. "He was being a bugger."

"Sure 'nough he was! Serves him right. I heard you bit him good."

I shrug, but a warmth springs up inside me.

"Drucker tells me you're staying the night here?"

"I am fine." I adjust the long switch so I can weave it evenly. "But I went black, and I think he wants to make sure I don't go silly."

"No rush," says Rutter through that lopsided grin. "I daresay even some of the common soldiers don't take on the old commission boys."

"I don't want a reputation as a brawler," I say, then fear I may have said it too primly. I scowl to make up for it. "Well, he asked for it. But I don't want to go my whole life looking like a—"

"A street tom?" His eyes sparkle. "Ah, Maki. A dandy, eh? Stars, but I forget it starts this early."

I shrug and turn my attention back to my work.

"I'll send you a bit of broth when supper's made," he says. "It'll go down easier than dried meat with that mouth."

"Thanks." I do appreciate it. I was not looking forward to trying to chew my ration today, even dipped in oil.

"Well, I only had a minute to come by," says Rutter, swinging his arms, "but I wanted to tell you bloody good job. At least you didn't get the stitches."

He leaves, and I am left with a quiet satisfaction. I could not have cared less for Rutter's opinion a few weeks ago, but I have rarely seen him grin like this, so I am glad.

I earned these bruises.

Willow whistles long when he sees me the next morning as I curry his horse.

"Maki, what in tarnation did you do to yourself?"

My pride in my accomplishment has all faded away. I do not know why, but I do not feel proud when I am rough and uncouth around Willow.

"A man was bothering me," I say quietly, concentrating hard on brushing the horse.

"So you fought him?"

"Yes."

"Why didn't you call for someone?"

"No one was around. I can take care of myself, Willow Tam." I give his mare one more solid swipe, then duck under her neck to the next horse.

I am horribly ugly right now. I do not know what a street tom is, but judging by the tone Rutter used yesterday, I am sure I look exactly like one.

"Well, I am sure you can, but have you seen what it did to your face?"

"I couldn't help it. He was rough and he didn't care that I was half his size. He was taking my snowshoes away just to bother me."

Willow looks hard at me, but I know in his eye he is seeing that man instead.

"Well," he says at last, "I hope you thrashed him good then."

"He needed to be sewn up," I say, and immediately regret it.

His eyebrows go up. "What did you do to him, Maki?"

"I bit him."

"What?"

My voice is tiny; he cannot hear it. I raise it miserably. "I bit him."

Willow's face twists perplexingly. Then he bursts into a laugh. "You bit him? Oh, Maki, you are a wildcat."

I don't want him to call me a wildcat.

I finish the second horse and move down, now two horses away.

"I will send you some broth." He lifts his head to see me over the horse's lowered neck.

"Rutter gave me some yesterday."

"That swelling will not go down in an hour. I can send you some tonight."

"I will be fine."

"Come now, Maki. Did I say something?"

I feel bad now. This is not a path I want to go down. I lower the brush and look back at him.

"All right, Willow. I would like the broth."

He does not smile, but he nods. He is not hurt by my words.

"I will send it, then."

It is just after dusk when Willow materializes out of the dark with a steaming pail of fresh broth. I am brushing down horses again, a job that takes me a bit longer in the dark.

"Evening, Maki."

"Evening."

"How much longer?"

I peer down the line. "Four more."

He sits down on a lump of log that we use sometimes for a mounting block. "I can wait."

A savory smell wafts through the darkness, and my stomach begins to growl. Rutter's was an onion-broth, but this one smells of meat. I have built up an appetite all day.

The horse I am brushing nickers to Willow, friendly-like. He switches the broth pail to his other hand and reaches out to stroke the horse.

"What did you do today?" I do not know why I asked. What do any of us do save travel and travel more?

"I whittled in the saddle."

"Whittled what?"

"I can't tell you yet. You must wait until it is done and then judge if it is any good."

"Of course it is good, Willow." He has shown me his carvings before, and they look like life.

His sad eyes smile, and a tiny feeling of regret starts in me like a tongue of flame. If Tsanu and I escape soon, as I hope, I may never see it.

"Well, I am no master. The man I learned from, now—he could do it better than anyone. He did a bird out of a dark wood once—a raven, life-size, and I thought at first it was real."

"Really?" I emerge from behind my third-to-last horse.

"You would like him. But alas, he lives far, far away."

But I could go with you.

The thought scares me, as it came out of nowhere. Until this moment, I'd never thought of leaving Uniap'nik to go anywhere, let alone with an Invader—even Willow.

"Perhaps I will travel one day, as you have," I say.

"Really? You would?"

"Perhaps. I am traveling now."

"Yes, but—"

"The sea does not frighten me, if that is what you are asking. It gives us whales to eat, and when it is frozen, my—I go out onto the ice and hunt seals. It is a fine thing."

"But dangerous."

I shrug. "Everything is dangerous."

"Ha! Perhaps that is why you are so brave, Maki. You think of all things as dangerous."

But they are, silly.

"Uniap'nik is a wild land, Willow." I brush the horse a little harder and move on to the next one. "Even those of us who are bred to it die by it. We do not fight with each other much, because we are too busy fighting the land. If a man has no food, we share. In the fall, we go out and hunt and dry our meat so that we do not starve. If we do not find enough, we may not live through the winter. Even hunters of many years go out and do not return. Children die because there is little medicine. We live with danger."

Willow is quiet. I hope that I have not offended him.

"But your home sounds wonderful," I say softly. "I do wish that I could see it someday."

"Do you?"

"I do not lie, Willow Tam. Ah!"

"What?"

"I should not talk anymore." I have bitten the side of my swollen mouth and I can taste the blood.

"Don't then. I will be quiet until you are done, and then you can drink the broth."

Rutter clomps up in his old, worn-out boots, the ones he always wears when he is doing a rough or dirty job. "Move along, Willow. There's work to be done."

"I was bringing Maki some broth. His mouth's swollen."

His mouth. For a few minutes, I had almost forgotten that I am supposed to be a boy.

Dangerous ground, Maki.

"Ah, so it is." Rutter takes the pail from Willow and shoos him away with his hand. Willow takes off, and disappointment seeps into me as I watch him melt into the shadows.

"You done yet, Maki?" asks Rutter.

"Just." Even my tongue feels thick.

"Well, come sit, lad. I went and fetched a little podge from the rations, my morning ration. Got permission, I did."

"For me?"

That was thoughtful. Very thoughtful, even. I rinse off my hands in a bucket of cold water and dry them slowly on my shirt.

I do not know what to think. Rutter is being kind to me.

Drucker comes by the picket line in the morning just to check my face and my head.

"Sound as a melon," he says. I have not the slightest idea what he is talking about, but it must be a good thing.

"Your face is healing well," he says next.

I do not know what he means by this either, because it is still badly swollen and feels far from well.

"What's he been eating?" asks Drucker of Rutter, who is lounging against a wagon nearby, as if watching Drucker examine a horse.

"Broth and podge."

I could have told him that. Why does he have to ask Rutter?

I swallow my annoyance and sit still.

"Good." Drucker looks me in the eye. "Keep at it, lad. You'll be sound in no time." He slaps me on the shoulder and walks on.

The slap was good and solid, and with it comes intense relief. Drucker seems the sort who would never slap a girl, even if he was pretending she was a boy. My secret is safe for now.

But—sound in no time? How long is no time? I am sick of eating liquid food and feeling like I have been stung by ground hornets. I just want my face back.

I find the leather harnesses that need mending and pick up a kit and the nearest piece of tack.

"What are you doing?"

I meet Rutter's eyes. "Starting this."

"Can't. We're leaving now."

"Now?"

"Captain's very insistent. And I don't want you putting that awl through your thumb."

I would laugh at this, but my face is throbbing. Instead, I pack the kit back up. It will have to wait until tonight.

Rutter sniffs the air and grimaces.

"It's powerful dry today. Back in my country we would cease all fires on a day like this. It's like tinder just waiting for a spark."

"We have fires here too," I say, shouldering my pack.

❧

Fredrico is covered in sweat. It is too dark to see, but I run my hand over his sides and find no new marks. The methodical crunch of hay should be a peaceful sound, but tonight it fills me with a feeling of anticipation, as if something is on the edge of happening. I do not know why.

But I mentally check the things I have packed for our escape, just in case.

"Evening, Maki." Willow walks by with his horse and ties it down the line. "How's the renegade?"

"This one?" I duck under Fredrico's head and start on his other side.

He only laughs. "How are you feeling?"

"Better."

"I am glad. I certainly hope Rutter will keep those characters clear of here. Many of those old commission boys are a bad lot. Too mean to set up a real life, and seen too much to understand one if they did."

I pick up Fredrico's leg and start to scrape the dirt and stones out of it. Willow is not looking for a reply.

"Fire!" The call comes from the center of the camp.

Fredrico's head snaps up and he jerks his leg out of my hands. Willow whirls around, and I raise myself up on my toes to look.

An unmistakable orange glow spreads over the tops of the tents.

Willow takes off running.

Iki gets slowly to his feet and Fredrico returns, a little nervously, to his hay. Everything feels still, though I see men running past me, hear as if in a dream the shouts for a bucket brigade. Now I understand my strange feeling of anticipation.

This is my last night here.

I run to Rutter's tent and pull out my pack. The horses on the line grow nervous, pulling at the lines, rising back on their hindquarters.

I had better hurry.

I run to the center of the camp, ignored by the men rushing past. They see only the flame and the water and the tents which must be protected. I scan the tents and wagons for Tsanu, hoping against all hope that he has not been chained up for the night. If he is still loose, we stand a chance.

I come around the side of one of the wagons and there, ten feet away, is Tsanu. He stands beside a man who carries a long strike-lock—the one they call a shotgun—in the crook of his arm. Both of them stare at the glow of the fire with wonder and horror on their faces.

Turn, Tsanu. Please turn.

He sees me. The firelight flickers on his face, on mine, and then he moves—swift, like the pounce of a wildcat—and the shotgun falls to the ground with a crack. For a moment the two men are locked in a struggle, and then Tsanu picks up a stone and hits him hard on the head.

He drags him over and chains him to the axle of the wagon.

"Now he will know how it feels." Tsanu dusts off his hands and picks up the shotgun. He reaches down and gives me a brief kiss on the head in greeting.

"This way." I take off at a run.

Iki waits for me beside Fredrico, whose head is jigging badly. I wish I could take him, but I cannot. It would make our situation far worse if I stole the captain's horse.

The horses on the line are frantic—I see a few snapped tethers where horses have broken loose. Pulling my knife out, I slit Fredrico's tether halfway. In another minute, he will pull himself free.

I slice a few more and loosen others to cover our tracks, then run to Rosita. She is fast, but she is fond of me, and I think she will be easier to ride than most of the other horses.

"Climb on." I reach for a bridle. A saddle we must do without, but I can get a bridle on her in moments.

I slip it over her head, and she only looks at me a little wonderingly, pricking her ears. I whistle to Iki, and Tsanu gives me a hand up.

Fredrico pulls loose, quicker than I thought he would, and takes off at a wild gallop out of the camp. I glance around—no one is here yet, no one has seen us—and one thought steals into my head.

I wish I could have said goodbye to Willow.

I dig my heels into Rosita's sides, and her hoofbeats are swallowed up in the roar of the fire and the thunder of many hooves.

NINE

A Girl Again

We stop seldom in the night, only long enough to navigate a couple slick-stoned rivers and skirt small outcroppings of forest.

By the time dawn spreads, pale and gray and promising sunshine, I slow Rosita to a walk to rest a little. Tsanu's chest is against my back, his heart beating into my shoulder blade. It is a comfort to my weary bones.

"How far do you think we have gone?" My voice sounds strange after so much silence—just hoofbeats and the pounding of my heart in my ears.

"Far enough. Almost a day's ride." Tsanu leans his chin on the top of my head.

"Far enough for them to not find us?"

"That is impossible to answer in a day."

I turn around to ask another question, but I see that he is smiling. "You did well, wolf pup."

I turn around to hide the grin that is spreading across my face.

"What do you say we break into your pack?" He ruffles up my hair. "I do hope that you remembered to bring provisions."

"Of course I did," I say with a sniff.

He pulls out a few strips of dried fish and hands one to me. I take a careful bite and chew slowly. It hurts my jaw, but I am so hungry I hardly mind.

Tsanu cranes his neck to look at me. "Maki, what happened to your face?"

I turn my head away from him like a horse refusing the bit. He takes the back of my head gently between his hands and turns it back toward him.

"It is nothing." I push his hands away. "I got into a fight."

"A fight? I hope you got the best of him."

A sly smile spreads across my face. "Yes, I did. He had to be sewn up."

Tsanu breaks into a loud laugh, and my heart hurts at the sound. Not because I am sad, but because I have missed it so very badly.

"You little wolf! You take care of yourself, don't you?"

"I told you that I would be fine."

"Well, it is over now," Tsanu says, reaching his arms around me and taking the reins lightly in his hands. "We are together now."

I sag against him, looking up at the pale blue sky above us. The birds are calm, singing and hardly minding our presence, and a *tuttik* grazes across the wide meadow.

Everything is going to be all right now.

"Where shall we go?" I ask. Tsanu has traveled much more in Uniap'nik than I have, and now that Tansilet is gone, well—

A sudden sadness wells up in me. I miss Kavik, I miss the simple life we had in Tansilet.

"I was thinking we could move east, toward the Jade Mountains. What do you think?"

"I would like that very much."

The Jade Mountains are not like the other ranges—they have high peaks, like the slate-purple and blue ranges, but they are greenish, like jade.

"It would be a quiet life, Maki. Lonely."

"I wouldn't mind."

"You say so now, but—"

"No, Tsanu, I mean it."

And I do. I am sick of being surrounded by many people. If I must choose, I will choose the solitude.

"Then it is set. Once we lose them, we will double back, southeast."

"First, we put meat on your ribs," I say. "Winter is coming."

"What, you think that I am too thin?"

"I know it. The captain said you refused to eat."

"Did he?" Tsanu sounds offended.

"Well, didn't you?" I know my brother.

He gives me a little smile, sheepish.

"Maybe I did sometimes." He clucks gently to Rosita, and she breaks into a trot.

We fall silent, because it is hard to carry a conversation while one is riding at a trot. The day dawns beautifully, cloudless and blue.

We really did it. We are free, we are headed away from the Invader camp. I am a little sorry for the few who were kind—and that I had to cut the tethers and run away with Rutter's favorite horse—but not sorry enough.

The Invaders should not have crossed us.

"Was it so bad, living among them?" asks Tsanu after a while, when we have slowed again.

I was not expecting this question. I must think a moment.

"No," I begin. "It was not so very bad. I worked hard. The worst part was not seeing you, hoping you were well."

He reaches out and ruffles up my hair. "What, you do not think I can take care of myself?"

I duck and giggle. It feels good to be able to laugh like a girl.

"I was made for that, Maki. I was a match for the captain." He sighs, and I hear the smile in his voice. "Not that I'm not glad to be done with it."

I feel him shift a little as he switches the reins to one hand. Rosita likes him. There has been no trouble with her.

"For all that there has been trouble, Maki, there is no place I would rather be right now than here, in this place, with you."

My heart swells. "Me too."

Rosita stumbles suddenly, jerking us forward. She recovers, but moves forward with a limp. I pull her up and slide off her back. My legs tremble, and I steady myself against Rosita's flank. It is not so easy as the Invaders make it look, this riding. Tsanu and I are both stiff and sore after our night on her back.

Tsanu slides to the ground behind me, taking Rosita's head, watching with concern.

"What is it?"

I bend down and lift her leg. A crack runs up her hoof, too deep to remedy.

"Bloody fool!"

"Maki, what are you saying?"

"Rosita has not been well cared for, and her hoof is cracked." I set her hoof down and straighten. "We cannot ride her fast. We can barely ride her at all."

Tsanu's face darkens.

"Tsanu, what are we going to do?"

He rubs his thin beard.

"Tsanu?"

"She cannot move fast?"

"Not for long. Only as fast as she can limp. And it will get worse."

He takes a deep breath. For a split second, there is indecision on his face. Then he smiles—just a thin one.

I am suddenly cold.

"Maki, listen to me carefully."

I don't want to. Not at all.

"We will split up. I will ride north, away from you. They will follow my tracks, not yours. You will go away to the south. Take the gun. Get away from here."

"No." I take a step back from him. "They will catch you."

"Maki, they can catch me alone, or they can catch me with you."

I clamp my jaw stubbornly.

Tsanu smiles and takes my shoulder, pressing his forehead against mine for a brief moment. "You are strong, Maki, but life cannot be bent to our bidding. We will wait for another day. It will come, I swear."

"We can't give up." I plant my feet hard. I wish I could plant them harder.

"This is not giving up, Maki. This is hoping for tomorrow."

"No, it isn't."

"Maki, Maki." He shakes his head, rubbing my shoulders in his hands. "I will be all right."

My lip quivers.

He leans down into my face. His dark eyes bore into mine. There is no sadness in them, only a straight honesty.

"I have not always able to protect you from trouble, Maki . . . ."

"I didn't mind that."

"But don't you see that this is what you expect of yourself? You cannot protect everything. It cannot be done. I will be all right."

"But the captain—"

"The captain wants the city, not revenge."

"But the city does not exist, Tsanu. I hate that story."

His eyes are suddenly sad. "I don't blame you, Maki."

He plants a kiss on my forehead. "I will see you in time," he whispers, and leads Rosita away. Iki whines, torn between the two of us.

He settles uneasily on his haunches at my side.

I watch Tsanu walk away as tears fill my eyes and run hot down my face. I want to run after him. Instead, I stand, sobs shaking my shoulders, until the tears hide my brother entirely and turn Rosita into a white blur.

When Willow finds me late that evening, trudging back in the general direction of the camp, I hardly care.

He draws rein beside me.

"Long way out, Maki. Especially with that pack and your dog."

I shrug. The tears are long gone, but I feel hollow, as if Maki has left me and I only look like her.

"Do you want a lift?"

I shake my head.

"Here." He pulls off a glove and reaches down to give me a hand up. I take it, putting my foot over his boot and letting him haul me up. All my bones hurt.

He settles me on the saddle behind him. The last thing I want to do is put my arms around his waist, but as he clucks to his horse, I am forced to hold on as the horse shifts below me.

Iki falls into step beside Willow's horse. He did not even give me the satisfaction of growling. Willow is no longer the enemy to him.

Willow leans down. "You have not said a word, Maki. Are you hurt?"

I shake my head.

"Were you looking for the horses, all the way out here?"

I shrug.

"I won't tell anyone." Normally a promise like this would make me bristle, but he does not sound like he is putting me under an obligation—he sounds like he is trying to prove himself.

"Are you hungry?"

I shake my head. We travel in silence until it is almost too dark to see. Willow stops us on the edge of the pine forest.

I stay on the horse and watch as he brushes away the pine needles to create a clear patch of dirt. The task of building a fire is one I know as well as the houses in my village, but I have no energy to move. I simply watch him as if I have never seen it done before.

The flame is steady and cheerful when he straightens and turns to me. "Are you going to come down?"

I sigh. I am so very tired. I want to come down, but I cannot muster the strength to do it.

He comes over and holds out his hand. "It has been a day, hasn't it? I won't ask questions, but please, come down and eat something."

I take his hand and dismount. The ground feels so hard.

We ride into camp the following night with a string of three horses, all tired and round-bellied from gorging on the late summer grasses.

Everything is as I left it, only a bit trampled, and there is a great charred patch where the fire burned. Captain Innes must be displeased with the delay.

Eyes follow us as we enter, but Willow pays them no mind. I try to follow suit.

"Where'd you find the lad, Willow?" asks one fellow.

Willow ignores him.

We stop near the picket line. From what I can see, most or all of the horses have been found.

"You are mighty late," says one of the men, someone I have seen around Laramie's fire.

"Had a ways to go and some horse to drag," Willow says matter-of-factly.

Another man comes up to help take the horses. "That *savet* disappeared the same night as this lad. How do we know they weren't together?"

I drop off the back of Willow's mare and pull one of the horses out of line.

"All the horse-boys were out looking." Willow speaks more sharply than usual. "If you're suggesting different just because he's native, I'd think twice."

He hands off the lead rope of one of the horses. "Besides, *that* one was found alone with a lame horse. Opposite direction."

The man shrugs. "If you say, Willow. Your word's good."

Willow dismounts and ties his horse up, removing the tack himself. I stand and watch, feeling oddly out of place, like I do not belong anywhere. Not here in the camp, not free out on the wide meadows.

"Goodnight, Maki," Willow says quietly, and walks away without saying more.

Much time has passed since I parted with Tsanu. I wonder how he is, and if the captain was very angry. I hardly have the strength to be afraid for him, or to be angry at the captain and the son of a devil's antler who did not treat Rosita's hooves.

Fredrico has been found again. He is at his picket with a new tether, eating hay like nothing happened. I stumble over and twist my fingers into his dark mane, scratching his chest in silent greeting.

He nickers to me. Normally I would not touch him much—he does not like it—but I lean against his dried-sweat hide and cry into his shoulder. Hard, silent sobs shake my whole body, and he just stands there, still save for the steady crunch of hay.

I hear footsteps behind me and I stiffen, holding my breath.

It is a man I have never seen before, but I don't like the looks of him. Just my luck to run into two bad characters in the space of two weeks.

I turn slowly so he cannot see that I have been crying, but he whips around the other side of Fredrico, startling him.

"Poor little native boy," he drawls. "Crying girls' tears."

He stops short and peers down into my face.

"You are a girl . . . by gar, you're a girl!" His face flies from incredulous to shrewd. "Wait till the captain hears this. That hostage didn't get away on his own, did he?"

I launch myself at him. I don't remember clearly what happened after that. I was on his back tearing at his hair and he was swinging at me over his shoulders when Rutter's voice broke in and rough hands pulled me forcibly off the man.

"Hey, hey! Maki, lad, what is this? Two in two weeks?"

"That's not a lad!" The man backs up, pointing a shaking finger at me. "It's a girl, a bloomin' girl."

I snarl at him.

"No, it isn't. You've lost your mind." Rutter doesn't even give me a glance.

"It is! look again." The man's eyes glint, taunting me.

I rush at him again, but Rutter holds me back. He looks down at me, and I see the realization slowly dawn on his face. "By thunder...."

The blood roars in my ears.

"Just wait till the captain hears about this." The man gives a sly grin. "The boys are going to—"

"The boys ain't going to hear of it." Rutter takes a step backward towards the wagon. "And neither is the captain."

"What do you mean?" The man's face is twisted in a sneer.

Rutter steps forward, his legs braced apart, his head cocked to one side.

There is a heavy click. My breath catches.

Rutter is holding his long gun, pointed at the stars, his finger on the trigger. "I said the captain an' the boys, they ain't going to hear of it."

Anger shoots across the man's face, but I see he is afraid now. A small crowd is gathering, four or five men.

"You bring harm to that girl—" his eyes go slowly to each of the curious faces watching us— "any man touches that girl, and I'll shoot him dead."

There is an uncertain silence.

"Now move on. There's nothing to be seen here."

A couple men, stir but no one makes a move to leave.

"I said move on!" The gun goes off deafeningly with a bark of flame. The men disperse quickly, muttering. They believe his threat.

Rutter drops his finger from the trigger and lets the gun fall against his shoulder. "Anyone touches you, says anything, Maki, you come straight to me." He swings the gun down and puts it back in the wagon, giving me a nod. "I will deal with 'im."

He stops. "It is Maki?"

"Yes." My voice sounds thin, breathless. I had not expected this of Rutter.

"Good. That makes it easy." He stomps pasts me.

TEN

Fading Gold

The river settlement of Heart's End lies just below us, beside the snaking Shakluk River. I pause, taking in the heavy smells of fish and oil and the warm, good smells of food. It is a reminder of what I want but cannot have. A sharp stab of regret enters my chest.

"What is this place called again?" asks Willow.

"Heart's End."

"Man must have been desperate to name it that." Rutter chuckles behind me.

I shrug. I have always guessed that it was named by some great man who had grown old and bitter by the time the honor of the naming was given him.

"Either that, or he was content." Willow lifts his face into the wind. "I could see a man looking down upon that river, full of good livelihood, at all the fine land around, and believing he need not go anywhere else to find such joy."

Even I had never thought of it that way.

"I don't know." I rub my sore shoulder. "It smells pretty bad here sometimes." It is a fishing town, after all.

Rutter laughs again, and his horse switches its tail in brief annoyance at the outburst.

But I see what Willow means. The whole river plain is beautiful from up here, the leaves going gold, the sun shining on the winding river and the mountains beyond. It brings peace to the heart.

Captain Innes has already started down the hill. I see Ransom riding back, probably to give orders to the wagons. I search for Tsanu, but cannot catch a glimpse of him. I have not seen him since our escape attempt.

I keep telling myself things will be all right—we will get another chance. But I cannot help wishing we had tried harder, done something more. Before, there was a chance that someone in the settlement might have recognized Tsanu and helped us. But he is too well guarded now. The captain watches him like a stalking wolf.

Tsanu told me to have hope, but I cannot feel it now. Not even for him.

I slide the captain's saddle off Fredrico's back. I would like to drop it in the dirt, but I spit instead.

I brush the wet patches from below the saddle while Fredrico shakes his mane out and blows loudly through his nose. Rutter says it is good when a horse does that.

"*Hagati!*" greets a voice behind me. "Welcome to Heart's End." A man of about thirty summers materializes out of the fog, his dark eyes twinkling over a black mustache. He wears a large tooth around his neck—a bear's, perhaps.

"*Kataya,*" I reply, pressing my forehead to his. "Thank you for the welcome."

"It is good to see the face of a brother. They said there was one of us among the men of the camp, but I did not expect him to be so young."

"It is good to see your face," I reply, biting back other things that I might say. The more people who take me for a boy, the better.

He looks at me like he is noticing my face—there is little swelling now, but it is still unnatural colors in places—yet he says nothing about it.

"When you have finished with your beast, come with me. You will be our guest for the time of your stay."

For a split second, I hesitate. Will Rutter worry, not knowing where I am?

I brush the thought off and accept the offer with a deep nod. I do not answer to Rutter.

"Your friend may come too, if he wishes. Your friend is our friend."

I turn, wondering if he speaks of Iki, and I see that Willow has walked up behind me. His face lights at the invitation.

I nod silently.

"Good."

The stranger waits patiently as I finish a few more horses. When I have done my share, I leave my bag of brushes and follow him. Willow has his hands in his pockets, looking unsure of himself, but he will find no trouble here. This is a river village. I am a guest of honor because I am like kin, but they will have entertained many like Willow in their day.

"Come inside." Our host gestures with some pride to a large house on the edge of town, built of sturdy logs and slat-wood. "For one night, you will forget the weariness of the journey."

I leave Iki in their dog-yard, wagging his tail and sniffing the other dogs cautiously. There is an unnatural stillness among them, but I can already tell there will be no trouble beyond a growl now and then.

I step inside and am greeted by the warm, homey smell of meat on a spit. Quiet talk fills the room, some half-dozen sitting comfortably about, speaking in the tongue of my people. On a rug in one corner sits a bowl of fresh berries and a flask of oil.

A large, quiet woman approaches us, her beautiful long braids adorned with beads and quilled wraps. "How long have you journeyed?" She looks at me as a mother might look at her small son.

The feeling is a jarring one.

"Four months, almost," Willow answers for me in the Invader tongue, and the woman nods, understanding.

"Poor lad. A while since you've been home?"

I nod. This much is true.

"Your name?"

"M-Maki," I spit out.

"And your friend?"

"This is Willow."

Willow steps forward with his kindest smile, bows to our host, and kisses the soft hand of the hostess—a tradition of the Invaders. "I am touched that you should share your home."

Our host presses his forehead to Willow's. His wife is blushing, running her big hands over her braids in girlish delight at Willow's foreign gallantry.

Something big and empty settles in my chest.

I run my hands over my tousled black hair. If only I had one of my whalebone combs. I know I am rough and thick-headed and less than four stone-weights of wolf-pup fight. But looking at Willow, I want to be more.

He and the host are laughing now. Whatever he has said, it must have been good. I had no idea Willow could do this with my people, laugh and talk and be friends. Why did he never do it in Tansilet?

The host throws his long arm around his wife's shoulders. "And I am Akak the hunter, and my wife is Taya. The rest—" he sweeps his arm to the other half dozen scattered about the house— "are kin and friends."

Taya leads me to the wolf-rug where the food is. "You are hungry, my boy. I see it in your eyes."

I give her a little smile. This also is true.

"And your friend, whatever happened to him? He has no meat on his bones!"

"He was sick some months ago. With a fever."

"Well, this food will be a beginning," she says briskly.

The floor is spread with meats and fish and berries, *muktuk* and seal oil.

I take a piece of meat first, and memories of Tansilet flood back so hard I almost cry. There is great emptiness in tasting what used to be and knowing it will never be so again.

Willow, cross-legged, seems to be enjoying himself. He dips some of the dried salmon in oil and eats it, listening intently as Akak speaks in a broken form of the Invader tongue. I cannot hear the subject of their conversation, the pleasant talk around me drowning out their words, but after a few minutes Willow's face breaks into a grin, and he and Akak start speaking very earnestly.

Akak clears his throat and the room falls quiet.

"It is good that you have come now." He gestures to Willow and to me. "There will be a herd passing by soon, probably three or four miles away, just over those ridges."

He waves his hand in the direction of the west, though one cannot see ridges through walls. "And I, Akak the hunter, will take you myself to hunt them!"

The mist clings to the ground like a child with its blanket on an icy day. The grass is brown and reddish now, still deep. It is sweet this time of year, and the herds will be ranging, fattening up before winter. I breathe the cold, crisp air deeply and grip my bow tighter. Willow lies beside me, a borrowed bow in his hands. He is admiring it, completely absorbed in figuring out how it is fashioned. He pulls one of the arrows from the quiver and stares down the end of it.

"Have you ever shot one of those?" I whisper.

He grins. "Last night. Akak took me out and we shot by firelight."

"Are you any good?"

"Enough to hit a *pannik*, I think."

I laugh softly and turn my eyes back to the ridge ahead.

"I told Akak I would let him try my strike-lock."

"And?"

"He wants to, very much."

"Are you going to let him shoot a *pannik* with it?"

"Depends on which way the herd is moving—whether we are set up well for it or not. I used to hunt back home, but just deer. They were not the size of these."

"They taste good," I say. I can imagine them now, raw or cooked, the rich flavor of true meat.

For Tsanu and I, the first *pannik* of the season was always for feasting. We would eat what we wanted and not stop until we were full. I can remember only once between the year of my mother's leaving and now that we did not do this. That was a thin winter, and I wonder in hindsight whether Tsanu had not hurt his main hand and hidden it from me, and that was why he caught so little that year.

But we did not starve.

A rumble starts in the ground, and the thrill runs through me like a river current. It is a big herd.

"Ahh!" Akak growls in pleasure beside me. "This will be good hunting!"

Willow scrambles up and cocks his ear to the wind. Akak listens to the ground.

"They will be breaking to the north," they both say, almost at the same time.

I quickly forget them and everything else around me. I can feel how close the *pannik* are to cresting that ridge. I can feel their thundering numbers in every inch of my body, and I—getting ahead of myself—I am tasting the fresh meat as I do every year when Tsanu brings in the first of the fall. I long with a fierce longing for things to be right again, for Tsanu to be back at my side, crouched here in the mist-damp leaves.

"Here they come!" cries Akak, and it does not matter, because the noise is deafening.

Hundreds break over the ridge, pouring like a waterfall down this side. I brace my feet on the trembling ground and take aim. Something must have startled them—the scent of wolves, perhaps—for they are running like dogs in the harness.

I spot one, a fat young male, running on the outside where he can be picked off easily.

Inhale, exhale, aim. Hold your breath.

The arrow flies from my bow like a part of me. I can almost feel as it drives true. The *pannik* falls, and a couple of his fellows veer around his body.

I aim and shoot again, bringing down a doe. The first one is for me, the second a thank-you to my host. Taya will be able to dry the meat, and it will get them through another week of the winter.

Almost as fast as it came, the herd is gone. The rumble is dimming now.

The mists are drifting off, weak and thin. Akak laughs, thrusts Willow's strike-lock back into his hand, and strides toward the body of one of the fallen *pannik*. I look to Willow in wonder and he only smiles.

Five or six carcasses lie in the grass. We have had a very good hunting.

Akak studies the kill. "We will get some horses from the town to help carry them back. But first we will dress them."

I pull out my knife and start on the young male I took down first. It was a clean kill, and that I am proud of. Tsanu would tell me I have done well.

I press my hand into the shoulder of the *pannik*. "Thank you," I murmur. Without their plentiful herds, we could starve. For this reason they are loved and honored by us, though we kill and eat them.

"You shot this one?" Willow stops beside me, gazing down.

"Yes, and that one." I point to the doe.

"Maki, I had no idea you were such a hunter!" Willow is laughing, truly laughing. A smear of blood and dirt on his face makes his smile even whiter.

"I suppose so." I shrug, but inside, my heart is singing.

"Do you want help dressing that?" He points to the doe.

"I'll do it."

"Is this yours?" Akak comes over too.

I thrust down my annoyance. I am the slowest, yes. But I am half their sizes.

"Yes, and that one beyond. This is mine, and that is yours. As thanks for your generous hospitality and food."

Akak looks at the *pannik* with pleasure shining out of his dark eyes. "It is well done, boy. You are a fine hunter for one so young. And your gift I will gladly accept."

I push my hair out of my eyes and strike bloody hands with him in agreement.

"My heart is sorry to bid you both farewell," says Akak.

The day is done, and word has come to us that the army will move out before dark. I am sorry about this, for I had hoped for another night with Akak and Taya and a continuing of the great feast we had today. It is the first time I have felt anything like home since Tansilet burned.

"In token of this time," he continues, "and hearing that you walk a dark path, I give you these."

He holds out a claw strung on a piece of hide string to each of us.

Willow pulls his over his head and it hangs just where his shirt opens at the neck. I tuck mine into my chest beside my pouch. I will treasure it. Not the token alone, but the memory of the home and the food and the hunting.

Willow bids Akak goodbye in the traditional way, then kisses Taya's hand.

Akak looks to me. "May the sun shine on you all your journey. May your hands be strong and brave, and whatever fear and darkness hounds you, let raven wings lift you beyond it."

"*Kuyanak*," I whisper in thanks. "Peace be to your house."

I bid Taya goodbye also and wave again as I run to catch up with Willow. I will miss them all, these people of Heart's End.

The camp is a stir of shouts and noise and the disturbance of moving out. Willow and I hear Captain Innes somewhere among it, shouting, and exchange a glance.

A voice hails me near at hand. "Where have you been, Maki? You look smug as a cat."

"Willow and I were in the home of friends." I find myself strangely warmed to see Rutter's lopsided smile. "And you?"

The smile gives an unpleasant twist. "There weren't enough provisions here to satisfy Ransom, and Captain Innes cannot wait long enough to fish for what we need. He hopes we'll find a better village northward."

"Oh." A pucker of worry starts between Willow's eyebrows, and my heart gives a twinge of pain. We were so happy for that night and day.

"And we were told that this winter will be brutal." Willow heaves a saddle onto Fredrico and cinches it tight, causing Fredrico to jump and pin his ears. "Headed into the teeth of winter with—"

He breaks off and sighs, "God help us all."

ELEVEN

When the Snow Flies

The wind howls, and I blink with an effort against its assault, straining to glimpse Tsanu's dark form up ahead. Clouds loom, blocking the sun and obscuring the path before us. Though it is mid-morning, it looks like dusk, and there is a feeling in the weather that I know well.

Snow is coming.

I glance up at Rutter, who is riding at my side, blocking the wind from one side. For once, I am glad that I am not allowed my own horse. He is bundled up, but his cheeks are an angry red, his hands chapped and bleeding.

He peers at the sky, puzzlement in his face. "What is this?"

Before I can answer, a single snowflake, driven like a bullet in the wind, smacks its tiny self into his coat and melts instantly.

"Is this snow?" He looks to me for an explanation.

"Yes, it is."

"But it's only—"

"The time of the leaves turning, yes. It is common for it to snow this early. I am surprised it has not snowed sooner."

"But we have so far to go, and it's bloody cold as it is." There is a note of worry in Rutter's voice.

"Does the world never freeze where you came from?"

"Only a little. We get snow, but we also have fires in our hearths and tea to drink scalding hot. We don't go about in it unless we must."

The gale picks up, sweeping icy fingers down every shirt back and up every horse's mane. Sprinkles of snow come on it, stinging little pellets of cold. I feel a little sorry for Rutter. He seems to dread the cold so, and he is in for a lot of it.

I turn my face up toward him so the wind will not dash my words away. "If you stop feeling your face, get off your beast and walk out of the wind awhile. It is warmer walking."

He shakes his head and burrows his face deep into his collar. "Wind aside, it's warmer bestride a beast, with their heat going into you. If I got off, I'd be shivering so hard I couldn't speak."

Well, he has opinions. If he freezes, it will not be my fault.

"Halt!" The captain's voice rings out.

What is it now?

Peering beneath the neck of Rutter's horse, I see the captain's tall shoulders hunch forward against the cutting wind. He is speaking to Tsanu, his voice carrying on the wind. "Is there no better way?"

We have come to a halt at the top of a small ridge. Scrambling around Rutter's horse, I peer over the edge.

The only way down is a deer path about three horses wide. Even in the dim light, I can see the steepness of the trail. Thank goodness it is Tsanu leading us. Any other path might have been deadly for the wagons, but here, with some care and some rigging, they will get down sound enough.

"This is the fastest way." Tsanu raises his voice to be heard through the wind. "We will camp below tonight easily. To go around would take two, three days."

Captain Innes nods, his sharp eyes studying Tsanu's face to make sure Tsanu is not playing him for a fool.

If Tsanu wanted, he could play him for a fool anyway. I know.

But Tsanu has always been honest, perhaps too much so for his own good.

Captain Innes straightens in the saddle, his mind made up. He tightens the collar of the wolfskin coat he traded for at Heart's End. "All right. Lieutenant, cover the descent."

Ransom salutes, and the captain follows Tsanu over the side. Ransom backs his horse out of the way, and the rest of the captain's party follows slowly behind.

When we reach the bottom and camp for the night, the damage is plain as day. Three of the horse-boys are shivering uncontrollably, their eyes bright with oncoming fever, and I hear wet coughs around the camp.

Laramie, ever fit and strong, dishes out a thin stew made of our combined jerky rations. He has added a healthy amount of chickory, as well as a hunk of my *pannik*.

Rutter's eyes light up at the smell. "What have you done, Laramie?"

"A body needs sommat warm and reaching on a day like this 'un. I used to march on the northern fronts—men that ate stew of nights lasted longer than the ones on dry rations." He looks at me and winks. "And our little *savet* has kindly given us some of his—erhm, *her*—own caribou."

The thought of giving my hard-won *pannik* to fill Invader bellies does not annoy me as much as it ought. They are so grateful, and Laramie speaks true. The stew will hold us in far better stead than ordinary camp rations.

"If we weren't setting such a terrific pace, we might be able to hunt too," mutters one of the men.

"We'll have to eventually." Rutter accepts a hot bowl in both hands and holds it like it is full of gold. "Unless we reach that settlement."

"The hostage says it's still quite a piece away."

"How far?" One of the horse-boys looks up, fear in his eyes.

I keep my mouth shut. It is far. If the weather was good, we might stand a chance of making it there, but with snow falling and possible fever starting among the men, I don't dare tell them how far.

Rations have dwindled noticeably this week, and in such cold weather, food is our lifeline. Any fool knows there is no chance of staying warm and well in the northern territory without enough food and proper clothing. The men huddled around the fire, shivering and gulping down Laramie's stew, are wrapped in wool, not fur. They will freeze in those thin, sorry-looking coats.

I shudder. I must start working on that *pannik* hide. Akak gave me the doeskin, but it takes time to make a coat properly, and I have not had the time. It is a good thing I am still small. Otherwise the coat would not fit.

Shouting on the other end of camp breaks the silence of fire-smoke and hungry men. An uneasy murmur ripples around the circle.

"It's the doctor," grunts Jeremiah. "He and the captain are at it again."

The fire crackles against the dark of the night, sending glowing sparks spiraling upwards. Rutter sits nearest to me, his thick-sleeved arms wrapped around himself as if to stave off the cold and hunger. He coughs once, but it is a healthy clear-your-lungs cough, not the wet, camp-fever kind. I fear the day Tsanu or Willow cough like that—like camp fever. The winter has already claimed many men, and I cannot stand the thought of losing them.

I have not seen Tsanu in two days; I hope he is keeping warm. I let my arm sit against Rutter's, and even through the layers of our coats, the touch brings warmth. Willow sits on my other side, further away. He has drawn himself up into his coat like a dog curls into a ball. I cannot help smiling when I look at him.

We are driving hard, the whole army, to the brink of a cliff. Tsanu is taking us on the fastest route to Kaquom, but we are still probably two or three weeks away in this weather, and I know we don't have food or strength to last that long. I feel the knife edge of desperation in the men. Some are close to breaking, others fighting to keep up hope against all odds.

I look up at the sky, faintly blue where the first moon is buried in the clouds. There are no stars tonight. I look up and whisper softly for something to save us.

What I want most is to hunt a herd of *pannik* and feast on the warm meat and show Willow how their coats are the warmest that can be found. I would make a coat for myself and one for Tsanu.

Rutter shivers through his coat and into my arm. Poor fellow—he should have stayed wherever he came from. Far off, a wolf howls, and Iki pulls himself stiffly to his feet, his nose tilted to the air. Wolves thrive on the cold. Their coats keep them warm and well, and they hunt down the cold and sick.

Captain Innes in his fur coat swims to my mind's eye.

Preying upon the weak and sick.

I wonder how Tsanu is. I am no longer just afraid for his life—I miss him. I miss how he teases me, how he laughs—too rarely, but wonderfully. I miss the strength of his arms, his stealth in the woods. I hate to see him chained like a hound and not a man, ever in the captain's sight, under his watchful eye.

"So solemn, Maki." Willow leans over and give my knee a push, painfully like an older brother. "What is it? Thinking of another frightful tale to tell us?"

I smile to indulge him.

But no—not only to indulge him. When he talks to me, I find myself smiling without meaning to do it. I find myself happy.

"No, I was not." I wrap my arms around my middle and lean forward to keep warm. "But I could think of another if you wish it."

Willow lets a long stream of breath out of his mouth. "Ah, singing seems more in keeping with this night, don't you think?"

"Aye." Rutter's voice is a little louder, rough as he tries to keep it from betraying his shivering. "Let's have a song."

"What say you to 'In the Falling Dusk'?" Willow leans closer to me. "You will like this, Maki."

He begins to sing, slow and sweet, of a hunter returning home from a long journey to a warm hearth and a happy family. The wistful tune brings a lump to my throat. My heart lights with longing, just as it does when I hear the songs of my own people in our native tongue.

When he finishes, the last note hangs in the air, quiet as the stars. I hardly breathe.

Rutter breaks the silence with warm praise. "That's prime. Makes you almost wish for home."

"Almost?" laughs a man from across the fire. "You mean so hard you're like to burst."

I glance up by chance and see tears in the man's eyes.

I expected to feel triumph when this moment came—when the Invaders found themselves crushed by the fierceness of this hard land. But I only feel sorrow for the man. We are, both of us, homesick.

"What is your home called?" I ask him.

The question comes out of nowhere, surprising even me.

"Blueheath. That is the town. I have, or had, a farm there. Three children, a wife."

"Why did you leave it, then?" A slight tone of reproach creeps into my voice.

And come to my land, I think, but do not say.

The man's face creases with trouble. "Three years of bad famine came. I was in debt to the landowner, and all the money I had ever saved was gone. I had a choice: I could lose the farm and everything I'd ever worked for, or

I could take commission with an advance—pay just enough for the farm and the family to survive. So I did that. If there'd been another way, I would have taken it. But in poverty, a man has little choice."

Gently I rub my stiff fingers. "How far away is Blueheath?"

He shrugs. "I am not a man of learning. I do not know how to read a map, save that of a farm plot."

"Thousands of leagues," Jeremiah says quietly. "And across a sea."

So many, come from so far. And for what? To burn Tansilet and to die in the wilderness.

Perhaps I should admire their courage, but I do not. My chest is too thickly tightened with pain and anger.

A little closer, the wolves howl.

"Bloody bruisers," mutters Rutter. "You don't suppose they smell the horses?"

Iki gets to his feet and growls.

"They won't come into camp." I rub Iki's back with my frozen knuckles. "There is too much man-smell. They will not dare even if they are starving."

Willow swallows slowly, a muscle twitching in his cheek. Is he truly scared of the wolves? Or is it that he is hungry?

He looks to me. "Maki, sing us one of your songs."

"Me?" I do not know what to sing.

"Yes, of course. You must have learned some songs in your village."

I have learned songs, many songs. But my heart has been heavy for Tansilet of late and cannot put itself into a song.

"Come on, Maki, sing something." Rutter turns to me and smacks me, friendly-like, in the arm.

"I have never heard one of your people sing," says Willow. "It must stir the blood."

He speaks true. Our songs stir the blood against the cold and keep alive the memory of things past that are no more but are worth the remembering.

I think of the stag on Tsanu's arm; of the girl-children of Tansilet dancing in the middle of the village, dark braids flying; of Kavik and his wolf-pack, running under the dark trees among the summer lights. All is gone now, living only in my memory.

I want to bring honor to the people of my slain village.

I lean forward and close my eyes. The firelight is hot upon half my face; the rest of it feels the smart kiss of the freezing air as I turn my closed eyes to the sky. I open my mouth and sing, a slow, chanting song.

It is in our native tongue, which most of the men do not understand. A song of courage—a young man bidding his home and family farewell before setting out upon the doomed quest that will kill him.

I finish and open my eyes to see Willow grinning. "That is beautiful. What is it about?"

I tell him and his face changes suddenly, sadly.

"That's bloody awful." Rutter wraps his sleeves around him darkly. "Who'd gladly walk into suicide?"

"The song is not about death," I say quickly. "It is about living."

"But he died." Sadness still haunts Willow's eyes.

"Only those who have lived well can accept death with such courage," I say.

"Or lived a rum awful life," says a man from across the fire. "Sometimes a man doesn't want to go on."

"But you should." I stiffen. "Evils that come your way are no excuse for giving up. To give up would be wrong!"

"And how do you know?"

I do not remember getting to my feet, but I am standing. "How do I know?" Anger rises within me, proud and hard. "My father died by the hands of your fellow soldiers when I was just a baby, so I do not remember him at all. My grandmother stopped talking. My mother, when I could only just go about on my own, ran away with a nomad to the mountains. Not even me, or my—family—were enough to make her stay. I lost my last living relative to you soldiers—and then you burned my village. I know."

Willow is gazing at me, his eyes dark with sorrow. He looks as I felt when he finished his song, unable to move or speak. The others shuffle their feet and clear their throats in the cold and will not look at me.

I do not mind. I do not want their pity. But I am glad that Willow understands.

"It was a fine song, anyway," he says. I give him a nod in thanks.

Rutter gets up, rubbing his hands together. "Well, I'm turning in for the night. Three hundred horse do not ready themselves."

"True 'nough," Laramie grunts, getting to his feet with a groan. "This cold will be the death of me."

"You coming, Maki?" Rutter crooks an eyebrow at me.

"I will be along soon."

The others leave, one by one, but Willow does not move from his place. He stares into the flames, his face etched with weariness. At last he says in a quiet voice, "I am sorry, Maki."

I am suddenly awkward and do not know where to put my hands. "It is all right," I say, as if comforting him. "We cannot always choose how life runs."

"But you have no family now? Is that why you joined this company?"

I sigh. It seems wrong to lie, but cannot tell him the truth. "Yes. Otherwise I would be alone."

"I always wanted a—" He catches himself and then smiles, shaking his head. "A sister like you."

"Well, you would make a fine older brother, I think." This is the most I dare say. I try to think of another thing to say before he asks me more about myself. "Do you have any brothers or sisters?"

"One younger brother. He died when we were young. By then, my father was dead, so—" He shrugged. "I used to have dreams that I saved him, but even those stopped eventually. It is good to forget, sometimes."

I nod, but everything in me fights this idea. I want nothing to do with letting go. I want to fight, fight and conquer. I want to save what I love.

"I cannot forget. Even if I wanted to," I say.

"You are young, Maki. There is time yet." Willow moves off the log and lies beside the fire, pulling his coat closer around him. Iki takes this as an invitation and relocates to lie beside him.

I notice afresh the hollows of Willow's cheeks. They are growing hollower, which means he is losing weight faster than most of the men in the camp. Good fresh raw meat would put color and life back in him, but we have none, and he is too thin. Not enough time has passed since his fever.

If we keep on starving, he may die. The captain is wagering the life of Willow Tam against the chance of a city of gold and jewels.

The captain is a fool.

"He is starving us, isn't he?" I say bitterly.

Willow sits up. "No, Maki. He just does not know Uniap'nik. He is a man used to conquering harsh conditions. But he was not expecting these winters of yours."

I put my face in my hands, savoring the thin heat of the fire. "What do you think of Inik Katsuk, Willow? If it was real, what would you think?"

His eyebrows go up till they cannot go any further. "What do I think of it?"

He gives me one long look, then wanders a moment in his own mind. "I say," he answers at last, slowly, "to be rich would be a fine thing. I have seen much sorrow brought on by poverty. And yet there are other things that are far more important."

He reaches out with a sudden smile and tweaks my ear. "And what about you? What do you think of Inik Katsuk, you sly weasel?"

I laugh a little and move out of reach. A moment ago, I had no clear words for what I thought of Inik Katsuk. Now they fly from my mouth before I can fully comprehend them.

"I hate it."

I expect some reaction from Willow, but he does absolutely nothing. My words fade from my ears long before he picks up his gun and runs his thumb over the shiny metal, rubbing away a blemish that does not exist.

"My mother told me that story the day she left me, and it has haunted me ever since. If it existed, I would run from it as far as I could, or I would hunt it down and destroy it."

This last declaration seems too much against Willow's silence, but I had to say it.

"I don't suppose I blame you any."

My eyes rise to his. "Truly?"

"No. All it seems to have brought you is sorrow. Sorrow and trouble."

"That is true." I find I can no longer look him in the eye—I fear if he looks into my face he will see the whole truth, Tsanu and all.

"For my part, I think Captain Innes should—"

He stops. He knows better than to speak against his captain. He thrusts his gun into its holster and gets up.

"Wait, Willow, are you going to leave?"

He stops. The fire pops and flares a little brighter on his face. "Do you want me to stay?"

I am on the edge of saying no, but instead I nod.

"Very well, I shall." He settles on the log across from me.

"I went too far into my own head," he apologizes. "I do not always see eye to eye with the captain, and—"

"You do not have to explain to me."

Willow reaches down and rubs Iki's ears, and I notice how the firelight plays on his face, striking it differently than a few weeks ago.

"You are too thin for winter," I say.

"Am I?" He smiles sadly. "There's nothing I can do about that."

"You need meat."

"Indeed, and so does every man."

"No, you."

I should not have started this. I am hungry, and that makes me weak, and I fear more for him. Most men who go into winter looking like that die.

"Do not worry about me, Maki. It cannot be helped."

"It must be helped!"

I get up. I cannot stand to continue this conversation, and I know Rutter will be freezing in the tent. "Think about it," I say. "We need fresh game, or we may die."

I call Iki and go to my tent. Rutter's muffled snoring sounds from the far wall, behind the blanket that has hung from the roof since the day he discovered I am a girl.

It is too cold in here.

"Iki!" I snap my fingers. In Tansilet, I never allowed the dogs to sleep with me, but tonight we need it. Unsure of himself, Iki tiptoes in and burrows between Rutter and me, halfway under the hanging blanket.

I fall asleep with my face and fingers buried in Iki's stiff fur.

TWELVE

The Gift of the Great One

The next day, we reach the sea coast, gray and cold and stern. The strong winds blowing off the sea are tinged with salt. I have only been down to the sea a few times in my life, and it was always the southern sea. I have never been this far north.

I think we would enjoy the view more if we weren't all starving to death. We are forced to make camp because it is dusk, but the sea-wind blows the tents out of their pegs and makes the horses nervous.

I am currying a couple of the big horses, two hours later than usual because of the wind, when Drucker, of all people, approaches me, his jaw like iron. What have I done wrong?

He opens his mouth, but nothing comes out at first. Then he says, "Do you know these parts?"

"These parts? Not really. Why?"

"Is there is game or fish in these parts? Anything?"

The rations must be getting bad.

I try to break it to him gently. "It will be hard to fish in the sea."

Even if it was not, there is no guarantee we would find anything fit for an army on this salty stretch. "The sea is icy and stormy this time of year, and, well—"

Hope lingers in his face. I cannot kill it.

"If we take time tomorrow to hunt, to look around, it may be possible to find seals—or bear, maybe, though the bears will be going into hiding soon."

"Seals." He latches onto the possibility. "Do they make good eating?"

"Yes." That is the truth, though we may not find a colony.

He nods vigorously. The hope in his eyes hurts me, just under the ribs.

"I will speak to the captain. We will arrange some hunting parties."

He leaves and I swallow hard, skimming just the dirt off the horses. I can't stand to take more of the winter fur off their protruding ribs.

Maybe this is it. Maybe this is where we will die.

I stretch high on my toes and gaze down the long, pebbled beach. A gull cries high above me, distant and mournful. I rub my arms and swing them a little. The wind off of the coast is needle-sharp, and a thin crust of ice edges the rocks by a quiet pool.

My breath streams into the frozen air as I rub my hands together to bring the blood back into them. It has been two long hours of searching for signs of seals, rabbits, or anything living, and fear has settled cold and hard in my belly. Fear of dying out here, a long and painful death filled with men raving and going mad. If it comes to this, I will run away.

And leave Tsanu?

"Is there any hope of finding anything along here?" Rutter pulls his horse up beside me and looks down the beach, shoulders sagging in dejection.

I shrug. "We have nothing to lose by looking." We can't afford not to look.

"Come on, Maki. I'll give you a ride." He hoists me up behind him.

Rutter is shivering, but we both warm a little as we ride down the beach. He is very quiet, and I know that he is unhappy—scared, even. I don't blame him. Poor fellow, far from home, half-expecting to starve to death now. At least Tsanu and I have always known this was a possibility—to die out in the middle of nowhere in the land that gave us birth.

Ahead of us lies a point where the trees grow out almost to the sea's edge.

I gesture to it. "We will go around the end, and if there is nothing, we can head back."

Rutter and I have switched roles this morning. I make the decisions, give the advice. Yet I admit I feel far safer for having him and his gun at my side.

He clucks to his horse and speaks to it under his breath as he guides it into the icy shallows. We round the point and see another length of beach stretching ahead.

"Hey now, what's that?"

I stop, follow Rutter's pointing finger.

Down the long stretch of pebbled beach, halfway in the sea and halfway out, lays a massive beast. We call them *ugut*—Great Ones.

I slide to the ground and break into a run.

"Wait, Maki, what is it?" calls Rutter.

"A Great One!" I shout back.

Please let it be fresh. If it has been rotting awhile, I will sit down on this beach and cry my eyes out.

I circle the beast. It is dead. No sign of disease. No sign of carrion-feeders. I approach and put out my hand, touching the thick, smooth skin.

It is fresh. Last night or this morning fresh. We are saved.

I jump into the air, whooping and shouting and reveling in the joy of it all. Now we will not starve, at least for a time.

Rutter finally reaches me and dismounts, tying his horse to a log of driftwood. "It's a whale—stars, I've never seen one this close."

"It is a miracle!" I shout.

"Why?"

"We can eat it," I say. How can he still not understand? "It is fresh."

"You can eat whale meat?"

"And the blubber. I can show you how to make *muktuk.*"

"So—all this is food?" Light grows on his face as he slowly comprehends.

"Most of it. It will be more than enough for us all."

Besides meat, I will have ivory and oil and teeth for fishhooks. If the captain can be convinced to stay until we harvest what we can, we will be rich. Even back in Tansilet, this would have been great wealth.

As it is, we will not die, and that is enough for me.

Rutter's horse snorts and blows long through its nose. It seems afraid of the whale. I throw back my head and laugh. In this moment, nothing can shake me from my joy.

"Well, I suppose I should tell Lieutenant Ransom." Rutter reaches out, very hesitantly, to touch the whale's skin.

"Yes, quickly. You ride to him. I will stay."

"We're out far—are you sure?"

"I will be fine. If there's a scavenger, I will climb on top of the whale. There is more than enough to go around."

Rutter shakes his head, but he goes to his horse, unties it, and rides for camp.

I look up and down the beast, my heart full. "Thank you, Great One. You have saved many lives by your sacrifice."

I am atop the Great One when Rutter arrives with a party from the camp. They see me perched high in the sky above their heads and begin to point and exclaim, their hands full of knives and hatchets and other tools. I only grin and wave.

I show them with my *ulu* how to cut the whale's skin so as to peel out the thick layers of blubber, and how to reach the meat underneath. I help them fashion makeshift hooks to hang the blubber on for *muktuk*, and I teach them how to spread the meat upon the pebbles to dry. They work fast and vigorously, motivated by the promise of food.

Drucker surveys the whale with his hands on his hips. "How long will this take?"

"Three days is best for the meat. But there can be other ways of drying it, if we prepare it carefully."

"And taking apart this whale?"

I shrug. That all depends on how fast we work and how much we want to salvage from the Great One's body. "Tell the men not to eat it all at once, or it could make them sick," I warn. Whale is wonderful and rich in fats, but one should not eat much of fat after starving for a long while.

"I'll tell them." Drucker grins and gives me a brief salute before passing on down the beach with his long-legged stride.

I have never seen him so happy.

I do not see Tsanu, but I hope the news has reached him. It pleases me that Captain Innes has not come down to the beach. Perhaps the smell bothers him.

From the ground beside the whale, one man strikes up a song and belts it out merrily. It is caught up like a summer wildfire and passed all the way down to the men drying meat on the beach. I join in heartily, and when I do not know the words, I make them up.

I have not been so happy since the night I ran away with Tsanu. In a way, I am happier. I am happy because I am alive and not dead and I am not going to starve to death. And I am happy because my hands are busy at their work, making food for another day, and because the Great One washed on shore at the very time we had need.

I work until my fingers are numb, take a break, and work again. Over and over I do it, until the morning turns to afternoon and the afternoon to evening and dusk steals over and it becomes night.

The moon is high and the last crews are leaving with food for the night when I pick up my *ulu* to peel off blubber for one last hook of *muktuk*. Most of the meat has been moved far down the beach, nearer to the camp where it can be watched, out of reach of scavengers who will be drawn by the smell.

As I hang up the blubber, my eye catches a movement in the shadow of the Great One. It is Willow, laying out more strips of meat.

"Maki?" He straightens to look at me.

His tone is different. He is talking to the girl Maki, the one he tells things like a little sister. The way Tsanu used to talk to me.

"Hmm?" I set down my ulu and rinse my bloody hands in the sea.

"Can I sing you a song, one I love very much?"

"Of course. If you like."

The blue moon is playing on the waves of the pulsing sea, and even though I can hear it roaring far out, the waves that lap the beach are gentle. It is a still and perfect night.

Willow clears his throat and hesitates, but I am standing watching him, my hands dripping seawater. He gives me a smile and begins.

I rode away from Ellerslea
Upon a morning fine
And told my Jennie I'd be home
Ere long to make her mine

But long's the way across the sea
That now between us lies
And long's the road that I must tread
Beneath these foreign skies.

156

Keep your lantern burning, Jennie

To your love be true

And one day I'll ride o'er the heather

Coming home to you.

"Do you have a girl like that?" I ask softly.

"I did."

"Did?" My heart almost stops. He sang so beautifully, and I cannot bear another sad ending.

His hand plays with a thong around his neck, and I see a brief flash of clear gold. "I got a letter last winter saying she died."

"Oh . . . I am sorry, Willow. I cannot tell you how sorry I am."

"I thought you would understand, Maki. I wanted you to know."

"Doesn't anyone else know?"

"Yes—I mean, Ransom knows, and Drucker knows—some of my friends in the camp. I was crushed for a while."

"Just for a while? Are you not crushed still?"

He smiles a little. I know him too well.

"I thought you would understand. Sometimes it takes a girl to understand."

I nod quietly. "Little sisters understand. More than people know."

He pulls the thong off his neck and holds the amulet out on his palm. "She gave me this before I left. It is called amber, and it washes onto our coast from far, warm seas. She said I would be like that amber when I returned home to her, coming from far seas."

"But our seas are cold," I say.

"Yes."

He lets out a sigh and bends to toss the rope over his shoulder. "You should finish soon, Maki. I do not like leaving you alone in the night."

"I have my *ulu*." I laugh.

"What, and you can peel the blubber off whatever attacks you? I think not. Come, there will be more help in the morning."

I wrap the *ulu* in its cloth and tuck it away in my bag. The world is cold, but I have worked all night and snacked on the blubber, and in my coat I am quite warm. I see only the beauty and stillness of the night.

I am so thankful for this Great One.

"Willow?"

"Hmm?" He pauses and adjusts the rope.

"Is that why you were so sick this spring?"

He does not answer immediately. "Not really. Not entirely."

"But a little?"

"Yes, a little."

"I am sorry for that. When you saved—the guide Tsanu's life, it was brave of you."

He looks at me in surprise. "Who told you about that?"

"I—" I stop.

It is better in this case not to fumble around. It is a night of trust. "I was there. I saw it all."

"What?"

"I—I was watching your camp that night. I saw it."

"Oh, I see."

Perhaps this is a mistake. A prickle runs up my back. What if I have done the wrong thing?

"It was brave of you," I repeat, hoping he will think no more on my reasons for being outside the Invader camp the night of Tsanu's capture. "You saved his life, that is a sure thing."

"You know I only did it because it was right."

"Yes. And that is why I admire you. You did not know him, but you did it anyway. It makes you different."

He shakes his head. "No. No different from any other man with honor."

I shift my feet stubbornly in the sand, let the warm air shoot out of nose like a horse's. It is different.

"Come on, little wolf," he says, and my heart nearly stops. "Let's get back to camp."

No one has called me little wolf since Tsanu. I sling my bag over my shoulder, and the pebbles crunch and shift as I walk over them.

The night is strange and pained and beautiful.

THIRTEEN

Trail's End

The wind knifes through my thin coat and I draw it closer around me, wishing I had brought that caribou coat I left in our home in Tansilet. It is now assuredly ashes, long since scattered in the forest. The snow is horridly deep, and the horses are floundering.

Some of the men did not take Drucker's advice and are still recovering, more than a week later, from feasting on the fatty *muktuk* for three days. But that is the least of our worries now. Two hours ago, we broke camp amid three or four feet of snow and vehement protests from Ransom and Drucker. Now, thanks to the captain and his bullheaded ambition, I am cold, wet, and on the edge of losing my fingers and toes.

My only comfort is that we are closer to Kaquom. And my stomach is full.

Rutter rides up beside me, puffing in the cold air. White spots have formed on his cheeks. He will have to stop and put his hands on them before the flesh dies for good and spoils his good looks—never very fine, to be sure, but surely he has a sweetheart or someone back home.

"Rutter!" I gesture with my hands to his face. His expression falls, and he fumbles with numb fingers to remove his gloves. He drops the reins and presses his hands to his cheeks. It matters little—even given its head, his horse could not get far in this thick snow.

Shouts and curses ring out ahead. I am not the only one suffering from the captain's stubbornness. Three or four wagons, the front of the line, have fallen into a hollow six or seven feet deep and are mired in the snow. Men gather, supplying boards, shovels, ropes, and muscle, making ready to dig the wagons out.

It is a lost cause, I could tell them now. But I am not the captain.

"All right, heave now!"

Whips crack and horses strain, but the wheels will not turn.

"Move that wagon up!" Captain Innes's voice is tinged with rage.

You cannot rage against this land and live long. He must give in or die in his obstinacy.

The wagon slides, balks, and begins to slide backward. "It is no use," Tsanu is saying over the shouts of the men and the nervous cries of the horses.

"What?" The captain rounds on him.

"It is no use. We never use wheels or the like in the deep snow."

"What do you use, then?"

I scoff inwardly. Our people know better than to migrate from place to place in weather like this. How does Tsanu keep his patience with this man?

"Dogs. But they cannot be the hounds you use. They must be bred to it."

Captain Innes's eyes fall on Iki. "Like him?"

A window shuts behind Tsanu's eyes. "Yes, like him. But this one will not be of any use to you. It takes six dogs to haul one man and a week's worth of supplies in this weather."

My heart gives a grateful throb in Tsanu's direction. Captain Innes swears under his breath.

"Captain." Ransom is ever even-tempered through the captain's foul moods; the sound of his voice is a relief. "I suggest we find a suitable place to build shelters. With ourselves and our resources safe, we may take the time to chart a better course."

The idea is not one that charms Innes, but he closes his eyes briefly and nods, giving in to the inevitable. "Very well, but move quickly! We cannot afford to lose time now."

Ransom wheels and rides back up the line, issuing orders. A swath of pine lies within bowshot to the east of us, and soon the sound of axes rings out in the frosty air. Others begin treading down the snow, testing the lay of the land to find a good place to make camp.

"Come, lad." Rutter sounds frozen and winded. "We must make a picket line for the horses. And a roaring fire." His voice warms at the thought. "The poor things will take a hot mash tonight."

Hot mash for three hundred horses is a daunting thought, but compared to bloodying one's hands chopping trees and building shelters, it has a certain appeal. I blow on my hands and trudge back to the wagon to get the first length of rope.

"Hot mash," I say aloud to warm myself in my mind. Even though it is for the horses, the mere thought of warm food thaws my insides.

Rutter sends me to start the picket line because I have snowshoes. By the time it is strung and the men are picketing the horses, a fire is already roaring in the middle of camp.

I make my way toward it, carrying my *pannik* skin over my arm. Across the camp, Drucker is shouting about someone's incompetence, and near at hand, Laramie clatters his pots. My shoulders are soaked with sweat, my face and fingers and feet unnaturally warm where the cold had been unbearably painful before. I stomp down a patch of snow near the fire and lay my *pannik* skin on the ground, hair-side down. It will make a good place to sit.

"What are you doing?" Laramie is brewing coffee. I could hug him.

"Thawing out."

"Don't blame you none."

I close my eyes, letting the heat soak into my bones. Laramie's humming and clanging and the crackle of the roaring fire drown out Drucker's voice. I breathe a sigh of relief.

A sudden shout sounds from across the camp, followed by quick, low talk.

Perhaps the captain has had an *epilepsy*. I nestle deeper into my coat, feeling smug. I don't know what the word means, exactly, but I have heard the men speak of it now and again. It sounds like the sort of thing that would serve him right.

Rutter appears from among the tents, plodding toward the fire, looking ready to collapse under the weight of relief. "We are saved."

He drops heavily onto the nearest log and motions toward the pot of coffee. Laramie is already ladling out a cup for him.

I scramble to my knees. "What is it?"

"Scouts have sighted the lights of Kaquom three miles away. When this infernal snow stops, we'll move down there, and word is—I pray it's true— we'll wait out the winter."

I wake to the sound of Rutter's voice, low and angry. "What does he think he's doing, trying to kill us?"

A second voice hushes him and replies in a tone too low for me to discern the words.

I shove my hand out from beneath my furs and stretch. The morning light is coming in the windows of the old fur-shed we paid too much to sleep in, an indication that I have slept longer than I should. But the sleep still hangs heavy on my eyes.

After two and a half days of snow, it took us all day yesterday to break camp and wade the final three miles to Kaquom. It was well after dark by the time we began bedding down the horses for the night, and the red moon was in the middle of the night sky by the time we finished. I count backwards—I have slept little more than a quarter of the night.

Rutter, on the other side of the shed, raises his voice again. "Well, I know people who've lived in this land, and unless you're one of them, you don't venture out into the wilds during winter. It's madness."

"Rutter, enough. There's enough men pinning that word on the captain without you adding your voice."

"I'm starting to believe it. Nolan himself says some of the captain's great conquests bordered on madness. And this—this city—it's the greatest of all his dreams, so he says."

"Have the horses been seen to?" I ask Rutter, stumbling a little as I stand up.

"They had mash so late last night I figure on waiting a little longer to feed 'em again." He glances at the man he is talking with and then back at me.

"Why don't you go see how they fare?"

I know when I am not wanted. Not that I would report them to the captain—I was the first to call him *wukuk*. Crazy.

✒

"Maki!" I am standing among the horses when Captain Innes hails me, wading through the deep snow with the vigor of a determined man.

I do not like my name in his mouth.

"Maki." He stops in front of me and smiles. "You have that wolf-dog, don't you?"

I nod.

"Do you know how to drive a dogsled? Do they do much of that down in—in—" He snaps his fingers, trying to remember.

"Tansilet?" I supply, trying to keep the disgust out of my voice. The man burns a village and cannot even remember its name.

"Yes, Tansilet."

I am starting to get an idea of what he wants, and I do not want to humor him. But I must be honest.

"Yes."

"Can you do it well?"

"Yes."

He sighs in satisfaction, looking off toward the center of town. "I need to hire some dog-drivers and sleds. The army has reached the end of the trail until winter is past. That cannot be helped. But I—I must forge on."

"It is not wise to go out in the winter."

"So I have been told. But I also know that your kind goes about all over during winter. If your people can do it—with a little advice, so can mine."

"Our winter is very long."

"That is exactly why I cannot afford to wait. And in any case, I intend to do it the right way—the way your people do it. That is why I need you."

I stand and stare. Let him explain himself if he wants—I am not going to help him.

He leans his arm on the rump of the nearest horse and fixes me with his gaze as though I am a man with whom he is preparing to do business. "I need you to come with me to the outfitters—the trading post, you know— and tell me if the drivers are trying to cheat me or not. I will pay you well."

He holds out two bits of silver as if that will tempt me.

It does not.

That is, it might have if it did not come from him. Still, any chance to take something from the man . . . .

I snatch the two bits indifferently from his hand.

"I will go with you. But if they refuse, I cannot change their minds."

FOURTEEN

Bound for the North

Smoke hangs about the ceiling of the Kaquom trading post, the smell of cheap fire spirits cutting through just enough to be noticed. It smells powerfully of dog, though there are no dogs inside. Somewhere a harmonica plays.

I have seen places like this before, but not up close and not without Tsanu. If Captain Innes were not behind me, I might be afraid. As it is, any man I encounter here is probably no match for the captain.

The thought both comforts and unnerves me.

Innes sets a hand against the doorframe and leans down to speak in my ear. "You keep quiet. I will do the talking, and you tell me if they are bargaining fairly."

I nod. I do not want to honor him with a spoken answer. And how am I supposed to know if a man is lying or not?

Our entrance causes only a slight disturbance. A few men turn to look at us, and one greets us with a brief word, but for the most part we are ignored. The captain approaches a young man who sits at the counter drinking coffee from a tin mug, his fur ruff pushed back on his shoulders.

"Morning." Captain Innes leans one elbow on the bar, his voice friendly and comrade-like. I have to admit, he is charming when he chooses.

The young fellow flicks his eyes sideways in acknowledgement. "Morning."

"Name's Innes, Roger Innes. I just got into town."

"You're the army man."

"So you have heard?"

"Not much." The young man takes another indifferent sip of coffee.

"I'm Kane."

"I am looking for good dog teams and savvy drivers."

"Well, my dogs are good." He turns his face to the captain for the first time, and as he does, our eyes meet. His eyes glint with recognition.

I have seen him before, passing through Tansilet on his way north. He is a good man. A foreigner—not big-boned like many dog-men, but he knows dogs.

I shake my head swiftly at him behind the captain's back and run my finger down the side of my throat, mouthing a warning. He does not want this venture.

"However," he continues without missing a beat, "I am already contracted out. Unless you are willing to wait a month."

Captain Innes shakes his head. "I am afraid that will not do." He leaves Kane and moves down the bar.

Kane makes eye contact with me again and gives a nod of thanks. He drains his coffee and leaves.

Reluctantly, I return to shadowing Captain Innes. He has found two more dog-runners further down the bar: a tall, scruffy young fellow leaning his back against the counter, and a broad-shouldered, dark-haired man twice the age of his companion.

"I've run dogs all my life," the broad-shouldered man is saying. "Ever since I could stand on the runners. Briscoe here's been going for what? Fifteen?"

The young man extends his hand to Captain Innes. "Name's Briscoe. And fifteen is about right."

"I am in need of some good drivers."

"Dog-runners, you mean?" Briscoe adjusts his elbow on the counter and leans deep on it.

"All the same, isn't it?" The captain's mouth lifts with humor. "Listen, I need someone who can get me through this snow."

"What does a stranger like you want that can't wait till spring?"

"I have a man who has seen Inik Katsuk, the Seventh City. That is where I am going."

Briscoe raises his eyebrows, and the older man laughs outright. "I do not know what man you have, but I'd bet my lead dog he is *wukuk*." He gestures to his head. His meaning is clear.

"He seems to be of perfectly sound judgment." Captain Innes may not be in his own territory, but he knows how to stand his ground. "I have heard the legends, and I deem the risk worthwhile. You may speak of madness, but are not all brilliant men a bit touched?"

He means himself, of course—not Tsanu. But it makes me think of Jeremiah's words.

The broad-shouldered man scoffs. "What makes you think that I, a man of this country, don't know what I speak of? We have many legends better to chase than that one."

"In the legends, there were six others—"

"Ha!" The man laughs harshly and downs his small glass of fire spirits. "And this old down-and-outer trap claims to be one of them!"

Innes glances around the room suddenly, as if suspecting the locals of hiding jewels somewhere within. "And how do you know?"

"I was born here, bub. They mined every last ounce of silver out of here five years ago. You've got the look of a starry-eyed foreigner. I've got a piece of advice for you—forget it."

Captain Innes breathes deeply. He straightens to his full height and stands on his dignity, putting the entire weight of his distant country behind his words. "I am a captain in the great Army of the Northern Frontier. We have conquered this land."

"Conquered it, have you? What's that sick bunch of lads out there? An army? No, bub. We don't use that word out here. Just doesn't suit."

The broad-shouldered man pours himself another glass of spirits, cutting it with a generous amount of water. "I'm surprised you got that rag-tag bunch this far. First I've seen of any of you green-coats this far north."

This gives Captain Innes pause for only a moment. Then it seems to lend him strength. "That's right. And I will be remembered for it. As for you, it is your choice whether or not you want to be part of history, and rich to boot. I can always find someone else to take my money."

"Look here." The older fellow pushes aside the bottle and glass and looks more attentive. "I still don't believe a word about Inik Katsuk, but you're talking to the most experienced guide in these parts, and by *gur*, a good dog-runner too."

"I want to leave soon."

"I'll leave tonight, if the price is right." He leans back to look the captain over better.

"Five thousand?"

The man flashes a smile, which makes me like him better than before, and pours a glass of straight spirits, holding it out to the captain. "Quniak is your man."

Innes downs the fire spirits with a straight face and grins. "Good."

He rounds on Briscoe immediately. "And you?"

"Well, chasing any kind of legend is better than poking around his hole." The young man unfolds his arms slowly and holds out his hand. "For the same price, I'll do it."

The captain narrows his eyes. "Four-fifty."

"What's Quniak got that I don't?"

"Experience." The captain is a shrewd man.

"Maybe, but you haven't seen my dogs next to his." Briscoe leans back, confident. "I've got a leader that could find Inik Katsuk with his nose."

"Let me see him and I'll decide."

"On it." Briscoe jerks his head toward the door, not bothering to put on his heavy coat.

We all trudge out into the cold, including Quniak, who considers this a personal slight against his dogs.

"See?" Briscoe stops in front of his dogs, all lean, iron-muscled beasts who strain in the harness at the sight of him and bark as if they cannot stand still a moment longer.

They are fine dogs, and I tell Captain Innes as much.

He refuses to decide on Briscoe's pay until he can compare these dogs to Quniak's. We slog through the snow to see Quniak's dogs, which are in a dog lot a quarter mile down the street.

The lot is noisy and messy, but Captain Innes presses on admirably until he reaches the corner where Quniak's dogs are. They are different from Briscoe's—bigger, thick-coated, and quiet. A good dog team reflects its master; Quniak probably has a quieter hand.

Innes leans down to speak to me in confidence. "Briscoe's seem the better dogs."

I shake my head. "Quniak's are good. Different, but good."

A furrow comes between his dark brows, but he nods, accepting my judgment. Deep down, I think he still prefers the livelier dogs. He extends his hand to Briscoe.

"Five thousand it is. Be ready first thing in the morning."

"I will. How many men will you be bringing with you?"

"Twenty or thirty."

Quniak shakes his head. "You will need more sleds and more dogs for that. I have three teams' worth, and Briscoe two, but you'll need about ten more."

"Where can I buy them?"

"Ask back at the outfitters, or around the lots."

"I cannot afford teamsters for them all."

Briscoe shrugs. "You won't need a veteran for every sled. A few of us should be enough to sort out your problems."

"This one knows how to drive a sled." Innes tips his head toward me.

Quniak peers down at me. "You run dogs, boy?"

"Every winter, most of my life. I've got a leader."

"Good. You keep him, boy." Satisfaction spreads across his weathered face. "Get you some more dogs and sleds, Captain, and we'll handle them."

"In the morning, then." Innes gestures for me to follow.

Ahead, a dog team swings into the lot fast and strong, like a herd of buffalo. I stop, watching in wonder as they weave in and out among the sleds and equipment and stop perfectly, within inches of the spot their runner directs.

This is a dog team.

"What is it?"

I start at the captain's voice. "His team—it's good."

Innes picks up on the awe in my voice and starts off through the snow at a terrific pace.

When we reach the newcomer, he is dropping a hook into the snow and stomping it in, talking to his dogs in a cheerful tone all the while.

"That is a fine team." The captain looks over the dogs with his best imitation of a critical eye.

"Yes." The man's voice is quiet and sad. "It is the very best."

"May I talk to you?"

"No."

The man pushes back his hood, revealing a middle-aged face with frosty blond hair and very thin lips—pale, as if the snow had drained the life and color out of him.

"I must tend to my dogs first. But if you'll buy me a brandy at The Pick and Collarbone at noon, I will speak to you there."

"Done."

Word of Captain Innes's plan races through the camp. Some men rejoice, others mourn. Some of those who are chosen think they will die, while some hope for extra pay.

Rutter and Willow are both chosen. It will be a comfort to have familiar faces along, but I am sorry they will not be able to wait out the winter here in the safety of Kaquom. And my plan—to cut and run with a dog team and Tsanu—would have been easier without their watching eyes.

I find Laramie shaking his head over the to-do and dishing out coffee to the horse-boys.

"Only a fool rails against his lot in life," he says. "I'm right glad to be staying here. In my mind, a man's best left on his own hearth when the weather howls like this. It ain't right ordering men out in the dead of winter."

"Amen," agrees one of the boys fervently.

"By all the curses since the fall of the devil!" Drucker is shouting again, his voice ringing halfway across camp. "You had better figure on knowing, sir!"

The whole circle freezes. The captain and Drucker are having it out.

"You'd best watch your mouth, Doctor. I could have you branded and whipped!"

"You try, sir, and you'll find yourself upside down and inside out like a gutted grouse! No one browbeats a man of the scalpel, you son of a devil's antler—"

A slow grin spreads across my face. Drucker picked that one up from me.

"And what about your sacred oath to protect? You dare make threats against your captain?"

"No, sir—"

You can always tell which voice is Drucker's because of the "sirs" sprinkled liberally among the insults.

"But I tell you this, sir. You'll not lay a hand on me. Out here it is the doctor, sir, and not the captain, who commands life and death. What's to keep me from doing you in instead of keeping you alive on that godforsaken trail?"

"You say that one more time, you—" here the captain inserts a word which I cannot and do not wish to understand— "and I'll see you face a court-martial when we return to Arislet!"

"Do so, but I will not leave my men!"

"Your men are going with me! There is a doctor here in town. The men will be in warm conditions. You want to sacrifice the men going north, who will have no doctor, for the ones here who will? Who is the fool?"

"By all the powers, sir! I will do what I think is best for my men and nothing more!"

"He's done." Laramie picks up the poker. "The captain has won."

I look up curiously. "How do you know?"

"He's made his point. Drucker will go." He stirs up the fire and drops the subject.

Jeremiah walks by, a satchel over his shoulder. "Laramie, you got some charcoal?"

"S'pose I do."

"I'm making more ink tonight."

Laramie looks up swiftly. "You going?"

Jeremiah nods.

Laramie doesn't answer—a bad sign.

"Don't worry for me." Jeremiah rakes the charcoal into the snow to cool it. "It was bound to happen. Captain needs someone to map all the land."

"Map it to somewheres that doesn't exist? Really, partner?"

Jeremiah shrugs, blowing on the hissing, steaming charcoal. "Might as well map something while we're out here. No other cartographers have been out that way."

Laramie pours out coffee for everyone, offering some to each man, Jeremiah last of all.

"Nah, I'm all right." Jeremiah wraps up his cooled goods in an old cloth bag. "See you around."

"Come back, now—hear?" Laramie calls after him.

Jeremiah gives the smallest of smiles and tips his hat in answer.

✦

We meet the third dog-runner at noon at The Pick and Collarbone.

"I could not help but notice your fine team this morning," begins the captain, when the fire spirits have been ordered and set upon the table.

Liar. I noticed them.

"Indeed." The dog-runner pours the spirits—*brandy*, the captain called them—into two glasses with the air of a man at a funeral. "That is to be expected, since they are the finest team north of Arislet."

Captain Innes leans back and folds his arms. "That is quite a boast."

"It is not a boast. You will know that once you see them in action."

Innes studies the man a minute through keen eyes, then takes a sip of his brandy. "I want to buy them."

I wince. *Wrong choice.*

This is not going to end well.

The driver gives the captain a thin smile. "Out of the question. They are not for sale."

"Anything is for sale at the right price."

"No, sir."

"Then perhaps you can help me anyway." Captain Innes tries a different tack. "I am the captain of the army encampment—and I am in need of good dogs and good drivers."

"Have you hired any yet?" The stranger is appraising the captain as much as the captain is appraising him.

"Briscoe, Quniak."

The man laughs softly through his nose. "Of course," he mutters to himself. "Of course."

Captain Innes bristles, but he is still trying to be polite. "I am putting together an expedition. I need more dogs, more sleds, and another experienced driver."

"Why do you want me?"

"Your dogs are good."

"That's right. The fastest along the whole route."

"I'm willing to pay."

The man rubs his chin, rough with faint stubble and old frostbite. "How much?"

"Four thousand."

"Pah. Not for my dogs. Seven."

"Four-fifty."

"Six."

"Five, and we'll call it even."

"Not so fast. I did not say yes to five. Five-fifty is the lowest I will go, and you can take it or leave it." The dog-runner lifts his chin.

There are patches on his coat, and the parka laid over the chair next to him is moth-eaten. He has fallen on hard times, but he is no less proud.

"Five-fifty, and don't you breathe a word of it to the other teamsters. I pay the best for the best."

A brief smile thaws the man's face and he holds out his hand. "Grim Halver. How many men you taking?"

"Roger Innes. And I am taking twenty-eight."

"And you have Briscoe and Quniak?" He rubs his chin again.

"And this lad has a leader."

Grim looks at me in the same appraising way, but I cannot detect any scorn. "I'll get you the rest of the dogs you need," he says, his eyes still on me. "I'll need an advance."

The captain pulls a pinch of gold out of a pouch and lays it in Grim's creased hand. "There it is. I want to meet an hour before dawn."

"Understood."

The captain gets up, and I follow.

"He's solid," says the captain. "It will be good. We won't have many officers with us, and he seems like he'll fill in well."

"Which officers are coming?"

He names them, but I do not hear Ransom's name.

"Isn't the lieutenant coming?"

"No." The captain looks at me in mild surprise. "Ransom is staying."

❧

"I am coming." Ransom fastens his bedroll with a jerk. He does not even look at me. "The army is here at a settlement. They have most of their officers, and they will not stir far in this weather. Little ill will befall them here."

"But Captain Innes—"

For the first time, I hear a bite in his voice. "Do you think I would let him take my best men and not lift a finger for their protection?"

I close my mouth. Of course not. And I want him to come. I would feel much safer if he were along.

"Sergeant Nolan is a competent man. Further, he is a peacemaker and will not allow the men to create any problems with the locals here. I have spoken to him already, and he has agreed to remain behind in my place."

I don't know why I feel so brave today, but I do. Perhaps it is that I have spent most of the day with the captain and survived. Whatever it is, I am brave enough ask Ransom, "But what will the captain say? Will he be angry?"

"Not as angry as you would think. My understanding of your tongue surpasses most. He—" His look goes straight through me as if checking me for hidden dangers. "He may rail for awhile, but he will see the sense in having a translator he can trust."

And he does not trust Tsanu.

I knot my fingers into his horse's mane.

The irony is that Tsanu is too honest for his own good, though they do not know it. This—this madness in searching for Inik Katsuk is the closest thing to a lie he has ever told.

Part of me wants the legend to be real, if only to justify Tsanu. Much as I hate Captain Innes, I would give him anything if he would only let me have my brother back.

FIFTEEN

Blood and Ice

The entire camp is alive, though only a fraction of it is leaving. Fires are stoked, hot coffee is being passed around, dogs bark, and the horses whinny in nervous reply. Ransom is packed and preparing to ride out with us, so I assume he has changed the captain's mind.

Laramie sends Jeremiah with more charcoal and with extra coffee from the secret stash he calls *contraband*. Rutter is making his way down the line, leaving instructions for his second-in-command and saying goodbye to his favorites, especially Rosita.

I say goodbye to Fredrico in the dark early morning while he is still sleeping in his straw. He is not interested in my attention, whisking his tail through the straw and shaking his head, but I am not to be put off. "You are going to grow fat and lazy without Captain Innes," I say, pressing my face against his, which he tolerates. "Enjoy it."

Packing takes me two minutes. I carry everything I own in one satchel, except the bone Laramie gave me for Iki. I think he has a soft spot for dogs.

I look once more around Rutter's tent. I do not know when or how I grew fond of it, but there is a small empty place inside me at the thought of leaving it behind.

Rutter ducks his head under the door. "Come on, Maki. Time to be off."

⟡

"So this is your dog." Quniak is eyeing Iki. "I've never seen one like him."

Pride warms me as I release Iki—I had him on a line in case he took ideas into his head—and he goes to meet the six other dogs that will make up his team. I dig my hands deeper into the pockets of my new parka—caribou fur with a thick ermine ruff. It is made for a boy, but it looks good on me.

"He'll settle in," says Quniak. "These are good dogs. A little less wolf in them, so he'll rise to the top. This is your sled. There's Fish, Aka, Nanook, Seal, Raven, and Tom. I'll leave you to get to know them."

"You name them all?"

Quniak grins. "I do. All these I brought up from pups. I know you will be good to them."

"I will."

Quniak stumps away. His mukluks are thick and heavy, and that bodes ill for this trip. If he is dressing warmly, the Invaders will freeze badly.

Ransom comes up, wearing bulky fur mittens. Frost whitens his beard.

"I am to ride on your sled." He sounds apologetic. "You are to show me how to run it before I take my own."

"I can show you now." We still have five minutes.

He steps back respectfully as I go to the handlebars.

"You stand here, your feet on the runners. It isn't hard to balance once you get the hang of it."

He nods, watching my every movement with intensity.

"This is the snow-hook, and this is the brake. They don't always work, but they help to stop the sled if you need."

He picks up the snow hook, and I stand on the brake as he shoves it back into the snow and steps on it. I teach him the dog commands, and he repeats the words softly after me.

"You know more now than most foreigners."

I smile, and the frosty corners of his eyes crinkle in reply.

"Come, I'll let you drive for a minute."

I show him how to harness the dogs, then whistle for Iki and harness him in the front myself. Balancing on one runner, I shift so that Ransom can stand on the other. "Come on, Iki!"

Iki looks back at me, then pulls into the harness, the rest of the team following his lead. We circle the lot once, twice, giving Ransom a chance to give the commands. He is a natural leader, and he is good with animals.

When he pulls up in front of me, clucking to the dogs and grinning broadly, I laugh. "Why are you not the captain, Ransom?"

He shakes his head, wry and disapproving. "I am not so brilliant at the coursework necessary for promotion. And I have never done anything heroic."

"You must have done something brave."

"I do not know about that."

But I know he has. Standing up to Captain Innes when no one else dares is brave.

"I am sure you have," I say emphatically, and he lets it lie.

Willow comes up, dressed warmly in furs, and looks at the dogs. He turns to me. "You ready?"

I nod. I am very glad that Willow is coming. To have an ally in this lonely land is a good thing.

"All ready?" Halver, the pale dog-runner, stomps up in his boots. "I will lead with the captain, and we'll space the knowledgeable runners at intervals. I want you behind Briscoe."

Again I nod.

"Questions?"

I shake my head. This is like the army. No go-as-you-can or catching up—everything is organized.

"Good. We're moving out."

Five days on the trail, camping out with nothing but snow shelters to sleep in, and already the men of the army are changed. Gone is any false bravado, or lingering weakness from riding horses. They are wind-burnt, snow-flecked, and tanned from sun and exposure.

Willow stands on the sled's runners, while I ride in the basket, uncomfortably cramped, but warmer for a while. I feel the ground through the sled's bones, the snow packed slick and smooth where Halver and the others have broken trail. Willow has learned the driving fast and does well on the flat ground, but once we hit the rough terrain, I will have to navigate again.

"Maki?"

"Hmm?" I angle my head so that he knows I hear him.

"Do you have any idea where Tsanu is leading us?"

I shake my head. I wish I knew.

"Nothing seems to live up here."

"Things do," I say. "Not all pleasant things. But there are seals."

A deep, savage sound rips through the frozen air like a knife.

I freeze, then scramble to sit up.

"What is it?"

"Stop the dogs."

The sled skids to a stop. "What is it?"

The sound rips through the air again as I pull myself to my feet. At the front of the line, Halver is shouting and the dogs baying.

"It's a *nanuk*," I say, breathless. "A white bear."

The roar comes louder. The *nanuk* appears from over the ridge, its large head swinging a little from side to side as it tests the air.

We are far from the bear, but three of the sleds are much closer—

Halver's, Drucker's, and the captain's. My heart drops to my mukluks. *Tsanu is there.* If the captain makes a wrong move, inexperienced as he is, Tsanu will be the first casualty.

Halver is giving orders to his dogs, slow and quiet, easing them gently away from the bear. The captain follows suit, imitating Halver's tone and easy movements, but his dogs are curious, not quite listening.

Again. Say it again, now. If you don't say it now—

The captain's dogs lunge. They set off barking, not quite daring to engage, but certainly arresting the creature's attention. The *nanuk* kind are hungry this time of year—they will go after anything, the easier prey the better. The captain shouts, ordering the dogs back, but they are torn, half of them turning to obey, half of them still bristling at the bear.

It is too late. The bear lumbers down the hill, tearing through the snow, silent now, which is more frightening than the growls.

Innes fumbles with his gun, takes aim. The shot cracks, but I see no spot starting on the bear's fur. Even if he has hit it, it takes many wounds to stop a *nanuk.* The captain tips the sled and turns to run. My heart races in my throat as I watch Tsanu struggle up from the snow—he was bound in the sled basket—and run after the captain.

The bear goes after them, or after the food in the sled. The dogs meet him, lunging and snarling, unable to get their teeth through his thick fur. It slows him only a little.

I am watching a nightmare.

Tsanu is running. He knows what *nanuk* can do. If he trips, bound as he is, he will not be able to stay ahead of it.

I wrest Willow's knife from his belt and take off running.

"Maki, stop! What do you think you're doing?"

"I'm going to help!"

It is a stupid thing to do, but I would rather die fighting than live with the thought that I could have changed something.

A hand jerks me back by the collar and I fight back, but not with the knife. "Let me go!"

"Maki, listen to sense!" Willow is shouting, others are shouting—guns crack the air.

The bear is roaring. Barks and howls and whimpers rise in a cacophony, and I whirl to see a mess of blood, men and dogs running toward and away from the bear.

My heart is pounding out of my chest. I can hardly breathe. Willow's bony hands still hold me back, and I turn and bury my face in his coat.

If I can't do anything, I had better not watch.

The thing is over in a few painful minutes.

"It's done," Willow says quietly. "It's dead, I think."

I push away from him and stand, panting. "I—I suppose I should thank you for saving my life." I lift my chin proudly.

He seems about to laugh, but his face twists suddenly and I fear he is going to cry instead. "You may want to stay here."

I shake my head. "I want to know now." I turn and run from him through the crunching snow.

The *nanuk* is lying in a pool of sickeningly dark blood. Tsanu stands panting, spattered in blood, a gun in his hands. I don't know where he got it. None of the blood seems to be his own—or not much of it. He looks at me, slowly sets down the gun, and nods.

Every nerve in me yearns to run and throw my arms around him. My head swims with giddy relief. I still have Tsanu and Tsanu has me.

Three dogs are dead, another may be too torn up to live. I don't want to look too closely. Drucker is on his knees, his gun on the ground, one hand pressed like a vice against the ice, and Halver grips an arm to his chest, his pale face even paler than before. Blood is running off his fingertips.

Sickness rises from my stomach into my throat. The only warm smell is that of blood and insides, and it contrasts strongly with the cold air.

"Who is hurt?" Captain Innes's voice cuts into the senseless scene, demanding order.

"Here," pants Halver. The sleeve of his coat and the shirt beneath hang off, revealing his torn arm.

"Rutter's hurt." For the first time I notice Jeremiah, half blocked by the body of the bear.

"Let me see." Briscoe goes over.

In a daze, I follow him. I have hunted many things, and I know what a death wound looks like.

Jeremiah has Rutter's shirt open. His head is tilted back, his breath coming hard. The bear must have caught him across the chest. He is bloody and very bruised.

"He's busted some ribs," says Briscoe.

Drucker grunts, tries to get to his feet, and fails. "I'll come see him," he says through gritted teeth.

Ransom gives Drucker an arm up and helps him, limping badly, over to Rutter. Another wave of sickness washes through me, making sweat break out on my face. Faults and all, Rutter has been good to me. I do not want to lose him.

Quniak is inspecting the dogs, and I hear the crack of a gun—probably one being put out of its misery.

How wrong everything can go in a matter of minutes.

Drucker rolls up his sleeves. Underneath, his arms are strong, strong like a warrior's. Yet until now, I have not seen him hold so much as a gun.

His long fingers range over Rutter's heaving chest, feeling, almost listening. Dark bruising is starting across Rutter's ribs, and blood drips from a hole in his side, just above his hip. His clothes are smeared with it, and the snow beneath him is stained red.

"I need my surgical kit, now."

A man runs for Drucker's sled.

"Sir," says Jeremiah. "You're bleeding, you should—"

"Put a tourniquet on it, then!" Drucker shouts. "This man can't wait!"

The surgical kit is brought over and Drucker motions to the man carrying it. "Morphine, now."

The man opens the kit and produces a bottle. Drucker drips it into Rutter's mouth, his hand shaking.

Jeremiah is persistent. "The tourniquet, sir?"

"All right, quick."

I watch in horrified fascination as they wrap a cloth with two sticks around Drucker's leg and twist it so hard he can barely breathe. "That's enough—" Drucker has no voice left. "The morphine must be working some now."

"Maki." Willow's voice is close behind me. "Come away."

I don't want to leave. Somehow I feel that if I know what is coming, I can will it not to happen.

"Maki." His voice is firmer.

I follow him, my eyes glued to Drucker as he takes out a knife and a swab and some clear liquid.

"Let's help clean this up," Willow's voice urges me, and I find myself mechanically following his lead, picking up the fallen sleds and gathering the food and tools scattered in the bloody snow.

As we finish, I see that the crowd around Drucker and Rutter is dispersing and Drucker is being helped to his feet.

"How far is the nearest shelter?" Drucker's face is drained. "Not camping spot—a post?"

Briscoe answers. "The next post is half a day away. If you think we can travel that far, doctor."

"We can travel that far if the ground is flat."

Halver nods, and Quniak confirms it.

"Let's go. A few of us have lost too much blood. And I want to stop every so often and check those stitches."

"Let me bury my dogs." Halver tips his head toward two forms stretched lifeless in the snow. His usual melancholy takes on a tinge of tragedy.

Drucker presses his lips together firmly and shakes his head. "It'll be you we're burying if we dally that long."

Halver gazes at the dogs for a long moment, then nods dully and trudges back to his sled. My heart aches.

I, too, hate to leave the dogs out under the sky. They deserved better.

We go on, painfully slow at first, abandoning the bear where he lies. It is a pity to leave meat to waste, but we have no choice. It is well past dark when we reach the post, a homey place run by a sturdy fellow of thirty or so. He looks weather-wise, and even his voice sounds tanned by the elements.

"Run into a bear?" he asks, dry and businesslike.

"Yes." Drucker leans on Jeremiah so heavily that he is practically weighing him into the ground. "We have some wounded and we need beds."

"You look to be one of them."

"Doctors don't get that distinction."

The man shows the way to three beds, one of them his own. The rest of us will have the floor. I hold my breath as they carry Rutter in and lay him down.

Drucker is white as snow, but he sits down in a chair at Rutter's side to check the stitches.

"They're holding." His voice is faint. "Keep ice on the bruising all night. I've got to lie down."

He limps three feet to the other bed and slumps onto it.

For a moment it is very still, and I am afraid that Drucker has died. But Ransom, ever calm, takes the chair and drags it over beside the doctor's bed.

"Get ice for Rutter, you heard him," he says quietly, and two men duck out the door. "Do you have hot water?"

Without a word, our host puts a pot on the fire.

If I must be still and wait, I should keep my hands busy. I stumble out into the dark to fetch a pair of snowshoes I began making in Kaquom and drop exhausted onto a fur in the far corner, near Willow.

Someone groans, and I flinch. It is a pitiful sound. I try to block it out.

"So much sorrow," murmurs Willow, tilting his head against the knotty logs.

The reply comes to my lips as though rehearsed, rising in a small burst of resentment. "If you Invaders had not come, none of this would have happened."

"Do you still call us that?" Willow looks a little hurt. "We have a name that isn't Invader, you know."

It was a stupid thing to say. It is the Invaders I am worried for now.

"What is it? The name of your people?"

"Irylian."

I force a smile. In my mind, I try the name on Willow and then on Rutter. "It's nice."

"I have always thought so. And you, your people—are Uni, or Uniak?"

I nod. "It means People of the White Land."

"I like that."

"Me too." I do not mean to whisper, but my voice has disappeared.

"Maki, I wish you would teach me some of your words."

My hands pause, the caribou sinew motionless in my fingers. I am torn between my old hostility and the desire to share with Willow.

I must have been silent a long time, because he says, quite softly, "Please?"

"*Upik*," I murmur, pointing to the shoes I am making.

"Upik," he echoes softly.

"*Thari*." I hold up the soft, thick skin. "*Qpi*." I hold up the caribou sinew.

He echoes these, taking pains to imitate my pronunciation. "What is dog?" he asks, his face alight with pleasure.

"*Quinip*."

"Quinip!" A grin breaks out across his face, and he snaps his fingers to the nearest dog—one of Halver's, for he has the bad manners to let them in the house. It comes over, wagging its tail.

It is always a good sign when a dog likes a man.

"Fire?"

"*Sagu*."

"Sagu," he echoes.

We go on like this for a while. He will not remember all these words, but he is enjoying it, repeating them after me.

The warmth of the room sinks into me and makes my eyes heavy. The words are coming slower and slower.

"Try to sleep, Maki."

I muster just enough strength to fetch one of our host's quilts from the end of the bed where Halver sleeps, a dog curled under his uninjured arm. Ransom is still awake, watching over Rutter and Drucker.

I lie on my back and stare at the knots in the wood. Tsanu used to say they were just knots, imperfections. But I always saw shapes in them. The wide eyes of does, running rivers, plump blueberries . . . .

Ah, but the fire feels good.

SIXTEEN

The Sign of the Raven

When I wake the next morning, there is a fire crackling in the hearth and I am comfortably warm. It is quiet, quieter than I would have thought possible with a cabin full of men.

I stretch long and yawn. Ransom stirs from his chair and looks my way. He is gray around the eyes; he has probably been up all night.

From where I stand, I can see Tsanu sleeping. I miss him so hard it aches. Willow is asleep beside me, his face buried in a wool blanket. His hair is messy, and something in me wants to take care of him, like a mother with a little boy. Does he have a mother still? And does she worry for him, far away in this wild, savage land?

I go to stand beside Ransom, watching Rutter for a moment to make sure that he is still breathing.

His chest rises and falls normally, save for a brief catch at the end of a deep breath.

"It's been quiet." Ransom stretches his arms, quietly cheerful.

"Are they going to be all right?"

He gives a weary nod and gets up. "I have to clear off the sleds—it snowed last night, and we will need the supplies today."

"Are we moving out?"

"I doubt it." Ransom thrusts his arms into his coat. "I will be back."

A gust of cold air enters the room and fades away as he shuts the door behind him.

I sit down in his chair and fold my arms, watching Rutter.

For so long, I was determined not to like this rough fellow, who is loud and hard and everything that annoys me about the Invaders. I take a breath and feel an almost physical crumbling inside me. I can't dislike him now.

The truth is, I do not know what I will do if he dies.

"Ah, you are up." Our host pushes through the door with an armload of wood. I jump, but Captain Innes jumps higher. He sits up with a low exclamation and dashes the sleep out of his eyes.

His eyes fall on Tsanu, safely beside him with ankles bound, and he immediately relaxes. My soft mood evaporates. I make an ugly sign in his direction and get up.

Our host steps over several sleeping men and says, to no one in particular, "I will have coffee ready soon."

A little while later, Ransom comes in, shaking the snow off his boots, and sniffs the air.

"Coffee?" He sounds hopeful.

I nod and wade through the sleeping men to the oaken table where our host is pouring it into blue tin cups.

"Get it while it's hot," he says.

It is so hot that it nearly burns me right through the tin, but I pull my sleeves over my hands and take a tiny sip. The taste makes me miss Laramie, poking and prodding his campfire into existence regardless of the weather. I hope he is warm and well by a hearth in Kaquom.

Briscoe comes in, covered in frost and dog hair. "Morning! Is that coffee?"

"It is." Our host pours out another tin cup. Briscoe pulls out the chair and takes a quick, hot gulp.

"Did you sleep with the dogs?" Innes is drinking his coffee standing by the fireplace, leaning an arm against it, one eyebrow raised.

"Yes, Quniak and I. It was too crowded in here."

"Is Quniak still out there?"

"Yes." Briscoe finishes off his coffee and holds out the cup for more. "He's feeding Halver's dogs."

"I am perfectly capable of feeding my own dogs." Halver rises from his bed like a dead man from his pyre, causing the dog that was on his bed to start and jump down. "He'll probably blubber them."

Briscoe snorts.

Halver stumbles around a little, adjusts his arm in its sling, and rubs his stubbly chin with his good hand.

"You want coffee?" asks Ransom, holding up the pot. "Got some left."

"Actually—" Halver holds up a hand, still a little unsteady, and indicates about an inch. "A tot of brandy would be of more use at the moment."

"This early, huh?" Briscoe downs his second cup.

"I don't happen to see any marks on you, Briscoe. Where were you, running from the bear?"

Briscoe slams his tin cup down, but says nothing more.

"I've got a little." Quniak stomps through the doorway, a small flask under his arm. He must have heard them through the door. "I was bringing it for the doctor to use, but I suppose it was bound to get to you eventually."

Halver has made it halfway across the room. Now he sinks into a chair, giving Quniak a wide, bland smile. "Too kind."

Quniak sets the flask on the table—dumping a large amount of snow along with it—and throws back his hood. "Four more inches since last night."

Tsanu stirs and sits up. Innes finishes his coffee slowly, then makes his way back to the corner to loose the bonds on Tsanu's ankles.

Cold hatred settles in my chest.

Tsanu rubs his legs for a minute or two, then gets up and limps to the table. With a swift glance at Innes, he pours himself the last of the coffee.

"Is it still coming down?" Innes asks Quniak, picking up the pot and preparing to brew more.

"A little. Not strong yet."

"Yet." Halver laughs bitterly.

"It may as well snow," says Ransom calmly. "I don't think the doctor or Rutter can travel yet."

Innes growls under his breath.

If only Rutter was hurt, I suspect we would leave today. But the captain is not willing to leave the doctor behind.

Tsanu is three feet away from me, just across the table. He watches me through quiet eyes as he sips his coffee, and my heart reaches out for him. I haven't been this close to him in forever.

I wish I could make him smile.

"How long'll it be?" The captain asks casually, as if he doesn't care, but a chill runs up my arm.

Ransom shakes his head. "You will have to speak with Drucker."

Innes pulls out a chair and slumps over the table, shoulders tight. Drucker is asleep. He probably took morphine.

"Where you folks headed?" Our host puts out a tray of dried salmon and bread. The table is silent, as if a nerve has been touched.

"Tlatlik," Tsanu says quietly. He gives a hitch to his sleeve.

"Tlatlik?" Our host looks around the table from face to face.

Briscoe slides his mug off the table and heads for the door.

"Is that a problem?" Captain Innes lifts his chin calmly.

"It's not necessarily my business. But I've never met anyone who went to Tlatlik of his own free will."

The captain leans back just a shade, and his eyes slide over to Tsanu. Something cold slips through my chest.

Tlatlik is the largest mountain in the Tanaka range, and it is called Black One for a reason. I do not know of any villages on or near it. Only animals live there: the musk ox and the buffalo on the plain, rangy wolves and bears in the foothills. And there are legends of strange and terrible monsters that live in the mountain.

Our host speaks true. I, too, have never heard of anyone who went willingly to Tlatlik.

Captain Innes points a small, patient smile in the man's direction. "Rest assured, we go in with our eyes wide open."

"I hope so. Nasty legends around that place."

I sense a stiffening in the captain's manner, a snake-like vigilance building between him and Tsanu. I do not think Tsanu is leading us to Tlatlik to die, but the captain does not know that.

"What manner of legend is it that you think a well-equipped company of thirty cannot reasonably face without fear of harm?"

"Harm'll find you on the trail just as fast," laughs our host. "It may be nothing. But the Tligit tribe used to send their shunned out that way. Trappers have disappeared. Wolves and bears out there are thin. But that could be explained by any number of things."

"Ah." The captain says no more.

Behind me, a bed creaks and Drucker drags himself to a sitting position. "The time?"

"Eight o'clock," answers Ransom.

"The patient?"

"Halver is here, at the table. I gave Rutter morphine two hours ago, as instructed."

Drucker shoves his hand up the length of his face and into his hair. "I'll see to him." He slides his leg slowly off the bed and limps to the chair beside Rutter. I turn back to my coffee; little will be gained by watching now. When he finishes, I will know how Rutter is.

The talk at the table goes on quietly, but I mostly listen to what is happening behind me, hoping to hear Rutter's voice.

Ransom gets up and goes to the bed, and in another minute, he returns with a little smile. He carries off a mug of coffee, and I turn. Rutter is sitting up, leaning against the wall, taking the coffee.

I abandon my mug and go to him.

"Are you going to get better?"

"Yes," Drucker answers for him. "He'll be good as new, provided he rests."

I look down at him doubtfully. In Tansilet, a wound like that would leave a man's life hanging in the balance for weeks, waiting to see if infection would set in.

"That was quite a hole you had in your side," I say.

"I didn't look," says Rutter honestly, taking a sip of his coffee.

Ransom clears his throat. "That antiseptic is powerful stuff."

"Ah." Drucker waves a dismissive hand. "Once I was sure that the stitches were holding, he wasn't in much danger."

"You weren't really worried, were you, Maki?" Rutter gives me his slow, lopsided grin.

"Doesn't matter now." I realize my brow is still furrowed. "You look fit as anything."

"Sure don't feel it yet," he grunts, finishing the coffee and handing the mug back to Ransom.

"Those ribs are what will hold you back awhile," Drucker says. "Nothing but time'll fix them."

"And that leg, Doctor," Ransom puts in wryly. "Haven't looked at that this morning, have you?"

"I'll look at it in a moment," he says.

It's an ugly wound, I can see from here. A tightly-bound bandage just above Drucker's knee, crusted in dry blood. His pant leg is cut away—I feel colder just looking at it.

Drucker gets out his kit and limps back to his own bed. Ransom cuts away the bandage, but it sticks to the wound. I shudder inside. I am used to blood, but bad wounds like this make me feel tingly in my fingertips and distant in my head.

The captain is watching too.

"What is the verdict, doctor?"

"Half a week, at least. Another day or two and I'll be able to give a more accurate estimate."

"Son of a devil's antler," mutters the captain between his teeth.

✦

"Where are you off to, Jeremiah?" asks Willow, whittling idly beside the fire.

"Going to map the area."

"Map it?" The snow has been falling steadily since breakfast.

"There's precious little else to do. You should come."

"Who is going?"

"Briscoe and Quniak, most of the men. We're taking the dogs out. They say there are hot springs around here."

"I should." Willow gets up. "You coming, Maki?"

I shake my head. Tsanu is not going.

"Then rest, huh?" He ruffles up my hair, and I shove his hand just for the show of it.

He goes out, and I lie down near the fire. I am a little cold, but it is mostly an excuse to be on the same side of the cabin as Tsanu.

Halver is snoring on his bed, a dog flopped on either side of him. Drucker and Rutter must be asleep too, for neither has moved in nearly an hour. Captain Innes and Tsanu are the only others here. The cabin is oddly

196

quiet and strange.

I pretend to sleep—I do not want Captain Innes to talk to me. Tsanu is drinking coffee and thumbing through one of Jeremiah's books. I do not think he can read it any more than I can, but he likes the beauty of the marks on the page.

The captain pulls out his pipe, holding it with his teeth as he rifles in his coat for his tobacco pouch.

It is empty.

I enjoy a smile at his expense. He deserves for something to go wrong for him once in a while.

He bites out an oath through his pipe-clenched teeth and goes outside.

As the door shuts, I sit up and Tsanu looks over at me. "*Kitaya*, Maki."

"*Kitaya.*"

"He has a small store of tobacco in the sleds. That is, if the men haven't taken it with them." A smile tugs at the corner of his mouth.

I grin. I can just imagine the captain stalking after them on his long legs, shouting at them to "come back here" by every threat and oath he knows.

Tsanu tilts his cup. "This coffee—it is not bad. Better than the camp coffee."

I wish he would just say what he wants to say. The captain—or anyone, for that matter—could come back any minute.

He sighs. It's coming now.

"I know it is useless to tell you that I did not want you to come."

"It is."

"I want you safe, Maki. And I cannot protect you from where I am."

The same with you. I fold my arms.

"But it is you and I or nothing, isn't it?"

I only nod in reply.

He sighs and sets aside Jeremiah's book.

"Why are we going to Tlatlik?"

Tsanu pauses before answering me. "I am trying to give us a chance, Maki."

"By leading us to a mountain surrounded by legends of terrible monsters?"

"Maki, do you trust me?"

"You said yourself that you did not want me to come."

He ignores me. "The captain is a shrewd and strong-minded man. He has seen more than I ever will, and it will take everything I know about this land to outwit him. You must trust me, Maki."

I do not like the way he says it. It is as if he knows that something terrible lies ahead of us—something he will not share with me.

But his dark eyes grab mine and will not let go. "Maki?"

I reach out and touch his hand.

"I trust you," I say reluctantly. I trust him to do good by me, but not by himself.

The door creaks, and I throw myself down in front of the fire just as Captain Innes walks in. I smell the pipe smoke the moment the door opens.

"What are you doing?" He glances at Tsanu with suspicion in his tone.

"Just getting closer to the fire." Tsanu shifts his shoulders. The captain takes a chair with a creak and a thump.

With a sinking heart, I go back to pretending to sleep in front of the fire.

It is blindingly bright the morning we depart from the cabin. The sky is as blue as the creek outside Tansilet on a fine day, but a shade paler, as if the sun has surpassed it in glory.

Quniak, who is used to this weather, is in a fine mood, but none of the other men are. Even after a week of rest, there is a sullen air about them, simmering just below a quick obedience.

Rutter comes out of the cabin a little stiffly; Drucker has wrapped him tighter than a baby against a napping-board.

I squint to look up at him. "Morning."

"Morning, Maki." He manages a smile. "Ready to be back on the trail?"

I nod, but in my heart, I am torn. Every day, every step, brings us closer to the end, to finding out if we live or die.

But I cannot say that to Rutter.

The cabin door creaks and the captain strides out, headed for the sleds. Drucker meets him halfway, leaning on a cane that Jeremiah cut him from a sturdy oak branch.

"Are we ready?"

"Ready," says Drucker wryly, easing slowly into one of the sleds.

"About time," mutters the captain.

His tone is not lost on Drucker. The doctor reaches a hand out and seizes the edge of the captain's coat. "And if I were still at North Stanton, I would have kept a man like Rutter or myself in bed another week, and then ordered them to keep to the house. Consider yourself lucky. We are leaving at the first possible moment I could manage for you."

The captain's eyes flash and he looks at Drucker, jaw tightening. But he turns away and heads down the line without another word.

Ransom sees the exchange, and his eyes grow wary.

One of the men beside me leans his head near to another. "He's driving too hard. Back when we crossed the Nuvian frontier, he wouldn't have pushed like this unless our lives were in danger."

The dog-runners are making small changes—adjusting the sleds, untangling dogs, checking the straps on the supplies.

"Ready?" The captain already stands on the runners of his sled. "We cannot delay."

Briscoe throws up a hand. "Dogs are ready."

"Supplies are secure," calls Ransom.

"Huup!" cries Quniak, and his dogs break into a run.

Our sleds lurch into motion, and we skim away across the snow. I look back at the homey cabin, standing staunchly under a few feet of snow, and lift a hand in farewell.

A dark bird flaps over us and into a near pine, causing the top of the tree to sway up and down.

"A raven!" Quniak points and shakes his head. "Ill luck—they mean mischief."

"In the south," says Halver, "the raven is an omen of trickery. Of something not being what it seems."

A heavy feeling starts in the pit of my stomach as I remember Tsanu's dire face. Quniak is right.

We are heading straight for trouble.

SEVENTEEN

The Killer of Men

The fire crackles in the hearth, glowing orange and blue. Quniak has made it to burn long and slow. We drove the dogs long into the dark tonight, a lantern hanging from the lead sled and others spaced at intervals down the line. By pure luck, we found this abandoned trapping cabin in which to take shelter.

Jeremiah lies on his stomach on the floor, a precious candle lit, working on his maps. Some of the men sit around him, watching the hills and rivers we traversed today take form under his pen. I lean against the wall and watch them, too tired and sick at heart to join.

"Blazes, Jeremiah," says one man in awe. "You don't forget a thing."

Jeremiah gives a gratified smile. "It's my job, after all."

"Willow, come and see these."

Willow is passing by, his blanket in his arms, and he pauses to peer over Jeremiah's shoulder. "They are very good." He gives a reserved smile before moving on.

"Aren't you going to stay?"

Willow shakes his head. "I have a headache. I am going to sleep."

"Wish I could," says Jeremiah, mostly in jest.

The men stay up a little longer, long enough for the fire in the hearth to die to down and for the dog-runners to head back outside to sleep with their dogs. They prefer it to crowded lodgings.

After lingering awhile longer, I lie down, but I am not interested in sleep. I wait until well into the night when all is quiet. Then I raise myself very slowly on one elbow.

Willow, closest to me, is fast asleep. I creep over to where Tsanu sleeps. The captain has chained Tsanu's ankle to one of his own with a long chain.

"Bloomin' wolf," I whisper, using one of Rutter's words.

Part of me hesitates to wake Tsanu. He looks so peaceful, and all the worry lines in his face are erased. But I lay two icy fingers on his collarbone and his dark eyes open slowly, fixing on me.

"The ptarmigan has its head beneath its wing," I whisper, flicking my eyes toward Captain Innes.

"You imp." His words have so little breath behind them that they are little more than mouthing. But he is grinning, white in the darkness. He finds it as funny as I do.

"He fusses, like a mother hen," I whisper back.

Captain Innes sleeps with the furrowed brow and pursed lips of a troubled *aaga*. Perhaps he will intimidate me again come daytime, but in the night, I laugh.

I reach out and take Tsanu's hand, savoring the comfort of being sister and brother again. "How much further to Tlatlik?"

His face darkens a shade. "Maybe a week or so beyond Chegak."

"Then we are not far at all."

He sighs and shakes his head.

"I wish you would not come, Maki. Perhaps you—"

He breaks off. I am glaring at him.

"You won't stay behind, will you?"

I shake my head.

He sighs. "It is only that the tales that gather around Tlatlik are ugly."

Despite my resolve, a shiver runs down my spine. "Can't we escape?"

"To where, Maki? Tell me how we'd manage with this snow."

"You know the land and how to live off of it, and—"

"And any one of those dog-runners could find us. And there would be no escape if we were caught again."

His dark eyes are grim. I look at his ankle, stretched as far away from our conversation as he can manage, and the captain sleeping, propped up on his pack. My brother, of all men, probably knows best how far the captain can be pushed right now.

"Maki." Even through the whisper, I hear sorrow in his voice. "I do not think there is any chance of escape. Not in the way you think."

"What is the other way?"

He does not answer me. More than that, he looks away. The light from the coals plays on the edge of his jaw and his ear.

"What is the other way?" I should not press him, but I must.

"Maki," he says softly, "do you remember when our mother left?"

I do not want to, but of course I do. "Yes."

"You remember I went after her, tried to bring her back?"

"You couldn't."

"That is true." His dark eyes search mine. "What I did not tell you was that she asked me to let her go. She said please—that she needed to go—and I knew she believed it to be true."

"Why did you let her go?" I feel a sickness in my stomach at what could have been—what should have been. "You could have stopped her."

"Maki, I do not believe she was right to leave us. And I miss her. Every day. But we cannot force the world to our will. And we cannot force others to do what we believe is the right thing."

Hot tears fill my eyes and slide down my cheeks. I hold my breath, trying not to cry in front of Tsanu.

"Maki." He leans close and looks at me. I can't hide them now. His rough thumb wipes a tear off my cheek.

He puts his arm around me and draws me against him, like he used to when I was little. I sob silently into his shoulder, my whole body shaking, barely able to breathe.

His arms tighten around me, and he rests his face in my greasy hair.

"Easy, easy."

After a while, my tears stop and my sobs still, but I don't want him to let go. I do not want us to part, maybe for the last time.

One of the snores across the room is interrupted, and we both start. Tsanu's arms loosen and I force myself to pull away from him.

"Go to sleep, Maki. Things will look fairer in the morning light."

I force a smile for his sake and do as he says—I go back to my sleeping place and lay down.

But I do not sleep.

Instead, I pull my coat off the floor where I was using it as a blanket, take Quniak's knife from his pack—if he wakes, he will not mind that I have taken it—and slip out into the night. I have not hunted in an age, and there is no better way to avoid my thoughts.

"But when's the right time is the question," a low voice drawls as I step outside. I freeze.

A dozen paces from me stand two men. I can only see them by the glow of their thick smoke-sticks and the faint red of the moon.

"Sooner the better," answers the second man. "The further out we go in this forsaken waste, the less chance we have." He shakes his long hair out of his face and I see the strong line of his nose, lit by the flare of the smoke-stick.

"You know," he continues, "I was with him west of the Rein and all through the Havast. Both times we almost died, all of us. But none of that holds a candle to this land." He leans against the handlebars of the sled and lets a stream of smoke out of his mouth. "What do you think of the lieutenant?"

"Can't expect help from that quarter." The first man shakes his head. "He won't turn."

The long-haired man nods slowly, studying the ground. "Never thought

I'd be having this conversation."

"Me neither. I'm a soldier, down to the bones. But I know the beginnings of a madman when I see them."

I step back through the door and begin to ease it shut, keeping the men in my sight. I cannot risk being found out, eavesdropping on mutinous talk.

"Hear something?" The first man stiffens, removing his smoke-stick from his mouth and leaning into the night.

"Must be wolf, or something." The second shoves his hands in his pockets. "I've been hearing something prowling around here of nights. Still, it don't hurt to be careful."

I lower the latch slowly and step back from the door.

Tsanu said to stay out of trouble, but this—this found me.

The sun glints off the fresh snow as we prepare to leave. I kneel in the snow beside Iki, checking to make sure the harness is tight enough. He slipped his line yesterday and tried to go hunting rabbit, which was a popular idea among the men, but not with the captain.

Captain Innes strides out with Tsanu at his side.

"All ready, then?" He whips a glance and a grin round the nearest soldiers. "We're one day closer to the mountain!"

He is in a rare fine mood.

Iki growls a little in his throat, probably at one of the other dogs, and I tug at his collar.

"Peace," I warn him.

I trudge to the back of my sled and stop short.

There is a raven's feather laying in the basket, on top of the supplies. I glance around, looking for a bird, but I see—and more importantly, hear—

nothing.

Odd.

Willow tosses up a hand in greeting as he passes. He is running his own sled today. He looks a little too white in the face and red in the lips. I hadn't noticed it earlier this morning—though, thinking on it, I do not recall seeing him this morning at all.

I look over the sleds for the men I heard talking last night, but there is too much activity, and everyone has fur ruffs pulled over their heads. Anyway, if they were to mutiny, it would not be here in the mid-morning sun.

I stop bracing against the dogs and step onto the runners. We slide across the snow, away from the cabin, the snow sparkling like all the stars have fallen from the sky.

I lean against the smooth wood of the sled and whistle absently to Iki. He looks back to me over his shoulder, his tongue lolling happily out of his mouth. We have pulled up on a riverbank some five miles outside Chegak— the ice is thin, Halver says, and we must take turns at the crossing.

"Good dog," I say, speaking my own tongue. His tail makes a brief effort at a wag, and then he goes back to panting.

"Eh, Willow!" I call. "Asleep?"

He hasn't stirred from his place for the last ten minutes. Maybe he is nursing that headache still. A prick of worry starts in my chest.

Willow shifts his weight and shrugs. "Tired," he says vaguely. "Old fever nags a little when I am tired."

His cheeks are red in his white face. He looks like a festival mask, not a man.

"Come on!" Drucker, who has been roughly organizing the order of crossing, comes limping from the bank. "You're next, Willow Tam."

He stops. "Say, how are you feeling?"

"A little off today."

"A little?" Drucker walks up and without invitation pushes the hood off Willow's head. A red rash covers his neck.

"You're sicker than a horse, boy," he says grimly. "Hang on."

He wallows back through the snow towards Ransom. I watch them with growing concern. From their faces, I can tell the news is not good.

"All right!" Ransom shouts down the line. "Pick up the pace!"

Drucker limps back to Willow's sled and takes the runners from him.

"Get in. You are not driving anymore today."

Willow obeys meekly. His wordless obedience frightens me. He must be really sick.

We arrive in Chegak just before dark. Willow has gotten worse in the last hour—he is shaking uncontrollably and coughing like his lungs are on fire, and the rash has spread to his face. He needs Drucker's help to climb out of the sled.

Two other men are sick as well. One simply fell from the runners a mile or so back on the trail. Drucker's face looks like a gathering storm.

He hands Willow's dogs off to Briscoe and heads into the town almost at a run, his stride catching slightly because of his leg. The captain trails close behind him, looking less hurried, but just as anxious. Likely he is worried that this fever will set us back.

The rest of us stand, unsure of what to do or where to go. Quniak starts feeding his dogs right in the middle of the street.

I grit my teeth, shivering. The wind blows mournfully through an old shed nearby, howling like wolves.

Drucker comes back, accompanied by a spry older man carrying a lantern.

"There is an old storage house we may use," the doctor says. "Follow him—we are taking the sick there."

When we reach the storehouse, I hang back. Some of us must care for the dogs and get a hot meal going, and I know very little about healing—at least Drucker's way of doing it. The man of the town opens the broad, creaky door, letting out the musky smell of whale oil. He hangs the lantern inside and I watch, as in a dream, while the sick men are carried in and laid on cots fetched from the supplies.

The doors shut, and now the only light comes from the cracks in the boards.

"Come, Maki." Rutter slaps my shoulder. "We have work to do. Drucker will do everything he can—he's one of the finest medical men in all Irylia."

"Really?"

"And he gave it up for this." Rutter gestures to the snow and the sleds with some contempt.

I drive my dogs around the side of the storehouse and tip the sled to keep them from running off with it. I am unpacking the sled so that we can make a hot supper for the dogs when the storehouse door creaks.

"How bad is it?" The captain, too, has been waiting for news.

"Bad enough."

Drucker's face is grim in the splinters of light from the door.

"It is a good thing, then, that we made it swiftly to Chegak."

Drucker stalks over to the captain, and I realize for the first time that the doctor is the taller of the two.

"And not a moment too soon," he says in a low voice. "It is the quaking fever. We do not stir one inch from this place, sir, until the fever passes."

The quaking fever—the killer of men.

He turns and stalks back into the storehouse.

"How long will that be?" calls the captain after him. There is a hint of desperation in his voice.

"Until doomsday, if need be, sir."

EIGHTEEN

Uncertain Hope

Rutter keeps me busy all the next day. I think he is trying to keep my mind off the sickness. I admit it helps some, but now I find myself on the edge of night, my stomach sick and in knots. I want to check on Willow, but I am afraid to; I want to look for Tsanu among those who are still well, but I am afraid lest I not find him there.

I slip through the door of the common house, straining to close it against the wind. When it finally thuds shut, I sigh and wrinkle my nose at the smell of must and stale fire spirits. Ransom has arranged for us to stay here until the men are well. It is not fine lodging, but it has four walls and a roof.

Tsanu is sitting with Jeremiah, leaning over a map—not at Captain Innes's side, for once. Jeremiah and I are on friendly terms, so I make the most of this excuse to sit down across from Tsanu.

I bend my head closer to the map, spread across the dusty table in all its glory. Jeremiah is like a magician. The land we have crossed so far is drawn out in neat, artistic detail, every river marked, the hills and valleys covered with notes and symbols that I do not understand.

"It is beautiful." I look up at Jeremiah, not even needing to pretend.

He gives a gratified smile and ruffles my hair with his big-knuckled hand. He points to a place on the map. "I inked in Inik Katsuk today."

My stomach turns a little. The map is upside down to me, so I had not noticed it. There it stands, cold and foreboding against the cream of the new paper.

"Tsanu was just helping me with the dimensions," he says brightly.

"Does it bother you that this map will be worthless?" Rutter stumps in and drops onto the bench beside me. Snow is caked on his boots and

210

caught in his hair, and cold air radiates off his coat and icy face.

Jeremiah reaches out with a long arm and brushes the snow away from his map. "Well, it can't be entirely worthless. I made it."

Tsanu glances up at me, and I get an odd feeling. I cannot read his eyes, but the map is significant somehow.

I do not like this. I am tired of hearing about Inik Katsuk.

Sometimes, I hope beyond the wildest hope that there will be treasure, and then the captain will be overjoyed and set Tsanu free. And sometimes I hope there is nothing, and that I can stand near at hand as Innes realizes he has been chasing nothing at all.

I just don't know. All I want is for my brother and I to be together, for Willow to be well, for things to be right again.

"Did you eat?" Rutter bumps my arm.

I shake my head. I am always hungry, but my stomach is heavy with worry right now.

"I'm getting some." He rubs his thawing hands together and gets up.

Tsanu studies the map casually. "Were you out with the dogs, Maki?"

"Yes. I was repairing harness, too. It's easier than horse harness."

"I do not doubt it."

Rutter comes back and plunks a wooden bowl down in front of me—*muktuk* and rabbit stew that Quniak has made. "Eat. You've earned it today."

"Have you been to the sick-house?" Jeremiah dips his pen in the ink and makes a notation.

"I have not." Rutter gives a shudder. "Last place I want to be. It's likely to be catching."

"Any more men sick?" asks Tsanu.

"A few more." Jeremiah dips the pen again. "Some are pretty bad, I hear. Doctor thinks they may not all live out the night."

Rutter whistles with rough sympathy.

My throat tightens so fast that I nearly choke on my stew. I set my spoon down.

I must see Willow. If he should die tonight, alone, with no one there—like his girl did in the spring—I would never forgive myself.

It is quiet, too quiet inside the sick-house. Drucker looks like a dead man sitting upright in a chair, asleep, his fingers still gripping the dipper to the water pail. The fever must be bad indeed if the doctor is so very weary.

He stirs and sees me.

"Maki, do not tell me that you are sick."

"No," I say quickly. "I came to see Willow."

"Willow . . . ." He draws out the name, searching the figures stretched on cots and wrapped in bedding on the floor. "Over here."

He gestures and I follow, paying little attention to the other men who are ill.

I am afraid of their sickness—afraid that it will happen to me, and that I will lie in a fever and waste away like they are doing all around me.

But Willow I must see.

"How is he?" I ask, though I am afraid to hear the answer.

Drucker shakes his head, exhausted. "He used to be a strong one, but he had a fever in the spring . . . he's very weak, Maki."

Willow is lying near the back entrance, bundled just enough against the cold to protect him from frostbite. His shirt is open at the collar, showing the piece of amber laying against his chest, and he is slick with sweat. My heart tightens. It must be a strong fever to make a man sweat like that in the dead of winter.

"Willow, you have a visitor." The gentleness in Drucker's voice surprises me.

Perhaps, I think suddenly, there is a reason for his usual harshness. When a doctor has buried patients, surely it weighs on him. Perhaps being a doctor is the heaviest job of all.

"Maki?" Willow's eyes flutter open. A small smile lifts the corner of his mouth. "Is it just you? Did you come alone?"

"Yes, Willow, I did."

What does he mean? Who would he expect to come with me? Not Rutter, surely.

"I am glad. I have been so ill of late . . . ." He shifts, restless. "I thought perhaps you would not come."

"And why wouldn't I have come?"

"Because I am so sick. I do not want you to have the fever."

I lean close and offer him my hand. "It is no matter. The doctor says your fever is only so bad because you were sick before this. That is all. It is no more catching than any other fever."

"I'm glad. For your sake."

He grips my hand tighter and I am suddenly afraid.

"Maki, can you sing the song I once sang? If you start, I will whisper the words."

I nod, my heart catching.

I glance around, but Drucker has gone, and there is no one here—no one who isn't laid flat by fever. I lean close and begin to sing.

"I rode away from Ellerslea upon a morning fine . . . ."

When I finish, he is relaxed, breathing straight and even. I wish I could do more for him, but sleep is the best thing I can give him, so I leave my hand in his and wait.

I am there until cockcrow, as Rutter calls it, when the hesitant sunlight filters its way through the grease paper in the window. I take a deep breath and let out a sigh of relief. I am still well, and Willow's hand is still warm in mine. The night did not take him.

Drucker is asleep in his chair again—the poor man must be beyond weariness. It is a miracle he has not become sick, too.

I slide my fingers gently out of Willow's grasp and get up. Walking past a covered bed, I realize that someone has died. The blanket has been pulled over his head.

I wish I knew who it was. I know all the men in this company now, if only by face. But I dare not look.

I steal out of the place and into the blinding sunlight. The street is silent—it is blistering cold this morning, and the town is covered in ice, like an elk that has been out in a snow-storm, with the snow melting off its back in long dirty icicles.

A low bird call breaks as I cross the deep snow between the sick-house and the place where the dogs are bedded. Iki, sleeping loose in the dog lot, raises his head and perks his ears.

The bird call sounds again, and I frown. It is the wrong time of year for that call.

Iki gets up with a whine and walks a few paces east, looking toward a stand of birches behind the sick-house.

There, standing just inside the shelter of the trees, leaning against a thin birch, is Kavik.

I stop short, rooted in place. My heart pounds up into my throat, filling my ears. *Kavik.*

Glancing swiftly around, I go to him. He straightens and I see that he has not put on any weight against the winter.

"You are changed, Maki." He looks me up and down, taking in my odd clothing, my short hair. But there is no displeasure in his face. The flint in his eyes is as soft as powder snow. He looks almost as glad as I am.

"You aren't dead," I manage.

"As you can see." He gestures with both arms, like a shrug. I throw my arms around his chest, grip him like I will never let go. The sight of someone so familiar is too much—I am crumbling like the antler of an aged *tuttik*.

Kavik shifts heavily on one leg. I pull back. It has barely been two seasons since he was hurt.

I take a deep breath lest my voice come out shaky. "How is it with you?"

"I am well. And you? Your brother?"

"We are both well."

There is a silence. It is as if we have nothing more to say, or do not know where to start.

"You were always rash, Maki." He leans against the young birch again. "I did not mean for you to go after Tsanu in my stead."

I shrug. "I could not help it. Had you gone after him, I would still have followed."

He smiles. If he did not believe it of me then, he does now.

"How did you survive?" I ask. "They burned Tansilet, and you were—"

"Ill, yes." He rubs his stubbled chin. "A good number from Tansilet survived. There was some—warning."

"Warning?"

His mouth gives a bitter twist. "The captain's second sent a man before they fired the place."

Bless that bloomin' Ransom.

Kavik spits. "What kind of man gives warning, but will not stop the destruction? Savages."

I open my mouth to protest. Kavik does not understand how it is with the captain. Ransom does what he can, and it is not always enough.

"But that is not why I came, Maki—"

One of the dogs stands up on his chain and barks. We both look over, but there is no one in sight.

"We must be careful." Kavik glances toward the sick-house. "I do not wish us to be seen."

"They are sick, many of them. Some are dying. We will be here a little while yet."

He lifts his chin and shifts his jaw, thinking.

Suddenly I remember. "Was it you who left the raven feather, then?"

Kavik smiles.

"Kavik, why have you come?"

The flint comes back to his eyes. "I am gathering men from surrounding villages, many from the south. We are banding together."

My mind shoots to Sergeant Nolan and the army in Kaquom—to Laramie, waiting out the winter sensibly.

"But the army is doing no harm in Kaquom, they—"

"No, Maki." He takes a step forward, almost laughing. "Not the camped army. This one. I am coming, soon, to free you."

My heart rises within me. For so long, I thought was alone in the world. Yet Kavik was there the whole time, gathering an army to come after us.

"So do not worry, Maki. I will make them pay. Every last man."

The world goes quiet, almost muffled in my ears. *I said that once.*

It sounds so savage coming out of someone else's mouth.

For what, exactly, would Willow pay? For hiding the fact I was a girl? Covering for me after our escape attempt failed? Or Rutter—for defending me with his gun and giving me his podge ration?

I shake my head, taking an involuntary step back. Confusion enters his face, an almost hurt surprise. He was expecting me to be glad.

And I would have been, not long ago.

"No, Kavik, please. Come save us, take us away, but do not make them pay. Some of them are good men."

"No one can be good if he is part of that army," he says softly, gently. "Perhaps they have been good, in their way, to you, but that does not wipe out the crime of who they are."

"No," I protest. He doesn't understand. I clench my fists and try to think of a way to say it that will drive the truth into his head. "It is not just being kind in their way. They—they covered for me when Tsanu and I tried to escape. They stand up to the captain, sometimes."

"They will never understand, Maki. The Invaders must know that we will no longer tolerate their oppression, and none more than the company of Captain Roger Innes."

My throat goes thick. "Please, Kavik."

He sets his hand on my shoulder. "Trust me, Maki. I am going to help set things to rights for you."

I don't need things set to rights. I need the fighting to stop. I need nobody more to die.

I hear the creak of one of the sick-house doors and Drucker's voice in the distance.

Kavik stiffens, taking a step deeper into the birches, poised to flee. "Tell no one of this," he warns. "Not even Tsanu, yet."

We do not even have time for a proper farewell. He disappears into the trees and is gone.

✦

I stay away from the sick-house only because Quniak comes and goes between it and the rest of the town so often, trading for medicines and comforts that Drucker wants. Each time, he tells me the Ash-boy or the

Birch-boy is still alive. I have told him three times that it is Willow, but he cannot remember, so he substitutes the first tree he thinks of. I have stopped correcting him. Right now I will laugh at anything, so long as it relieves my heart for a moment.

Briscoe is sick. Quniak is caring for his dogs. Peck, the man who does most of our cooking and circulates most of the gossip, says that two men have died now. He tries to tell me about a time when the camp fell sick in hot weather and there were so many dead they couldn't bury them all at once, but I walk away.

When a man talks about things like that, I have no trouble being rude.

Night is falling, and my stew is sitting in front of me untouched. I should not let it get cold—I am cold enough already—but fear takes the hunger from me. When Tsanu was first taken, I thought things could not get any worse, that I could not be more afraid than I was. But it was not so.

I am afraid. I am afraid that Willow will die, that Tsanu will die, that my kin will slaughter my friends—that I will be able to do nothing at all as everyone I have left in the world dies, killing each other.

"So serious, lad." Rutter comes up and shoves my shoulder. "You look healthier than anyone else in the camp. I swear, if we all go down with this fever, you will be the last of us all!"

I force a smile, but my heart is not in it. Getting sick is the least of my worries—though I must be honest, it is still a worry.

I do not want to die, either.

"Where have you been?"

"For to see Willow," says Rutter, imitating my figure of speech, and it warms me.

"And?" My heart climbs to my throat and stays there. My stomach is glued to the top of my ribs.

"His fever has fallen. Drucker thinks it will not rise again."

My spoon falls to the floor with a clatter. I scramble to my feet, tripping over the bench, almost falling but catching myself on the edge of the table.

I must see Willow. Tears are filling my eyes, and I cannot let Rutter see.

"Sorry, I will be back for the stew," I say gruffly, holding onto my steady voice for just a moment longer.

I walk outside, and seeing no one, run to the sick-house. I cannot tell Willow any of these things that worry or frighten me, but somehow knowing that I have one more ally, that one worry is past, makes me dizzyingly happy.

I slip into the sick-house and am relieved that Drucker is not paying attention. I do not know why, but I am embarrassed that anyone should see exactly how happy I am.

I make my way to Willow's bed and stand above him quietly.

"Willow?"

His eyes open. He looks as he did the night I first saw him, wasted and gaunt, but my heart warms at the sight of him, and I don't care that he looks terrible.

"I—" I twist my hands together. "I heard you beat the fever."

"I think it's on the run," he smiles.

A soft laugh—almost a sob—bursts from me. A tear slips down my cheek and I do not wipe it away.

"You were here last night, weren't you?"

I nod.

He reaches out his hand, then pulls it back, remembering he is sick. But I reach out and take it anyway.

It is cold, but I feel his pulse beating, and the life of it fills me with strong, heady hope.

He looks me in the eye. "Thank you."

A sudden rush of emotion wells up in my chest. I try to wipe the tears away, but they do not stop coming, no matter how hard I try to hold them back. My face must be turning red.

Why, of all times, do I lose my head now?

"Sorry, I don't know why—" I drop his hand and turn away a little.

He doesn't say anything.

I drop into the chair and hide my face in my sleeve. I cannot stop.

"What is it?" Willow asks at last. I still can't breathe, but the heaving sea of emotion has settled.

I shrug. "I was just so—I am relieved, Willow. I was afraid . . . ."

"It is all right, Maki. It's over now."

I nod, let go another sobbing breath, and wipe my face on my arm, only to hear a loud footfall directly behind me.

Drucker.

"You are not sick, are you Maki?"

I shake my head. Poor fellow, that is his first question.

"Willow must rest."

"Yes, sir." My voice is thick—anyone could tell that I've been crying. I take a deep breath. "I'm sorry, I—"

"Don't mind me." Drucker cuts me off gruffly. "I've seen too much to care one way or another."

❧

There is a little wind, but the sun is out as we stand around four long pine boxes in the snow. The wind blows some snow off the nearby trees, making it look like it is snowing from the blindingly blue sky.

The captain stands like some tall, dark figure of omen, his hands folded, an expression of grim sorrow on his face. It is Ransom who holds the little book, his voice carrying in the wind like a mournful reminder that we are all

220

still very much real and alive.

Earth to earth, ashes to ashes, dust to dust . . . sure and certain hope . . . .

At last he closes the book and folds it safely in his coat pocket. "We cannot choose the time of our deaths," he says. "But we can live in such a way that when our time comes, we are ready and without regrets."

I clench my fists at my sides. The sense of life and death before me is very strong. Willow is beside me. He is nowhere near fat enough for the winter, especially now that he has been sick. We are to leave tomorrow before dawn, and I am afraid for him.

Tsanu stands across the circle, staring into the brilliant blue sky. We of Tansilet always look to the sky to respect the dead. The Inv—the others, they look at the ground.

I raise my eyes to the painfully bright sky and take a deep breath. If Tsanu can honor them in our way, so can I.

"And so it shall be with all of us one day," Ransom says. "God rest their souls."

"God rest their souls," murmur the rest.

The circle of men begins to disperse, and the captain's voice breaks in like a storm after a fine day. "Now, men—since we've been spared to live this day, let's put our backs into our honest work! Back to it!"

The men break up faster, going to their tasks, and I catch Tsanu's eyes. He slides his expression behind a mask, but not before I see what was in his face.

His eyes were grim, undaunted, resigned. He has death on his mind.

I will never forget that look as long as I live.

✦

I stand in the grove of birches, shivering in the early morning. The

221

world is still dark and mostly asleep, and while the air under the stars is still, it is shatteringly cold.

The chances of Kavik being out here, within earshot, are slim.

I raise my head and give the bird call. Silence.

Once, twice more I give it, and then wait.

I hear the sounds of preparation down by the sick-house. I wonder if leaving four of our company buried here has made the men more bitter. It must be terrible for the mothers, sending their sons off to be buried in the middle of an unknown country, among strangers.

A faint cracking sound catches my ear. It is the *kitya nitkas*, the lights drifting over the snow. Green and blue and white, tinged with pink and yellow. In the winter, they make noise as the air freezes their dampness into crystals. I bend down and reach my hand among them, admiring my mitten, lit by the gentle blue light.

"Maki?"

He is here. It would have been hard to see him an hour ago, when the last moon of the night was setting, but now I can see the starving lines of his face, his jewel-blue eyes, his sharp nose, all lit with the gentle, moving colors of the lights.

"We are leaving."

"Yes."

"We are going to Tlatlik."

There is a look in Kavik's eyes I do not understand, dark and strange.

"Please, come for us, and be careful."

"It will be a fight, Maki. I would rather you were not in it."

"But I am with them."

"I will leave you a sign." His eyes sadden. "You will know when we have come."

My teeth clench, but not with cold. "Then I must leave and you will fight it out? With strike-locks, you could all be killed."

"Perhaps. But they will all be dead as well."

A world with no one flashes before me. Part of me almost wants to tell him not to come at all.

But I can't do it. I want Tsanu back.

"If you see a young man with a piece of amber hung on his neck, tall like an aspen and just as thin—by the memory of Tansilet, do not shoot him."

Kavik sighs but nods. "If he does not shoot, I will not shoot him."

He looks down at the colorful light snaking through the birches. His face is drawn, but there is a fierceness in it born of long weariness.

He peels a strip of bark and rolls it gently in his fingers. "You have a warrior's courage, Maki. Hold on to it just a little longer."

I do not want to hold on a little longer. I want to keep my courage, and most of all, I don't want killing. But swallow back my protests and clasp his hand, maybe for the last time.

"Be well," I say, all other words sticking in my throat.

He grips my hand tightly, as he would a man's and not a girl's, and presses his forehead against mine. "Be well."

I part from him, but cannot seem to leave.

"Go on, Maki," he urges, but not roughly. "It is time to go."

I force myself to walk away. When I am nearly out of sight of the birch grove I stop, turning to look behind. Kavik is still there, watching me out of sight.

He raises his spear in a sign of respect, and I press my fist to my chest in reply.

NINETEEN

Mountain of Fear

Drucker slams his hand down on the table, sending dust into the stale air of the common house. "I say again, he is not well enough to go!"

"What in the devil's name is that supposed to mean?" The captain's eyes kindle.

"It means you leave him or you wait here."

"I will not leave him. The trail is going to be worse from here, not better, and we cannot do without his dogs. And neither will I wait! If there was a problem, you should have told me earlier."

Drucker's voice is flat and cold. "I did tell you earlier."

In the corner, I set aside one dog harness and pick up the next. Captain Innes has tasked me with helping the dog-runners check their harnesses before we leave, and I prefer the smell of dust and fire spirits to the howling wind outside. Halver took great offense at the suggestion that his harnesses might have something wrong with them, but the captain is too far gone this morning to reason over it.

"The fever took him almost a week ago." Innes paces like a wolf in a dog run. "He says he is well enough."

"With all due respect, sir, I am the doctor, not him."

I toss down the fifth harness—it is tight and strong. All of them are. Like Halver, I think this is a great waste of time, but there are more important things at stake than a little of my time, so I will not complain.

Briscoe gets up from the table, staggering a little. "I have led you a long way. Either I go with the dogs or you pay me now, but I will not send them on without me."

"Stay out of this, Briscoe," snaps the captain.

"Stay out of it?" Briscoe's voice turns sharp. "I think this concerns me!"

Drucker shouts again. "As a doctor, sir, I say he stays here!"

"And I say unless he chooses between you and the dogs, he will not see a red cent."

Dead silence falls, followed by Briscoe's disbelieving laugh. "I have already traveled two months! You have used my dogs, and you will pay me what you owe me."

"I control the purse," says the captain coolly. "You choose."

Briscoe's voice is hard as ice. "I'm sorry, Doctor. I will go on. And Innes, let me hear you threaten to cut my pay one more time, and as there are stars in the heavens I will tell my dogs what you are and see if you get away from them alive."

"Is that a threat?" The captain's low voice sends a prickle of sickness through my middle.

I do not stay to hear the answer. Filling my arms with leather, I carry the harnesses outside to trade them for more.

The sleds are lined up behind the building. I want to help Quniak, because he has the most to do, but I cannot find him. Setting the finished harnesses in one of the sleds, I start around the side of the building. As I round the corner, a low voice stops me in my tracks—one of the voices from outside the trapper's cabin, two nights after the *nanuk* attack.

Four—no, five men stand a short distance from the building, holding smoke-sticks in their chapped hands, their fur hoods pushed back on their shoulders. The one talking has hair to his shoulders and a beard covering a hard jaw. I slink back toward the sleds and crouch where I cannot be seen. If I am discovered, I will seem to be gathering harnesses.

"They always ride the same sled," says the long-haired man. "If we just—" He shifts the two fingers that hold his smoke-stick to one side in a sweeping motion.

One of the others leans in, eyes bright. He is young, younger than

Tsanu—perhaps not many years older than I am. "But where?"

"Sea ice, if there's a chance. If they end up in the open water, there'll be no evidence."

"What about the lieutenant?"

A new voice speaks up, the deep drawl I heard that night outside the cabin. "If it looks like an accident, there won't be any trouble." The speaker is a deep-eyed fellow with hair like autumn grass and a drooping mustache.

One of the soldiers takes a long breath on his smoke-stick and lets out a stream of smoke. "So it's mutiny."

The long-haired speaker shakes his head, almost regretfully. "No it ain't, not here. I've followed Innes well-nigh to the gates of hell, and I ain't never seen him like this. No legend of gold's worth freezing to death trying to get to a place even the natives won't go to. It's lunacy."

"Especially when some of the company's barely well enough to be out of bed, let alone traveling in snow up to a man's waist," adds another, shaking his head.

"We get rid of him, we get rid of the guide," says the man with the drawl, "and the trouble's gone."

Tsanu.

My heart hammers like a drum in my ears. I have heard enough.

Slowly and silently I stand, gather up harnesses from two or three more sleds, and steal back to the common house through the soft snow.

✐

Beyond the town is three days of sea ice. This, maybe more than Tlatlik itself, is the dangerous part of the journey. The ice can break and carry you out to sea with no hope of rescue. Howling storms cling to the ground, twenty or thirty feet high. Above them it is calm, but you would never know from inside. You might be lost in such a storm for days—or wander until you froze to death.

Tsanu has his own sled now—a necessity, as he will be leading the way. Looking at Tsanu like this is a lonely feeling. For the moment, I do not exist. His mind is on the task ahead of him and on Captain Innes, who stands on the second sled, ready to shoot down the dogs with a gun if Tsanu tries anything. In the last few weeks, Tsanu and the captain have taken on the stance of two stags, constantly locking antlers.

Neither one is willing to let the other go.

"Are we ready?" Tsanu looks back with insolent brown eyes. I hope the men understand how dangerous this is. We have to follow our guides almost to the inch, or we could be dead.

He gets no answer, but he does not seem to expect one.

"Stick close," he mutters. "This isn't Kaquom anymore."

He calls to his team, and they tear down the narrow path.

For the first time since leaving Tansilet, I am afraid in a different sense. I am afraid of Tlatlik the black mountain, I am afraid of sea ice, I am afraid of the stories of monsters.

I am afraid of the unknown.

We meet our first storm by mid-morning. It is clear one moment, and there is almost no wind. Then, out of nowhere, the wind picks up and snow flies into my face.

"Stay within sight of each other!" shouts Halver, in front of me.

I lean over my sled. "Iki!" I can just make out his shape in the whirling snow. "Follow, Iki!"

I hope he understands. He has good instincts, and he was made for this weather, but the thought of being lost makes me cold to my bones.

I wonder if Willow is all right. I twist to look over my shoulder in the whirling white. All I can see the black nose of someone's lead dog, and it does not look like Willow's. I face forward again, narrowing my eyes into the wind.

My face feels like it is being torn off. Numb-fingered, I crouch down behind the sled where it is less windy and let Iki lead for a while. He is the one following Halver—I cannot see a thing. There is no sense in torturing myself for nothing.

A sled shoots by me, silent, and my blood turns cold. All I can think of is the conversation I overheard in Chegak: *Sea ice, if there's a chance.*

For three days, I have watched for a chance to warn Tsanu, but the captain circles him day and night like a wolf with a fresh kill. I would shout now, but I know it will do no good. The wind howls so loudly that even Iki, with his half-wolf ears, can barely hear me.

I shout to Iki and break my sled out of line. If I cannot warn Tsanu, perhaps I can stop the mutineers.

A gunshot—two—break through the roar of the wind, and Iki shies off.

"Iki!" My voice cracks with the force of my shout. If he loses the rest of the company, we may never find them again.

He hears me and veers back. The thought of being so nearly lost makes my knees tremble. I grip the sled's handles tighter.

We come upon the scene a moment or two later. The shouts are barely audible above the wind. Two sleds are tipped, the rest of the line stopped behind. The captain's gun lies smoking on the ice.

Halver is trudging over to the wreckage—in this wind a man can do little more than walk.

"Just let me go after them! I have been out on sea ice before. If anyone can make it, I can!"

Tsanu is shouting—at the captain.

"Out of the question! Or do you forget yourself?" Innes's voice is like the roar of a bull elk in the wind. "His stupidity is on his own head."

"How can you say that about one of your own men? He knows nothing. He and his dogs will freeze!"

"I cannot risk anyone to go after them, most of all you. No one life is worth endangering this quest."

"If I go, perhaps no one dies." Tsanu's voice is stinging, like the snow driven on the wind. "I swear I will not escape—just give me a leader."

"No. He is probably lost already."

Halver is checking over the dogs carefully. "Who was it?"

"One of the men—Thompson, maybe. We won't know until we get out of this storm."

"What happened?" Ransom strides over, his face white with ice.

Captain Innes raises his voice to be heard above the wind. "Some fool broke line, cut right across my team."

"Who shot the gun?"

"Captain did," said Tsanu, his face white. He is angry. "Spooked their dogs. I think he was aiming for mine."

Ransom's mouth is a hard line.

"I think the man can possibly be saved," says Tsanu. "But the longer we wait—"

"No one is going out there, no one is risking their lives." The captain bends down and picks up his gun. "Let's get moving."

I move close to Tsanu. For a moment, in the swirling storm, no one is paying attention to us.

I grab his shoulder and stand on my toes to speak in his ear. "There was a plan—to lose you and the captain on the sea ice. I think that was it."

Tsanu's face turns even grimmer than before. He nods, understanding.

Many a man's plans have been thwarted by sea ice.

"Back in line!" roars the captain. He comes up and gives Tsanu a shove.

He speaks only for my brother to hear, but the wind carries it to me as if it was spoken in my ear: "Next time, think before you oppose me. I will not tolerate it a second time."

My brother's eyes are like stone.

"He shoots off his bloody pistol and then acts like it's everyone else's fault," says Rutter, shoveling a bite of stew into his mouth. He shoves it to one side of his mouth and talks around it. "I'm hanged if I can take much more of it."

"Pipe down." Jeremiah raises his head to look over the circle.

But the captain is well out of earshot, I know. He is still standing like a brooding eagle over his sled, where Tsanu is.

Quniak has built a fire on the ice, over which Peck made the stew. Many of the men look stiff with cold, but inside my parka, with the fire to heat my face and hands, I am warm.

Jeremiah pulls a cloth out of his shirt. He keeps his inks wrapped against his chest to keep them from freezing. By the light of the fire, he maps the territory we have crossed—swiftly, before his inks harden in the frigid air. He is the only one of us who seems unruffled by this afternoon's disaster, though I saw him earlier, as we were making camp, staring back over the ice with his hat over his heart.

His hands must be cramped with cold, but he says nothing about it. I watch as the sea ice, fading into unknown ground, takes form under his fingers. He ignores the rising complaints around him, and the others, wrapped in their wretchedness like a forlorn blanket, ignore him.

I like watching him. He is not happy, but he is content.

Sea ice does not take long to sketch. Jeremiah soon closes his inks, wraps them, and puts them back in his shirt. He folds the maps tenderly.

"Night, lads," he says, and strides off ten paces to sleep.

I follow suit. Sometimes I think Jeremiah is the wisest of us all—there is little to be gained from listening to men in their misery.

As I lie down to sleep in the shelter of my sled, Willow comes and settles down nearby. Iki wriggles to make room, and I throw my arm over his furry body.

"*Hagati*, Willow," I greet.

He touches his forehead. "*Kitaya*, Maki."

We lie silent under the dark sky.

I am glad that Willow is here—that it was not him the captain abandoned out on the sea ice. Guilt makes the loss sit heavier in my stomach. Thompson was one of those I'd heard talking out behind the common house in Chegak—the young one. My ears have strained all day for the baying of dogs or a voice out of the wind. I would not wish such a death on anyone.

Well, maybe Captain Innes.

I thrust my arm under my head and tilt my chin up to the sky. Streaks of blue and green are starting to weave their way over the stars, like *mudi* on a black stone.

"What is that?" Willow murmurs. "Does it have a name?"

"*Kigyat*," I say. "The sky is singing."

A faint breath, like laughter, comes from his nose. "The sky is singing."

The green spreads gently across the sky, pulsing in and out like a living thing.

Willow turns his head to me slightly. "I am glad that you were not lost. It could have been anyone. And—you do reckless things like that sometimes."

I can't deny it, though I wish I could. I take a deep breath, letting the air out in a long stream before I answer.

"I am glad it was not you either, Willow Tam."

His eyes crease into deep laughter lines, but he says nothing.

Willow's face is gently pink and green from the brilliant *kigyat* above us. "What do you think lies at the end of all of this?"

My heart jumps. For a moment, I do not know what to say.

"I don't know."

"Hmm." His face is gaunt, but the old Willow has returned to it.

I lay my head on Iki's back and he shifts under me. "Freedom, I hope."

The wind has blown the snow off a whole ten or twenty mile stretch of our trail, and the sea beneath our sleds is a dark blue-green. The ice is clear—you can see straight down to the water itself.

I do not know which is more terrifying: a day where you can see nothing, or a day where you can see too much. Dizziness spins in my head as I look down through four or five feet of ice at the water that goes on far, far deeper.

"Is it safe?" This is the captain's first question of the morning.

"Safe enough," says Tsanu. "If we let the dogs have their heads, they will keep us away from the thin ice."

A shiver runs up my spine anyway. If the wind is hard enough, we could be blown straight onto the thin ice, fighting all the way. But Tsanu does not mention that.

"Well, let's get moving."

I call to Iki, and we take off.

The world is lovelier and less savage today, but I try not to look down as we travel. I am not really afraid of the sea, but I have never been on easy terms with it. When Tsanu would take me on seal hunts, I was always afraid of falling into the hole and drowning the cold, dark water.

A few hours into our day's journey, I hear a commotion just ahead of me. One of the men is calling, pointing to the ice. I see a great shadow beneath him, and my blood goes cold. It is a *ska-ana*, a black kind of Great One, and the best killer known to Uniap'nik.

It swims along on its side, one eye fixed on him, keeping easy pace with the trotting dogs.

"What is it?" the man calls. I can see that he is both curious and a little afraid. I would be too.

"Keep moving!" orders Quniak. "Do not slow down!"

This sobers everyone, and we quicken our pace. The *ska-ana* loses interest in that man and drops back to eye Drucker. Its sleek black-and-white body slides beneath us, its beady eye fixed on the doctor and his dogs.

I wonder if four feet of ice is thick enough to hold.

A heavy jolt almost knocks me from the runners and my dogs stop short, skittering away. Drucker is calling to his dogs to steady them; their ears lie flat against their heads, their tails tucked between their legs.

Another jolt, and I see it this time: the *ska-ana* banging upward against the ice with its great pointed fin.

"What is happening back there?" Ransom shouts down the line.

I raise my voice to call, but it sticks in my throat.

"The black thing is hunting us!" bellows Drucker, his breath hanging in the air.

Another jolt shakes us, and the dogs veer off at an angle. The *ska-ana* follows us easily, rolling upside down beneath us, showing a smooth white belly longer than the span of my sled and dogs put together.

Ransom slows his dogs, falling back to see for himself. The *ska-ana* hits the ice again, and he falls off the sled. His dogs take off running, and I slow mine to pick him up. Briscoe and Halver are both beyond us; the dogs won't get away.

"What is it?" Ransom dusts the snow off.

"A *ska-ana*. They are very large and dangerous."

"Can it break the ice?"

I shrug. "It will need air soon, so maybe it will leave. But if it is here, there must be open water not far off."

I shudder at the thought of open water and a *ska-ana* waiting in it.

"Hold on—where did it go?"

"It probably went to breathe." As I look out to the west, I see a black fin rise and fall. "There!" I point just as it goes down again.

"Let's get out of here."

I call to Iki, and we race forward across the blue-green surface.

The *ska-ana* follows us on and off for the rest of the day. Once, the ice cracks above his fin, and we move further inland. Even though it lengthens our route off the ice, Captain Innes does not argue.

Perhaps it cannot get to us, but it is a bad omen. It is like the trials of Nanik, beset by monsters and dangers on his journey.

"Look!" On the sled ahead, Willow points to the horizon.

There is land ahead.

As we leave the ice field behind, I look back one last time. The *ska-ana* has vanished into the deep.

Tufts of grass jolt the sled through the snow, and for once I am grateful to feel them. I have never been gladder to leave a place behind.

"What is this?" Murmurs break out among the men, and the sleds come to an uneasy halt. A great red and white mass lies to the northeast of us.

"It's a *nanuk*," says Quniak. "It's been slain."

It can't be. Nothing can kill a *nanuk*, not one so large as this. It must have died, and scavengers have had at it.

Quniak approaches the carcass with caution, Ransom following a little slower behind him. I tip my sled and follow.

This *nanuk* is one of the largest I have ever seen, larger even than the one that attacked us. Something has torn it at the throat—just at the throat—and left. It is a death-wound, not scavengers' work. Wolf tracks circle it, but do not come within more than ten feet of the carcass.

A prickle runs up my arm.

"I don't like this." I jump as Rutter's voice echoes my thoughts. Several others have gathered around. "I do not know where we are or what we've come up against, but there are tales about this place. And I, for one, want no more of it."

"Aye!" agrees Peck, who has a very loud voice. "I say we go back while we can!"

Across from me, on the other side of the *nanuk*, stands the man with the drawl and the drooping mustache. He looks to his friend, and they exchange a meaningful glance.

Close at hand comes the click of a shotgun. "Say that again, boys," says Captain Innes grimly.

Peck swallows hard.

The captain fires the gun into the air and several men jump, already made nervous by the sight of the carcass. "I said say that again!"

"You're captain." Rutter wisely chooses to avoid the danger standing before him rather than the nameless dread of dark tales. "What you say goes."

"Sounds mighty nice, don't it?" The captain clicks something on the gun, and a hollow fragment of metal drops onto the icy tundra.

"Onward! And the first coward who dares turn back, I'll shoot!"

TWENTY

The Pack Gathers

"All right, men! We're settin' down camp!" Innes's voice rings through the frozen air. It is not dark yet—and the days are short here in the north. Even the captain is becoming wary in the shadow of the mountain.

I do not blame him. Now that we are off the ice, nothing stands between us and Tlatlik but rocks and dirt, and those will not keep anything away.

The men grumble openly, not even trying to hide their unhappiness. It has grown worse since the plan to be rid of the captain on the sea ice failed. If Innes notices their resentment—and he is far from blind—he says nothing. He only stands warily, as he has for the past two weeks, with a shotgun cradled in his arms, watching Tsanu take care of his dogs.

The closer we get to Tlatlik, the more he seems to fear that Tsanu will disappear into the night.

Snowflakes blow gently into my face. The faint wind promises a still night—we will be able to hear for a long distance. And if we can hear, so can anyone or anything else.

Beside me, Iki stiffens, staring into the forest. Even I can sense something wrong, but his senses are far keener than mine. His ears prick up, and cold fear threads down my spine.

I leave my sled, using all my willpower not to run, and find Peck, who is fumbling with his flint.

"Peck, hurry with the fire."

"Eh?" He squints up at me.

I have never given orders before. But the feeling in me is strong, almost desperate.

"Hurry."

"Why?"

"I am not sure yet. But something is wrong." I pass him and find Ransom unpacking his sled.

"Ransom?"

He straightens and turns to me.

"Ransom, I think we should circle our sleds, make a few more fires."

He jerks his head back a little. "Do you have a reason?"

"Just—just a bad feeling. I feel like we're being watched."

"Was it the bear back there that made you feel that?"

I shake my head. It is more than the *nanuk*, more than the *ska-ana*. Nothing feels right or safe about tonight. "There have been many bad omens today. I think we will all be safer with more fires."

"I agree with the boy, Ransom." It is the captain, unexpectedly agreeing with me. "Set the men to working on the fires. And we will double the watch."

Ransom looks at me and shrugs. "If you think so." He slaps my shoulder.

I think he would rather show agreement with me than with the captain.

I lie in my sled, under my furs, staring up at the sky. The stars flicker like a thousand watchfires in the distance. My mind goes round and round; I cannot sleep. Danger is near.

If only I could talk with Tsanu. He would know what to do. But Innes has too close a watch on him now, and his grip on the rest of the company is tightening. Soon it will be too late for all of us, and I do not know what to do to stop it.

I pull the fur tighter around me and tilt my face nearer to the stars. I should be sleeping.

I have never had trouble sleeping before.

"Maki, you are still awake?" Willow stops beside me and looks down.

I shrug. Telling him I can't sleep would sound silly, like a little child talking to its mother.

Willow is wearing his pistol in a belt across his chest, and even in a parka, he looks thin. If there was food to spare, I would try to put meat on his bones. A man should go into winter a little fat, not twenty pounds below weight.

"What are you doing up?" I am proud of myself for finding the perfect reply. "Shouldn't you be resting?"

"No, this is my watch. Halver has the other side."

"Oh." Of course. The captain has doubled the watch.

I sit up on one elbow. "Do you want company? I cannot sleep."

He smiles. I wrap the fur around me and step out onto the snowy ground. A fresh inch or two has fallen since I climbed into my sled.

We fall into comfortable step beside each other.

"Maki, may I ask you something?"

I do not like his tone. I steel myself, not looking up at him. "Go ahead."

"You do not seem well. Is there something the matter?"

"Tonight?"

"Since I recovered from the fever. You have been avoiding me."

"I have not meant to," I say quickly. This is the truth.

"But something is not right."

I shrug.

The snow crunches under our feet, and it is so still that I can hear the gentle falling of the fresh flakes. It is a beautiful night, more beautiful because we are both still alive—we are all alive.

"Is it about Inik Katsuk?"

"No. Well—perhaps. Not really."

He stays quiet. I look up at him and he is watching my face patiently.

I find my fears coming out of my mouth, telling him things I hardly knew before. "I am afraid that we will all die. And if only I knew what to do, perhaps we wouldn't. But—but I do not."

"What makes you think you could cause or stop all our deaths?"

I pause. Why do I think it? Because I alone know Kavik plans to attack? Because the captain will kill Tsanu if we do not find Inik Katsuk? Because my heart is full of dread tonight, and perhaps if I knew why, I could stop whatever terrible thing is coming?

"I do not know. But I feel it."

"You are the smallest person in this camp, Maki. And other than perhaps Lieutenant Ransom and the doctor, I think you are the only one who loses sleep over protecting us all."

I glare at him. "I will not be little forever. One day I shall be tall, tall as the trees, and girl though I be, I shall walk as a hunter among them."

Willow chuckles, but his eyes are serious. "Why, Maki, I did not mean it to be an insult. I think you are perfect the way you are. I daresay I'd pit you against any man in the camp for your grit alone."

This comforts me. Grit has kept me alive and a good many others before me.

"But why should you feel this way? After all, you wanted to destroy us all when I first met you."

A smile pulls up the corners of my mouth. Was it only this past spring that I was such a spitfire? But the merriment leaves quickly.

I do not know how to answer him. Even if I could speak freely of Tsanu and Kavik, I do not know if I am willing to open these places in my heart.

Instead I talk of Inik Katsuk, try to make him understand. "This is my land. I know it. I belong to it and it belongs to me. This journey is so much more than keeping my head down while the captain searches for a—a legend. Every day I say to myself, *I hope he does not find it, and I hope I am there to see his failure*. And every day I reply to myself, *But I do. I hope he finds what he wants and is happy again and will go away and leave us alone*. Every day I say this."

"But why?" Willow pauses and looks down at me.

I open my mouth to say it, but there is nothing. I cannot say it.

"Because I do not want the people I care for to die," I manage at last.

He lifts his head and walks on, clasping his hands behind his back. I wish I knew what he is thinking, he is so quiet.

"Did it ever occur to you, Maki, that maybe the world wasn't made to be carried by you?"

I stop. The snowflakes continue their slow, gentle falling. It is really, suddenly, a new thought.

He faces me. "Especially not on your little shoulders."

"But if I could do something about it, and I didn't, I couldn't live with myself."

"Do you think you control all this?" He gestures at the snow, the dark, the sleeping camp, with a long arm.

I shake my head.

"Then do not act like you do."

I nod. Panic and relief both clamber over me. I could not go on in life if Tsanu was dead. I couldn't. Yet what a blessed thing it would be to not have to be afraid or to worry.

I am so very tired of being afraid.

We turn and walk back the way we came. In the distance rises the bellow of a bull *bisgak*, and some of the dogs in the camp growl. Willow raises his head and lays his hand upon his pistol.

The noise dies away and slowly he lets his grip relax. "You should sleep, Maki. Save your strength for another day."

"I can't, Willow."

"You can." He sets both hands on my shoulders and looks into my face. He knows I am not telling him everything. We are both tired, and I think we both wish nothing was hidden between us.

"Maki, go to sleep. There is still tomorrow." He reaches into his belt and hands me a knife. "Keep it. I think everyone should have something to their defense now."

My eye catches movement in the dark. I freeze, laying my hand on Willow's arm.

"What is it?" He tries to turn around, but I grip his arm, stopping him.

The patch of darkness is changing, materializing. A shape emerges—the leering face of an unnaturally large wolf, green-eyed.

Wolves are not supposed to have green eyes.

"Willow, wolves," I breathe.

I hardly dare move. Willow's hand goes to his chest, very slowly. I hear him cock the gun with a muffled click.

He whirls. A gunshot splits the night. The wolf stumbles, retreats.

"I—I hit him square on . . . ."

Another gun goes off in the darkness—Halver, on watch.

"Wolves!" I scream, rousing the camp. "Wolves!"

Willow cocks his gun and fires again. I run to the fire and grab a brand, the dogs around me starting up with barks and growls. The noise is deafening. The men are rising quickly, pulling their guns out. I reach Willow's side with the brand, and in the light of the fire, my heart nearly stops.

Fifty or more shapes with glowing pairs of eyes stare back at me—not low to the ground, like the wolves around Tansilet. These stand as tall as Iki, perhaps taller. Watching those eyes advance on us chills me to my core.

Captain Innes rushes forward to the circle of sleds, slamming to his knees and taking quick aim. "Fire on them! Do not wait! Fire!" He empties his two small guns into the blackness with a roar, and a pair of eyes goes out.

Horrid snarls answer the deafening noise of the strike-locks. I have never seen a pack of this size or number in my life—the fifty have more than doubled in number, surrounding the camp. The men spread out in a thin circle, and the dogs bay and yelp, mad with frenzy to meet their renegade kin head-on.

"Maki!" Rutter is stumbling toward me in the firelight, carrying a box in one arm and a shotgun in the other. He is bleeding from a shallow gash in his arm—at least one wolf has already come too close.

Rutter is lucky. In a split second, these wolves can take an arm straight off, or so the stories go.

He drops to his knees and pulls three pistols from his belt. His hand trembles as he fumbles with the box of bullets. "Help the men reload—I'll show you how—"

But I already have one of the strike-locks in my hands, and I am opening it as I have seen Willow and the others do time and time again.

Rutter's face goes slack with astonishment.

It makes me want to laugh—these Invaders expect all people to be as they are, paying little attention to the world around them. Did he think I could live among them for months without learning by sight how to use a strike-lock?

Time does not seem to pass at all as we load and reload, Rutter dropping a little blood into the fresh snow. Every time a man throws down an empty gun, we have a freshly loaded one ready. Tsanu has a gun, too—I think the captain has been too busy to notice. Innes has been "pouring lead into them," as Rutter says, since the fight started and has not so much as looked around him once.

Ransom kneels nearby, firing his long rifle over the top of the sleds, and Peck and a couple others throw firebrands. The deafening crack of guns makes my ears ring.

Innes stumbles back. My heart jumps, looking for a shaggy beast—then I realize no wolf touched him.

The long-haired man stands facing Innes and not the wolves, his pistol smoking. He has shot the captain.

The clamor of barks and howls fades from my ears as I see him cock his gun again and aim for Tsanu.

But Tsanu sees. His gun is leveled on the man already. The others are still fighting the wolves.

Innes hauls himself to his feet, gripping his left arm tightly. The long-haired man gestures with his gun. "Don't move or I'll shoot the guide."

"Are you out of your mind?" Innes bites out.

"You're the one out of your mind," says the man through shut teeth. "We're taking over."

The wolves are thinning, retreating, and slowly the men are turning back to the fires, realizing what is happening.

"Are you sure you don't want to rethink that?" The captain's voice is tinged with his old charm and confidence. He speaks like a man who has done this a dozen times. "Days away from being a glorious part of history, and you want to turn back? Can you not feel the weight of this honor?"

The man keeps his grip on the gun, torn between covering the captain and Tsanu. Behind him, almost a dozen others gather, led by the man with the drooping mustache. If we lose these men, we will no longer be able to drive our supplies.

We cannot afford to lose so many.

In one swift motion, captain lets go of his wounded arm and reaches down, snatching up his pistol.

"I am giving you to the count of five to drop that gun, Wade. Drop it, and I will consider not putting a bullet through your skull."

The long-haired man laughs grimly. "I'm for the good of this army, I am. I have followed you through death, but this time—"

The captain's arm is soaked. It won't be long before there is not enough blood in him to keep him on his feet. "Have I asked anything of you that I am unwilling to do myself? Yes, the journey is dangerous, but so much greater the honor!" His voice turns to steel. "Men, I am giving you one chance to redeem yourselves. After that, I'll give you nothing but lead."

The men behind Wade begin to murmur, backing off, taking on the look of cowering dogs. Only his friend with the mustache stays, uneasily standing his ground. Innes strides toward the mutineers, his gun-hand steady, the other running with blood.

It is not a sight any of us will forget in a hurry.

Innes's gun goes off between Wade's feet, sending up a stinging spray of rocks and pieces of pebble.

Then he fires again, knocking the gun out of the man's hand. There is a snap—I think Wade's hand is broken.

"Anyone else?" The captain's voice echoes into the night.

Even the dogs are silent.

The captain turns, meeting every man's eye. "I said anyone else?" His voice is a roar now. "If you have complaints, speak them now!"

The only sound is of men and dogs, breathing hard.

The captain raises the corner of his mouth in disgust as he jams his gun back into the holster on his leg. "Get to cleaning up this mess."

The men move immediately to obey.

As Wade limps away, cradling his hand, the captain rounds on Tsanu.

"You said you knew this land! How is it that you did not warn us of the wolves?"

Tsanu stiffens. "Wolves are a danger everywhere we go. If you assumed we were safe because I did not mention what is as clear as the two moons, that was your fault."

Captain Innes strikes Tsanu with his unhurt hand, leaving a smear of his blood on his cheek. Tsanu does not move a muscle.

Innes turns and swears through his teeth. "Drucker, get over here before I bleed out!"

Drucker comes striding through the darkness, already pulling bandages from his bag. For the moment, Tsanu is forgotten.

But I meet his eyes, and we stare long and hard at each other.

Those wolves, vast in number, large as young buffalo, with unnatural eyes, are only known to us in legend.

A shiver runs up my spine. The story of Tslaniq is coming true—to us.

I take a deep breath and gaze at the black, towering mass of Tlatlik above me. Today, five days out of Chegak, we finally set foot upon the mountain. The ground is pathless and rocky. Where the rocks are not, scrubby trees and deadwood crowd thickly. The supplies we do not need stay below in a base camp, guarded by Halver, three soldiers, and almost half the dogs. They are happy to stay, I think, and I do not blame them.

I whistle low to Iki, and my sled lurches forward.

It is impossible to ride the runners on such uneven ground without damaging the sled, so I walk behind the sled, keeping the dogs at a slow pace. Iki whines and pulls a little against the harness in protest, but he listens to me. The trail is rough, the black rocks jutting from the white snow, the trees brown and bare in the middle of it all.

It is so desolate.

I see now why stories have been started about Tlatlik. It must be barren even in summer. Now, in the dead of winter, it is fearsome.

Up ahead, on a high, flat stretch of ground, Jeremiah stands on his long legs. He looks back down the steep, rocky slope, making measurements with a glass tool. A smile grows on my face. It never seems to bother Jeremiah that his whole task is to create a map to a city he does not believe in. He maps the land as diligently as if he has been promised the world at the end of it all.

"It will be a hard job getting the sleds over the edge of that shelf." Tsanu, walking just ahead of Iki beside the captain's sled, gestures to the plain where Jeremiah is perched, scribbling notes.

A hard glint enters Innes's eyes. "It must be done." Beyond the bulge of the bandages under his sleeve, he does not act like a man who has been hurt. He does all he did before—and with more determination, if that is possible.

"It can be. But we must be careful, or we risk losing supplies."

"I cannot tolerate delay. It must be done in good time."

Quniak, in the lead, calls his dogs to a halt. "We will rig ropes. Unhitching the dogs and pulling the sleds from the top, we will make it up. I have done it many times in places steeper than this."

The captain nods briefly, his jaw tight. We unhitch the dogs and run ropes through their collars. I lead some of them up the ridge myself, tying them to a tree on the plateau so they cannot run off. All good sled dogs are half wild.

Quniak shows the men how to rig the sleds with ropes and assigns a team to haul them up the slope. I lean against a tree to watch and wait, throwing an arm over Iki to calm my nerves. His muscular flanks heave as he pants, ears pricked to the shouts of the men.

As they are pulling the last sled up, the rope shifts and goes slack. The sled tilts and begins to career back down the way it came. If it falls from this height, it will be smashed on the snowy ground below.

"Hold!" Briscoe shouts, running over to grab one of the ropes. "Hold it!"

The sled skids, wavering between staying and plummeting. Jeremiah and Rutter catch hold of the stays and drag it back.

"Will we have much more of this?" The captain turns on Tsanu as if he is to blame for the lay of the land.

Tsanu nods. "Eventually we will have to pack our supplies on our backs."

The captain's fingers fondle his gun. "I swear, *savet,* if we reach the top and this is some trick you have played, I will put a bullet through your worthless head."

Tsanu doesn't flinch. His dark eyes are emotionless. My hand clenches Iki's fur until he shies away in protest.

Not an hour later, Quniak calls a halt, and the dogs pull up, slowly and uneasily. The snow before us is churned with tracks, as if many beasts passed this way at once.

"What is it?" demands Innes.

Tsanu stoops, examining the tracks and the dirt and leaves mixed into the snow. "Probably *bisgak.*"

"What are they?"

"Buffalo—the big deer. Short horns, heavy fur on their shoulders, tails like cows."

The captain leans against the handlebars of his sled, favoring his left arm. "Are we in any danger from them?"

Tsanu shakes his head. "This happened yesterday. The herd will have moved further down the mountain."

He drags his fingers through the snow a moment longer before getting to his feet. The company moves on.

But I stop a moment where he was kneeling, and there, with his hand mark cutting through the center of it, is a perfect footprint.

Kavik is ahead of us. I look up the slopes at the perfectly still trees and the towering rocks and shiver.

TWENTY-ONE

A Place for Remembering

Iki shoves his panting face into mine and I wake damp with sweat. It is still dark, but a foreign sound plagues the night—the sound of dripping water.

I lie, staring up at the murk of the sky—there are no stars, and the moon is hidden in a sea of reddish cloud—and count the days and the weeks backward to Chegak, then to Kaquom, then to Heart's End.

It is not yet the time for thaw.

I undo the bone fasteners that hold my parka closed and shove it off. The wind brushes under my hair and against my neck, cooling it. I wipe the sweat off the back of my neck. My hair is getting long again—perhaps I will not need to cut it this time.

Iki sniffs around suspiciously, and I snap my fingers for him to come back. The wind blows powerfully over the rocks, pushing against me, sounding mournful and alone. I feel rested, but that is no guarantee that daybreak is near. With the moon covered, I cannot tell.

Getting to my feet, I reach out for my sled, only to remember that the sleds now lie half a day behind us, awaiting our return.

If we return. Only yesterday, Quniak came to me and said in his low, rough voice, "There is someone else on this mountain." I nodded, wide-eyed, wondering what was in his mind.

"I heard the call of a snow fox," he continued under his breath. "I am *Koqebani*, and we use that call. I know the difference between the fox and my brethren."

I do not even remember how I answered him, I was so shaken.

I fear Kavik has not taken my pleas to heart. I fear what he may do, seeking vengeance for Tansilet. Doubtless the *Koqebani* and the others with him have grievances of their own—this is not the only company of Invaders on Uniap'nik soil.

I wander a little way from the others. It is not safe to walk alone on the mountain in the dark, but Iki is beside me. His pale fur stands out against the dark shapes of the rocks, so I will not misstep in the dark and fall off the edge.

Finding a flat rock, I lay my hand on its smooth surface. It is wet, not icy. We are in a thaw.

I sink down on the rock. Iki leans against my leg, then lies down on my feet with a sigh. I reach over and ruffle his ears. "Are we mad, Iki?"

He lifts his head and thumps his tail.

I should be frightened. I am days away, perhaps less, from knowing how all this will end. But right now, I am not afraid. The thought of death is distant, and I cannot bring it close enough scare me.

I strain my ears for anything unnatural, and I hear nothing but the powerful, world-drying wind.

Iki lifts his head, scenting something.

"What is it, Iki?" He gets up and trots down the rough trail to a stand of trees not a stone's throw from our camp. As I come up beside him, my leg scrapes against something in the dark. I trip, barely catching myself.

My eyes examine the shape in horror. Stretching before me in the dark are the remains of a bull *tuttik*, picked clean, some of the bones scattered. But solidly attached to the skull are a set of badly misshapen antlers.

Devil's antlers.

Our legends say that a beast with devil's antlers cannot be killed—it simply wanders into deep mists and disappears forever. But this is as real as the ground under my feet.

A moment later, a voice makes me start. Lantern light quickly follows it, and I let out my breath in relief. It is Peck, complaining about the impossibility of a fire in this wind and damp.

"Never mind that," the captain answers. "We will not need it. Have the men eat the dry provisions, and then we leave."

I reach into my pouch and pull out a hunk of dried salmon, settling back down on my flat rock. No sense in waiting until the captain orders me. I want to stay a step ahead of him today.

"Morning." Jeremiah materializes out of the dark. He too has set aside his coat, and his long arms are folded, something I rarely see. He is always sketching or doing something with his hands.

I move over, making room on the rock, and hold out a piece of salmon.

He takes it with a nod of thanks. "Can't sleep?"

I shrug.

"Me neither."

He takes a bite of the salmon and chews quietly.

"It's oddly warm," he remarks. "This happen often?"

"No. But it happens. Then it will freeze again, and we will be miserably cold again."

He gives a rare grin and squints up at the sky. The clouds are clearing, revealing stars and the reddish sliver of the last moon. "You know, I first traveled with Captain Innes when I was fourteen."

That is not much older than I am. "How old are you now?"

"Thirty-two. I marched west of the Rein with him and mapped it all. Havast, Nuvia."

"What do you think of the captain?"

Jeremiah dismisses this question with a wave of his hand. "A captain's a captain. But the land . . . of all the territories I've surveyed, this is the one that calls to me most."

"Really?" I look up at him swiftly.

"I'd stay here the rest of my life." His eyes kindle. "The love of the land is written in you, too. This land and its people are very alike at times."

I have always been proud of being Uniak, but the way Jeremiah says it—it feels like a great honor.

I shove my lengthening hair out of my eyes and smile, feeling shy. "Thank you."

He stands up and dusts himself off.

Without meaning to, my eyes wander back toward the trees. I cannot see it in the dark, but I know the dead *tuttik* lies there with its devil's antlers. A shiver runs through me.

But I am not as afraid as before; Jeremiah's words have taken some of the fear out of me.

I cannot tell if Tlatlik is angrier than usual or guiding our steps. The sky has lightened, and the threatening black rocks have given way to green moss. But there is also an uneasiness in the air, a tightness—like something is coming.

Perhaps it is only my imagination.

Willow walks beside me, his gaunt face tighter than usual. He has not said much this morning. I look over at him and he smiles, a little strained.

"What are you thinking about, Maki?" He looks me in the eye as if piercing straight into my mind.

"Nothing."

"Let it be."

I draw in a deep, life-filled breath. "There."

"Courage," he says with a smile, and I nod. If only he knew.

We stop to catch our breath on a plateau just big enough for all of us. Beside us, Tlatlik's face is a sheer wall, impossible to scale. Before us is the nearest thing we can find to a path—a long, winding way up around the mountain's outer edge.

The captain is displeased that we have stopped, which is incredible, for he is wearing a sling and has had to use only one arm all this way. He does not even seem winded, as the rest of his men are. But he sees the sense in taking a short rest.

The men all sit down, exhausted from the steep climb, but as Tsanu begins to sit, the captain kicks him.

"Not you."

Tsanu straightens, and I see that proud, grim look in his eyes again. I do not know what he means to do, but I do not think it will end well for everyone.

If he is preparing to die, I will be so angry with him.

I force myself to look away. If I am to pick a fight with Captain Innes, it will not be on a plateau barely big enough to hold the company.

I settle down on the edge and hang my feet over. It is a painfully long way down, but not the sort of drop that would kill a person. Trees darken the mountainside below, and far off, on one of the foothills, a herd of *bisgak* picks at the snow-covered grass.

Willow sits down beside me. "Some view."

"Yes." I lean back and close my eyes as the wind runs over my face and through my hair. "Willow, this is my land. I belong to these wild hills, and nothing can change that."

"I think I understand that. It is good to love your land."

"There is a beauty to the order of things. The wind races through the pines and the pines run to the river. The salmon run red in the river and the river runs to the sea, and the sea gives life to the seal."

"The seal?"

I nod.

"Why the seal?"

I scratch my head. "I suppose it stands for all food. It is what keeps us alive. We mention it particularly."

"It is good." He picks up a bluish pebble and turns it in his hand. "Seals."

"You think it is funny."

He tilts his head down a little as he thinks. "No. But I do think they are rather sweet little things to be using as a symbol for food. It would be like— eating a dog pup."

"No!" I shake my head vehemently. "Nothing like!"

He has obviously never seen a seal hunt.

"To each his own." He tosses the pebble up and pockets it. "As for me, I—"

"On your feet!"

It is the captain. Does he never grow weary?

Willow and I scramble up, not eager to provoke his ire while sitting on the edge of a precipice. A cold drop splashes on my hand; rain is coming.

"We cannot delay," the captain says, adjusting his sling and looking up the mountain's forbidding face. "If the weather turns, we do not want to be out on these rocks."

What he says is true, but I know that he does not care one whit what dangers we face, so long as they bring us nearer to his city. And further up the mountain he will only find more rocks.

We have walked only a few steps when Willow leans close to me. "Maki, what is this?"

He is pointing to a mark on the mountain's face. I reach out and brush my hand over it with a thrill of awe that he should have noticed it, so old and faded it is.

A bird, upright with wings outstretched, its mouth open proudly.

"It's a Thunderbird," I whisper.

His eyes are fearfully earnest, waiting for me to explain.

I drop my hand from the rock face. "It's just legend. Some say perhaps it was only eagles they spoke of."

But the hair stands a little on my arm. It is odd that we should find a carved likeness of the Thunderbird here, on this mountain where so many dark tales gather . . . .

A blinding light splits the sky and a thunderclap answers immediately, shaking the mountain. I grab Willow instinctively, startled out of my balance.

This is winter. The sky is not supposed to be doing this.

"What was that?" demands Jeremiah, clutching his instruments in case the sky were to do it again.

The captain rounds on Tsanu. "What is it?"

Always it is Tsanu's fault, as if on this deadly mountain he could be expected to keep us from all trouble. My hand settles on my knife, though I dare not do anything yet.

Quniak looks up at the sky. "The Thunderbird is angry that we have set foot on his mountain."

"And what does that mean?" Hope sounds in the captain's voice, as if the anger of a Thunderbird can only mean that we are treading close to Inik Katsuk.

"It means we must halt and find shelter," says Quniak. "Perhaps his anger will pass."

As if on command, the heavens split again with blinding light and crashing thunder. Even I shudder. Several men glance upward, faces slack with terror.

But Captain Innes is smiling, fearless, raising a defiant face to the sky as if daring it to do worse. He believes we are near the Seventh City.

"Find shelter!" Ransom shouts, seeing the captain will not give the order. He runs up the path in search of safer ground.

Thunder shakes the earth again, rattling rocks and sending pebbles and stones the size of my fist tumbling down toward us. Rain lashes furiously down on us in pulsing sheets. Ransom comes running back. "The rocks are sliding! Back, before we are buried!"

Inik Katsuk matters to none of us—none but the captain, who is only now noticing the imminent danger to his life. He faces into the storm as if it comes against him alone, and he would conquer it.

Someone slams into me, trying to flee back the way we came. A few men are breaking away and running, perhaps believing what Quniak says— that the Thunderbird is angry.

But Tsanu told me when I was very young that it was just a story, and until I see a Thunderbird, that is what I will believe.

Tsanu is standing now, staring grimly into the rain as it streams down his face. It is as if he is looking for someone. Or something.

Lightning strikes again, leaving colored spots in my eyes. If we do not do something, we shall all die here upon this mountain, trapped by the stubbornness of Captain Innes.

One of the elders of Tansilet used to say—speaking of Barbarian, whom he had set his mind against—"This is the tragedy of a madman: He never destroys only himself." This, here and now, is truer than the sky above.

The captain has all but destroyed us.

"Look!" Jeremiah is drenched, the rain pouring like a river off the rocks and soaking him. I push through the rain, shading my eyes. He stands half inside a cracked rock—no, in a gap between two rocks.

"I think it's a cave," he says, peering into the musty blackness.

"A lantern!" I shout. No sense going in if we all fall a hundred paces straight down and break our necks.

Drucker has a lantern in his supplies, and Rutter comes running with it. The storm howls around the side of the mountain like a great wolf, and the men crowd against the steep face, covering their heads for protection from rain and stone.

Jeremiah strikes a match, sheltering the flame, and holds it inside the lantern. He ducks his head into the cave.

"All clear, there's a floor!" he shouts back. And then he goes strangely silent, just standing in the doorway.

"Move on, Jeremiah!" shouts one of the men over the rain. "Let us in!"

"It's powerful strange in there," says Jeremiah, a little faintly. "Not like any cave I've seen before."

"Hold!" The captain runs up, shoving Jeremiah out of the way by his shirt, and in the space of two heartbeats, he is in the entrance, holding the lantern aloft. He stands for a long moment—I cannot see his face—and then takes three unsteady steps forward.

I follow him. Iki squeezes past me and begins to sniff the ground diligently.

It takes a moment for me to see, even after the lantern light strikes the inside of the cave, and a moment more for me to understand what I see.

A vast underground valley drops away from the place where we stand. Below me, stretching as far as the light reaches, is smooth rock, covered in a clear, shivering blue like sea ice. Bright, twisting halls lead off from the great expanse beneath me; salt crusts the walls like blue glass, shining in millions of splintered pieces from the lantern's flame, taking my breath away. The ceiling of the cave, higher above me than the tops of pines, sparkles where the light hits it. All of Tansilet could fit inside this place.

And then I see them.

Ancient structures, white and blue and red and black, carved out of stone and cedar wood. Towers of memory, row after row, with fading, peeling paint. Carved ravens, proud eagles, men, seals, and *nanuk* with hideous tongues curling out of their mouths.

They are *totem*, and they are made to record brave deeds and remember great heroes. My mother's words come to me—*the good live there*—and at last I understand.

This is Inik Katsuk, the great Seventh City. Not a city for living in, but for remembering.

Behind me I hear the shuffle of the men's boots as they come in out of the rain, the gasps, the shouts as their eyes adjust.

Spears line the walls and the carven path leading down from my feet, standing as if their bearers had gone but a moment before, save for the rust upon the heads. Pottery jars, finer than anything I have seen in any of our villages, sit in clusters at the feet of the *totems*, like memorial gifts for the dead. I crouch beside the nearest vessel and peer inside.

It is filled with gold and jade and garnet.

I stand slowly, taking in deep breaths. The captain is turning in a circle with the lantern upheld, taking in every inch of the place. He has forgotten all else in his wonder.

The place is filled with legend, each *totem* telling a story, each gift left by a mourner or a friend who built a monument to some hero's memory.

A place where only the greatest of men live.

Tsanu has come in, too. He drinks in the sight slowly, and for the first time, I realize that he and the captain are paying no attention to each other. He comes over and takes my hand, holding it tightly.

"Maki—"

The captain's incredulous laugh echoes beside me, first disbelieving, then jubilant, then hysterically, wonderfully happy.

I did not know if I could live with Captain Innes getting what he wanted after treating Tsanu so horribly. But now, with my brother's hand in mine, feeling the warmth of his presence next to me and hearing the thunder dying away over the far side of the mountain, I have my answer.

I only feel delirious joy.

Tsanu reaches out and touches the nearest spear with reverent fingers. He is touching history—our history, and we both know it. His hand closes on it, testing, and he almost lifts it. Then he gives a start, as if remembering himself, and releases it.

It has been ages since he has held a spear—I suppose he misses that feeling very much.

A slow movement at the mouth of the cave catches my eye. A raven's feather, large and glossy black, drifts to the ground and lands. My heart gives a thump.

I watch, frozen, as if time is moving without me.

"Maki," Tsanu is talking to me, but I hardly hear. "I must tell you, now that we can—"

A splintering crack shatters the happy noise of the men. An arrow lies broken in the doorway, fletched with black-and-white.

"You are surrounded, *kannuk!*" The voice echoes from outside. "Do not come out unless you wish to die where you stand."

It is Kavik.

The captain swears loudly, pulling out his pistol. He rushes towards the entrance of the cave but stops within a safe distance. "Who dares challenge the Army of the Northern Frontier?"

"I, Kavik of Tansilet. I hold every man of you guilty, and you will answer for the burning of my village."

There is an uncomfortable murmur among the men.

"And what of your attack on our camp?" Innes shouts back. "Is there not guilt to spare? Surrender now, before we blow you to pieces. We have guns, fool!"

From outside come three loud reports of a gun. The echo dies, and after two heartbeats, I hear Kavik's voice again.

"We have guns also, and a hundred warriors to man them. Now, you will send out those of Uniap'nik. I know there are some in your midst."

Captain Innes tightens his grip on his gun. "No chance."

"It will be the worse for you if I must fight you for them. I said I want them, and you will turn them over now."

"Says the hunter to the bear!" Laughter rings in the captain's voice. "No! I am prepared to wait you out. You may have the entrance, but we have the ground. If any man of you so much as pokes his head through that hole, we will blow it off!"

Tsanu's grip on my hand tightens faintly. The silence stretches long, and my throat is so dry and thick I can hardly take a breath. At last, Kavik shouts through the mouth of the cave. "If you do not surrender, I will burn you out of your den and cut your throats one by one."

"No!" Innes grinds his teeth. "There will be no surrender. We are fully prepared to wait you out and to spill every drop of our own blood if necessary!"

Heavy silence falls on the men. The blood pounds in my ears.

The captain presses against the wall, brandishing his gun. "And as for the *savets* you want back, if you do not surrender yourselves this moment, I will shoot them all in the head! There is my bargain!"

Tsanu grabs me and shoves me behind him.

A gunshot thunders behind us. I feel Tsanu stiffen, but there is no impact.

Ransom steps up from some ten paces back, cocking his shotgun as a metal shell falls to the rock with a clang.

"Roger Innes, you are relieved of duty."

TWENTY-TWO

Waking the King

Captain Innes whirls, his face white with fury.

"Lieutenant Ransom, is this mutiny?"

"You cannot abuse your power in this way." Ransom speaks quietly, as if to a frightened horse. "You have long since exceeded your orders, sir."

"You have no right," Captain Innes snarls through his teeth. "By the oaths you have taken as a soldier—"

"These oaths I have kept, and am keeping now as I protect my men from you, Roger Innes. And now you will drop your gun and step back."

Captain Innes looks from Tsanu to Ransom. He grips his pistol like a lifeline, his knuckles white, like a drowning man clutching the last solid thing in his possession.

"Set down your gun." I wonder how Ransom can stay so masterfully calm.

A muscle hardens in Innes's cheek and a spasm crosses his face. He pries his fingers off of his pistol and steps back.

"Cover him," says Ransom briefly, and Willow steps up with his pistol.

Ransom steps up near the entrance of the cave. "Halloo, Mr. Kavik!"

A gunshot blasts the ground a few feet from him. Ransom doesn't move a muscle.

"I want to talk peace, Kavik. This is the acting captain, John Ransom!"

"I hear."

"I wish to make reparations on behalf of the army. We will pay you back double for what was lost in Tansilet, and more besides. If you want help building homes before next winter, the army will send men. It is only right that the wrongs done should be repaid."

"They should be repaid in blood," Kavik calls. "That is what your army has cost us."

Tsanu leans down to whisper in my ear. "Maki, go now. Ransom will not stop you."

I grip his hand harder and shake my head.

"I understand this." Ransom leans nearer to the entrance. "Great wrong has been done. But hear me—if you shed more blood, these men's comrades and kin will wish to avenge them, and when they are avenged, your kin will rise against their kin, and so it will go down through the ages. A man will never see just retribution in the shedding of blood when it is his own kin who are sacrificed."

Silence.

"I cannot agree to this, John Ransom. Your promises are hollow."

"Let one of us stand as a pledge, then, that you may see our promises are true."

Tsanu glances down and motions for me to go. But I cannot leave him. Kavik will not dare open fire while I am here.

Iki returns to me, and I thrust my fingers into his thick coat.

I stop short. His ruff stands high above his back, and his lips are pulled back in a snarl, his eyes locked on the darkest end of the cavern where the lantern light barely reaches.

"Tsanu?" I call, horror climbing my throat. He turns and sees Iki.

Then we hear it.

Faint whuffling. A distant grunt, echoing off the vast chambers of the cave.

Tsanu freezes. His eyes meet mine as we hear the sound again. "Maki, Kavik will not fire on you. Lead those men out if you want them to live."

He bends down and presses his face against mine.

"Wait, Tsanu—!"

A roar rips my ears apart. Not even the thunder of earlier could match it. There is only one thing I have ever heard of in life or in legend that this could be.

The Tiriarnaq.

I know now why the huge *nanuk* was dead by one blow, why the wolf tracks circled round and round it and did not dare come near.

Tlatlik is its mountain.

"Tsanu!" I start after him. He is pulling down spears from the wall. I can't leave him.

He turns on me, gives me a firm shove. "Maki, there isn't time. You are those men's one chance of surviving." He swallows. "We do not all have to die."

But why you?

He clasps my hand firmly. "Go, Maki."

I hold onto his hand one second more, my sight blurring. "I can't—"

He smiles, and I know every goodbye is in that smile. "You can, Maki. It's all right. You will survive." He is not talking about the bear.

The shouts of the men fill my ears. I hear their terror.

I let go and step back.

The roar comes again, closer—more deafening, if that is possible. The world slows as Tsanu hefts the spears over his shoulder and walks toward the darkness.

"Where is he going?" Rutter's voice is shaking.

"To buy us time." I look up into his white, rigid face. "We have to go now."

"But those warriors—"

"Kavik is my friend and my kin." I set off toward the entrance at a run. "Stay behind me, and keep your hands off your weapons. Willow!"

I whip my glance around, searching. The whole place is in confusion, men drawing their guns, men pressing towards the entryway, afraid of stepping into sight of the warriors outside. We may only have a matter of seconds left.

Willow is still guarding the captain with a pistol, but he is torn.

I cannot lose him, too. "Willow, come!"

Captain Innes stands up and straightens his crooked uniform.

"Give me the pistol, Mr. Tam." He holds his hand out.

Willow hesitates.

The captain's jaw hardens, but his voice is still calm. "Give me the pistol."

"Sir—"

"I set out to find Inik Katsuk, and I did. It's done. I've never sent a man where I wouldn't go myself, and someone's got to get out of this death trap if the truth of my conquest is to be known. I'll buy you some time." He grabs the pistol out of Willow's hand and jams it into his own belt. "Tell those doubters I did it."

Willow swallows, a muscle in his cheek twitching hard.

"Run, fool!" the captain shouts. He grabs a shotgun from the dirt floor and follows after Tsanu.

The men crowd around the entrance. I force my eyes forward, trying to still my heart in my throat so I can speak. "Stay behind me. Do not touch your weapons."

I step out onto the open ground, blinking in the light. A shot lands near my feet, and I throw up an arm angrily. "*Kannuk!*" I shout, giving them all the strength in my lungs. The insult in our own tongue gets their attention. "Do not shoot, or you answer to Tsanu!"

Kavik will listen to that. I am trembling from head to foot, but I force my steps to be steady, crossing the ground as fast and calmly as I can.

"Kavik!" I cry, but another roar rips the air.

I do not need to explain the king of the bear-kind. He explains himself.

Kavik's face changes only a shade as the roar echoes deep in the mountain. He throws up a hand and jerks his head to us to come over.

"It is not to be that we fight the Invaders today," he says to me with wry smile. "The king—he has other plans."

My throat aches so hard I can hardly speak. "Tsanu stayed behind."

Kavik lifts his chin. "He made his choice. Like Nanik, he chose a worthy end."

Guns echo inside the mountain.

"What is it?" Rutter's voice is low. "Is it a *nanuk*?"

"It is a Tiriarnaq. Like in the legends."

"You never told me that they were real!" He sounds betrayed.

Tears fill my eyes. "I did not know."

Cold wind blows through our hair; we are upwind of the creature. This would be an advantage if it was deer or *pannik* we hunted, but the Tiriarnaq hardly needs the help of the wind to make an end of us.

"Courage, men!" Ransom calls, and the army men pick up his shout.

My heart stands still as the Tiriarnaq emerges. Its pale, malicious head snakes out of the cave, its long teeth bared, its piggish eyes staring at us— and now it moves, not lumbering like a bear, but long and lithe like a weasel, emerging and emerging, its great mass seeming to come on forever.

"Good hunting, my brothers!" Kavik shouts, raising his spear.

"To glory!" echoes down the line.

The Tiriarnaq roars, drowning the shouts, and chaos breaks loose. Screams, bellowing, strike-locks firing, a clamor I will never be able to erase from my ears. Not even the destruction of the *nanuk* came close.

To think—all the time, it was going to end like this.

The beast has blood-lust in its eyes and a score of wounds along its body. One leg is dragging. The wounds have made it more dangerous, not less. I adjust my grip on my spear and take a breath, and wild confusion gives way to a tiny moment of deadly clarity.

I see a gap, just behind the shoulder.

Once I throw this spear, I have no defense. Yet—I must do it now.

Tsanu has already gone before me. Perhaps this is how it should be, in the end. I, Maki, meant to go down in battle like Nanik, dying the hero's death.

The beast turns, looks at me, and charges.

Pressing my fist to my chest and raising my spear high, I shout the war cry of my ancestors as Kavik and Tsanu have before me: "*Tagli yanika, auta!*"

I should be scared, watching it come for me, blinded by rage and maddened by blood, but I am not. The world has gone very still, perfectly still, and I can see the entry point by its shoulder where a good clean kill should be.

I pull out my knives—I will not have time to draw them from their sheaths, so I thrust them both in my thick leather belt.

I watch, make ready. Count the heartbeats, my last heartbeats, and calculate the distance between my spear and the creature.

Arrows, bullets, spears continue to fly—they are like snow on the wind, meaning nothing now.

I kneel down and brace myself. I have only one chance. If I miss it, I could be dead in an instant.

It is probably better to die instantly, but I must take it down with me.

I aim and thrust, bracing the butt of the spear against the ground, feeling the tearing of flesh as it strikes true.

One word sears through my brain. My name. Tsanu, no—Willow is shouting it.

I am knocked over before I can reach my knives. The world upends in a churning mass of fur and dirt and hot, sticky blood.

TWENTY-THREE

The World Is Full of Strange Things

One moment there is nothingness—I remember nothing, and I open my eyes to stare at an empty sky.

I cannot breathe, either. My chest weighs a hundred pounds. Every breath hurts.

"Easy now," soothes a voice I know. "Hold still. I'm right here to help you."

A pained grunt. The heaviness is replaced by a light, cool sensation and searing pain. I gasp, and the gasp makes it worse. My eyes focus on a rough, familiar face. Ran—no—Ru—

"Rutter?"

"There you go. I think you've got a busted rib." He grins at me as if a smile will cure it. "Not to worry, they heal up. Personal experience, you know."

He helps me sit up and leans me against something—something warm and soft. I shudder hard, more from instinct than anything else.

The slippery smell of blood is hot and sickening, filling my nostrils. I twist my head a little, trying to catch the fresh breeze, but without moving my ribs. Blood is soaked into my clothes and smeared on my arms. I let out a moan, trying not to be sick.

"It's all right, it's all right. He can't hurt you now."

"It's not that . . . ." I am trying to remember.

The fight, the bear . . . Tsanu.

I look up at Rutter. He is spattered with blood, too.

I stumble to my feet, ignoring the pain in my chest, and am sick in the nearest patch of reedy brown grass.

The horrid taste is almost better than the blood smell.

"Maki—" Rutter has followed me. "Maki, are you all right?"

I grab a handful of slushy, half-melted snow and wash my face with it. I am used to blood, but being covered in the blood of the Tiriarnaq . . . . I shudder.

I turn back to the massive carcass stretched out on the rocks, its pale fur matted with dirt and snow and thickening blood. Before I lose the courage, I draw my knife and kneel down to take a long, knife-like claw from the beast's paw. I have to saw awhile to get it off.

"Whatever are you doing?" Apparently, Rutter does not know of this custom.

"I killed him—or, I helped." The claw finally comes free, and I sit on my knees, staring at it. "This is my trophy."

I have nothing to wrap it in, so I clutch it by the smooth part. I will clean it later.

I lean back against the beast to steady myself. "Rutter?"

He looks down at me.

"Who's dead?"

His face falls. "A good many, Maki, a good many. He went through men like a wild horse. Quniak the dog-driver, Peck, Jeremiah—"

My hands are shaking.

"What about Willow?"

Rutter's face grows dark. "Lands, I don't know about him! I haven't seen him."

I have to find Willow. I push myself up on one hand but don't quite make it. I settle back against the damp ground.

All around me are signs of the fight. Dead men lying where they were killed, some helping others up, blood and broken spears everywhere.

I have to go.

"Don't you think you should rest?" Rutter protests as I start to get up.

"I can't wait. I have to find Willow."

Right now I do not want to think of anything else.

✦

The makeshift hospital is a mess. Men, mostly Kavik's warriors, lie everywhere, bleeding, some unconscious, some groaning, and some—I can tell by the hue of their skin and the dullness in their eyes—waiting to die.

I almost turn around and run away again, but I see Willow nearby, cutting bandages.

"Willow!"

He turns quickly, and his face goes slack when he sees me.

"Do I really look so terrible?" I ask.

"Yes—I mean, you are covered in blood." His eyes look me up and down once or twice. "But I am glad you are alive."

"It is not my blood," I say. I am too tired to say more.

"Has Drucker seen you yet?"

"No."

"Hurt any?"

"A rib, I think. It hurts just here when I breathe."

He reaches out to ruffle my hair like a brother, but stops short. "You're a tough one, Maki," he says finally.

Drucker approaches, up to his elbows in blood. My stomach turns strongly. It is not the blood itself that makes me ill—the sight is no different than when we clean a *tupak* or a seal to eat it. But this is not the blood of animals on his hands. It's the blood that was flowing inside men's veins minutes before—men I know.

His face is expressionless. It is as if he cannot find even one emotion to fit this moment, so he has decided to give way to none at all. He sways a

269

little, but not, I think, from weariness.

I am glad Willow is not one of those men lying there so hurt that they wait only to die. I cannot think of a worse fate than that.

"You, I have something for you," Drucker says.

Without a word, he walks down the row of injured men and stops before a makeshift bed.

Tsanu lies on it, his leg swathed in bandages. He is white, like all the life has been drained from him. A double claw mark runs down his neck—deep enough to be sewn, but not touching the vein that drains men's blood away and makes them die.

"Most of the trouble is in his leg," says Drucker. "I have saved it for now. Another week or two will decide whether or not he keeps it. He's blooming lucky—he'd have been dead if it weren't for the fact the captain was dead on top of him—cut off all the blood to that leg."

I nod, unable to speak.

Drucker stops and looks at me oddly. "He is your brother, isn't he?"

"Yes," I whisper.

When he is gone, I sit down cross-legged beside the bed and take my brother's hand. "Tsanu?"

At my voice, his eyes open. On seeing me, he is alert, like himself. "Maki!"

He leans forward into my face, a relieved laugh in his voice. "I told you to get out of there!"

"I did."

He grimaces and shakes his head. "Oh, Maki. My little wolf pup."

I put my arms around him, biting back a gasp at my ribs. For once, pain only makes it better. We are alive, *alive*.

It was he and I against the world, and we lived.

His hand is in my short hair, soothing me, though it is he who is crying;

I can hear it in his breathing. "I do not want to lose you ever again, Maki."

"Nor I. Let's build a cottage and go live alone like Barbarian."

"Don't you think that is taking it too far?"

I shake my head vehemently and he laughs. "I will give you time to change your mind on that score. Now go on, Maki. I must rest a while longer."

It is true. He is not well, and I think the doctor has given him morphine. His eyes are dulling.

I lean his forehead against mine, then kiss it. "Don't leave me, Tsanu."

"I will not, Maki."

He closes his eyes again, and I leave him be.

I find myself walking up to Drucker. "May I—"

He looks down abruptly as if truly realizing for the first time that I am here. "What?"

"May I help in any way?"

He stares at me for a long moment, as he used to stare at the captain while thinking of a scathing reply. But when he answers, his voice is weary, and there is a note of kindness in it.

"This way. I could use another hand."

It is dusk when I finally leave the hospital. The sun is setting behind Tlatlik, its golden rays reaching out like a crown around the sides of the mountain.

Iki has found me. He is limping on three legs, but after examining him, I do not think it is serious. He will begin to walk on four legs again in another day or so.

A bird calls to another somewhere on the mountain. I love that about the birds—every thaw, even in the heart of winter, they come out again and act like it is spring.

A small stream trickles through the rocks from the mountain, clear and cold, full of the melting of the snows. I kneel beside it and plunge my hands in, leaving them as long as I can stand. I rinsed my hands in a bucket back at the hospital, but somehow this feels cleaner.

I wipe my hands on Iki's back, which seems a better place than my bloody clothes. He shoves his wet nose in my face, thinking I am petting him, and I throw my arm over his neck in reply. The golden rays of the sun bathe everything around us in one last display before the night and the stars take over. I lean my head against Iki's shoulder and bury my fingers in his fur.

I wish I had a mug of Laramie's coffee.

I stare down at the overturned dirt and imagine the faces. Peck's thin, odd face under his curling gray hair; Quniak's broad face with his short, stiff black hair and crooked smile; the way Jeremiah's face would remain calm and thoughtful long after everyone else had become short of temper. It was because he was always studying the land and not paying attention to whether or not we were in danger of dying.

Word was he'd gotten in four rounds of shots and saved a few men before he went down.

I miss them all.

It is quiet around the small circle, the mixed few who are well enough and can be spared to pay homage to the dead. Ransom and Kavik are both here; Ransom's arm is in a sling, and Kavik has a large bandage under his open shirt.

There is a tenuous peace in the camp. The need for vengeance is subdued by the need to survive—and, I think, by the bond men grow after fighting together for their lives. Ransom and Kavik have not needed to break up any fights; they almost seem now to be allies. If anyone is the leader of all, it is Drucker, with his scant supplies for healing and his urgent mission to save as many lives as possible. No one refuses Drucker a thing.

Ransom reads aloud from a book for his men. Kavik lifts his eyes to the clouded sky and speaks the customary words of memory we used for the dead in Tansilet.

"If anyone wishes to remember the dead, you may speak," says Ransom.

For a time, only the wind replies. The air is frigid, the ground frozen again—we buried the dead only just in time.

Wade, who shot the captain the night the wolves attacked, clears his throat. "Y'know, I had the honor of marching with the captain on a number of his campaigns. He wasn't perfect—" He glances down at his gun hand. "No, he wasn't. But he could sure lead men. He had a way about him—he was brilliant."

Jeremiah's words come back to me: *All brilliant men are a bit touched.*

I can hear his voice in my ears like it was yesterday.

Beside me, Rutter shoves his hands in his pockets. "I recall saying to Jeremiah once, when I powerful frightened, that I was surprised he looked so calm. He said he figured our days were already set out for us, and we'd live up to them, just as we were meant to. And I said, 'How do you know?' And he said, 'I've seen too much to think this can all be an accident.'"

He drops his eyes to the dirt patch in front of us.

"I can't help but think he'd be the first to say it was all right he had to go."

Rutter swallows hard, and the wind takes up the silence again.

"God rest their souls," Ransom murmurs, and the men repeat it. I swallow back a thick, hard feeling in my throat that will not turn into tears.

The men disperse around me, some with heads down, some shaking off their sad manner as if they have devoted too much time to thinking about death and cannot endure anymore.

I stay.

I don't know if I will ever come back here, and it seems wrong these men should be buried without a *totem*.

Perhaps I will come back one day and raise one. Tsanu and I.

I like the sound of that.

I look up at the clouds and see a white bird, wheeling on the moving wind. Back in Tansilet, they are signs of fair times. I take a deep breath in through my nose. I feel so very alive.

"Maki, will you come here a moment?"

Ransom thrusts his head into the makeshift tent, and Iki takes the opportunity to push a cold, wet nose in after him. I get up, dusting the frozen dirt off of my hands, and shove Iki's curious nose away.

Three days have passed since we buried the men, and it has grown colder still. Frost hangs in the air and sticks in Ransom's beard.

"I have something to show you." The edges of his eyes crinkle slightly, as if he is hiding a surprise.

I follow him, our footsteps loud against the hard, frozen ground.

We go to the shelter that serves as a common area for the few of us who do not need to stay under Drucker's watchful eye. Kavik is there, sitting on the ground and polishing his spear. Even wounded, he is organizing a group to go out and hunt the great *bisgak* so we can have something to eat out on this terrible mountain.

Terrible—but less so, now that the Tiriarnaq is dead.

Kavik gives me a nod and something almost like a smile.

"I was looking through Jeremiah's things," Ransom says, picking up a cloth packet from the top of a small trunk, scattering a couple sharp pens and a sextant. "And I found this."

He holds out the cloth packet. Pinned on the front is a small piece of precious paper.

Wolf Pup

I finger the paper gently, feeling the slight prick of the tears I could not feel earlier.

"Open it," prompts Ransom gently.

I turn it over and unfold the cloth with one hand. Inside is a folded square of cream-colored paper. I set the cloth down and unfold the paper in my hands.

It is a map, a map of Uniap'nik.

I trace my fingers over Arislet by the coast, a small circle marked Tansilet, and further up Kaquom and Chegak, shadowed by the mountain, Tlatlik.

Here lies the great Seventh City, he has scrawled beside the mountain. Along the coast he has written, *Here a Great One was found, saving the company,* and north of Kaquom are markings that read *Way Cabin, Hot Springs, Here a nanuk was killed.*

And suddenly I realize what makes this map different from the others. I am reading it all in my own tongue.

Tears sting my eyes and fill them. I duck my head so that Kavik and Ransom cannot see. All that time, Jeremiah had been making two maps. I had always seen the one with the clear, precise markings of an army surveyor. But this—somehow the savage beauty of the land has been captured in every stroke, and I am, for the first time, seeing my whole land in one glance, from southern Arislet to the wilds around Tlatlik.

I take a quick breath and sneak my hand up to wipe away my tears before they fall on the map.

"It's yours," says Ransom. "He made it for you."

I fold it methodically, my fingers doing it without thinking, and tie the bundle up again.

"Thank you," I whisper to Ransom. But I am not really talking to him.

Spring has come to Kaquom by the time we return. It was a long while before all the wounded were well enough to travel, and by that time, the ice was breaking up and we had to find a new route home. Among Kavik's men, there were some who knew the stretch of land well, and though we broke a few sleds on the bare rocky ground, we all arrived safe and sound.

From Kaquom, Tsanu and I will go our way. Perhaps we will go to Tansilet—to the place where it stood—and help rebuild. We have not spoken of it between us, but I think we are agreed.

Ransom has given us horses for the return journey, and of all the horses he could have chosen for me, he chose Fredrico. I think he noticed that I am fond of him.

The lazy brute will not be scolded by me. At least, not much.

Tsanu has Rosita, whose rider died from the Quaking Fever in Chegak. Rutter says she deserves a quiet hand.

Kavik appears from behind one of the tents, slowly leading a horse, preparing to set out with us. Ransom is with him, keeping pace with his hands clasped behind his back, head cocked to one side as if considering something.

It is a thing I never thought to see: Kavik and Ransom talking peaceably in the heart of camp. But over the last few months, as we traveled together, they have found much to admire in each other.

"For my part, I would be happy to withdraw our fighting men," Ransom says. "But I must admit, this land has begun to call me."

Kavik sets his hand on his horse's shoulder. "This land is powerful. It is made for brave hearts—like yours. What you did upon Tlatlik was good, and in peace I would welcome you."

"As for what I have done, it was what any good man would do," says Ransom. "They are my men and I must do everything in my power to do right by them."

"Even so it is with me. Where do your orders take you?"

"Captain Innes vastly exceeded his orders, so we will be marching back to Arislet. After that—" He only shrugged.

"I wish that in the course of time, I myself may come to Arislet with the leaders of the villages, and if it seems reasonable, we may talk of peace, that you may take our words back to your own leaders and it may be established."

"I should be honored."

Ransom holds out his hand for Kavik to shake, and Kavik clasps it.

Rutter comes to say goodbye with saddle oil on his hands and dirt on his face from currying the horses.

"Well, Maki, I hate to see you go." He puts his hands on his hips, shaking his head as if pronouncing a horse lame.

My heart warms at the sight of him. Since the finding of the city and the slaying of the beast, I have come to believe that however hard we try, we can never know much about what will happen, or what will come of it. If Innes had not been so cruel, Ransom and Kavik would never have come to understand each other. And in a strange way, even while my heart was set on Tsanu, I was there on that mountain so that those men in the camp—men like Rutter—could live.

The words stick in my throat a little. "I hate to leave you. And the horses."

"Don't lie. You're taking Rosita and the big 'un—there's no need to miss any other flea bag around here."

"I will miss you, though."

He jerks his head in agreement and looks away briefly. "I'll miss you too. You are a gutsy little thing."

I reach up and press my forehead against his in farewell.

"If you are ever out Tansilet way, please come by."

A lopsided smile spreads across his face. "To be sure. Take care of yourself, Maki."

He slaps me on the shoulder, scratches Rosita's mane once, and strides away.

Last of all, holding onto Fredrico's bridle at the edge of camp, I bid farewell to Willow. He has not put the weight back on as I should like, but then again, I never could convince him to drink seal oil.

It is silent between us for a moment. The wind blows a little, filling my ears.

"Must you go with the army?" I ask quietly.

He has said before that he should like to settle—settle here, perhaps—and I want to ask him to, but I am afraid he will simply say no. If he does not say no, I can keep on hoping.

He nods. "I am contracted to the army. I couldn't stay if I wanted to." He drops his gaze and then lifts it again. "But my service is up in two years. If you promise you won't forget—"

"Willow, I would never forget you."

A smile breaks out across his face. It is easier to see how gaunt and bony he is when he smiles, but I do not care. "The world is full of strange things. Maybe I will come back."

He presses my hand in his and turns away abruptly, before either of us can lose our nerve. I watch him go, striding across the brown grass, gold in the sunlight.

Why didn't I say anything—not even a farewell? Where did my tongue go?

I stand on my tiptoes, cupping my hands around my mouth. "I shall count on it, Willow Tam!"

I watch till he disappears among the tents.

✒

Fall is coming on. The leaves are beginning to turn, and the *pannik* are passing by in roving herds, fat and carrying thick coats for winter.

I look up from the new parka I am stitching as Tsanu comes in the door, a string of fish in his hand.

He still limps; even after three years, it has not quite faded. Perhaps it never will. The trout are fat and fine. That is what I like about fall. Every year the land gives us a fighting chance to hunt and store up for winter.

"I see you did not fail."

He laughs and hangs the fish up on a peg out of reach of the dogs. "Have you so little faith in me?"

I grin and look back at my work so I do not prick my thumb.

"Maki, when did your hair grow so long?"

The braids are halfway down my back right now. I look up and smile.

All around me are memories. Jeremiah's map is tacked on the smooth walls of our new home, Fredrico and Rosita whicker to each other outside, and Iki is in the house with me. Even Tsanu, with that permanent, twisted

279

mark on his neck, is a constant reminder of what I have.

Oddly, that is what I remember. Not what I lost, but what I gained.

"I have something for you, Maki," Tsanu says, pretending to be very serious, though his eyes sparkle.

"Oh? And what is that?"

He holds out his hand and drops into it a piece of amber, strung upon a thong of deerhide.

"Where did you—?"

I get up swiftly.

Willow is standing in the doorway.

With Thanks

Writing seems like a solitary pursuit, but I have found it to be quite the opposite.

To my beta readers, Mollie, Schuyler, Lucy, Audrey, Elizabeth, Lincoln, Kenzie, and Justin. Your feedback and support are invaluable, and you are brilliant at identifying the places that need fixing without discouraging me.

To Katie Phillips—not only my editor, but my cheerleader. Thank you for taking this journey with me.

To my wingmen, Elisabeth, Lydia, and Scott, who always have my six. I would walk 500 miles for you, and you know it.

To James Egan, thank you for bringing Maki and Uniap'nik to life in the gorgeous cover.

To Esther, Emilie, and Lydia, who used their design skills so brilliantly, thank you. You bring this world to life under your fingers!

To my proofreaders, Anna, John, Ethan, Alice, Elisabeth, Lucy, and Elizabeth. Thank you for your tireless efforts in abolishing the typos. And to my jellybean buddy Meredith, who would have found all the typos if she could have.

To my street team: We may be few in number, but we are fighters, all of us!

To my family: Thank you for everything, from peace and quiet to treats on late work nights. Your love and consideration truly make this possible.

To my readers and you lovely people who ask how I am doing: Thank you for your love and support. Your enthusiasm keeps this author going!

And to my Heavenly Father, who has given me this blessing, thank you. This book is all grace from you.

EMILY HAYSE is a lover of log cabins, strong coffee, and the smell of old books. Her writing is fueled by good characters and a lifelong passion for storytelling. When she is not busy turning words into worlds, she can often be found baking, singing, or caring for one of the many dogs and horses in her life. She lives with her family in Michigan.

Connect with Emily!
Website: emilyhayse.com
Instagram: @songsofheroes
Twitter: @theherosinger
Facebook: /theherosinger
Goodreads: /theherosinger